## "Uh-oh," Colby said. "We've got a second one on board."

Ian stood to the side of the cow, the drama of the situation making him tense. Colby helped to pull the first calf forward until it finally slid onto the straw in a heap, and wonder assaulted him. He thought about his own son's birth and how incredible it had been to hold the tiny body in his arms. He recalled the instantaneous love he'd felt for him, and his chest ached with the memory of it and a yearning for things to be right with Luke again.

"Let's get the other one," Colby said, and when it emerged, the same sense of wonder washed over him. This one was noticeably smaller, its eyes round and startled. His heart contracted.

The calf raised its head and let out a halfhearted bleat. Colby laughed. "Looks like she arrived with an appetite."

The cow weakly reached around to swipe the closest calf with her tongue. "These three have some bonding to do." Colby wiped her damp forehead on her shoulder, then looked up at Ian and smiled. "Thanks for being so patient."

Ian didn't remember a smile ever affecting him quite the way hers did in that moment. It made him feel as if he'd witnessed something incredibly special. He couldn't remember one incident during his entire career that had made him feel this way. And he had no idea what to make of that.

## ABOUT THE AUTHOR

Inglath Cooper's fascination with romance novels began
the day her mother first took her to the local bookmobile.
"A librarian handed me a Janet Dailey Harlequin Presents,
and I've been hooked ever since," she says. Now, she
writes as well as reads them.

Her second novel, *The Last Good Man*, is set in Virginia,
where Inglath lives with her husband, Mac. She'd love to
hear from her readers and invites them to write to her at:
P.O. Box 973, Rocky Mount, VA 24151-0973.

## Books by Inglath Cooper

HARLEQUIN SUPERROMANCE
*(writing as Inglath Caulder)*
609—TRUTHS AND ROSES

# THE LAST
# GOOD MAN
# Inglath Cooper

# Harlequin Books

TORONTO • NEW YORK • LONDON
AMSTERDAM • PARIS • SYDNEY • HAMBURG
STOCKHOLM • ATHENS • TOKYO • MILAN
MADRID • WARSAW • BUDAPEST • AUCKLAND

ISBN 0-373-70728-2

THE LAST GOOD MAN

Copyright © 1997 by Inglath Cooper.

This edition published by arrangement with Harlequin Books S.A.

® and TM are trademarks of the publisher. Trademarks indicated with
® are registered in the United States Patent and Trademark Office, the
Canadian Trade Marks Office and in other countries.

Printed in U.S.A.

To Mac, for the pink Jeep dream
and
To Michele, sister, best friend

Thou art the star for which all evening waits.
—George Sterling
*Aldebaran at Dusk*

# *PROLOGUE*

IAN MCKINLEY HAD finally made it. Reached the pinnacle. The top rung of the ladder. Tonight represented the crown jewel in the career he had spent seventeen years of his life building. Thirty-nine years old, and by most definitions, he had it all. Money. Success. A teenage son. A beautiful woman to whom he had become engaged a couple of weeks ago.

Having just brought on board the biggest client CCI Investments of Manhattan had ever represented, he was a hero among men. His partners had thrown a party for him at the Waldorf-Astoria and invited enough people to sink a small ship.

Standing there among trays of champagne and tables loaded with exotic-looking foods, he should have felt nothing but exhilaration. But somehow, he merely felt tired. Bone weary. He thought about the routine of his life, the predictability of it. Every single morning he bought his breakfast at the same bagel shop on Sixtieth Street, ate it at his desk with exactly two cups of coffee, no cream, no sugar. Every single day he ran six miles at noon. He couldn't remember the last time he'd done anything remotely spontaneous.

But this was the life he had wanted. This was what he'd worked so hard for—to prove that a poor boy from the wrong side of Third Avenue could make it

to Park and Sixty-first. His only regret was that neither Sherry nor his mother had lived to see his success. He'd promised them both he would make something of himself one day. He wondered if they would
have been proud of him. But then, if Sherry had
lived, maybe he wouldn't have been quite so driven.
Maybe he wouldn't have buried himself in his work.
Maybe life would have been more normal. For him
and for Luke.

He wasn't sure he even knew what normal was
anymore.

For the past three weeks, he'd gotten no more than
five hours' sleep a night. That could explain his fa-
tigue, but part of him felt as if he'd been tired for
years. Maybe he needed a vacation. To take some
time for him and Luke. He couldn't remember the
last time he'd taken one—or the last time he'd spent
more than an hour with his son. Guilt gnawed at him.
He would plan something for them to do together.
Soon. This time, he would make sure he followed
through on it.

"Why is it you look like a man headed for the gas
chamber instead of the man of the hour?"

Ian swung around to find Rachel looking up at him
with inquisitive eyes and a smile on her lips. "Hi."
He put a hand on her shoulder and gave it a squeeze.
"A pillow and a bed sound pretty good about now."

"I could go for that. Anyway, I've been getting
just a little jealous of the stares half the women in
the room have been sending you all night." She
leaned in to kiss the corner of his mouth, her right
breast pressing against his chest. He waited for the
surge of arousal that should have followed her delib-

erate provocation and decided, when it did not come, that he was more tired than he'd realized.

"Hey, we can't have any of that." Curtis Morgan clapped a hand on Ian's shoulder. A short man with a receding hairline and an expanding waistline, Curtis was one of Ian's partners at CCI. "Not until after the wedding, at least. Ms. Montgomery, you'll have our guest of honor ducking out before I've had a chance to make my toast to him."

"I suggest you hurry up and do it," Rachel said with a raised brow. "I'm afraid he's nearly dead on his feet."

"No wonder. You really gave this one everything you had, Ian," Curtis said. "Our firm will see the benefit of it. We're all very appreciative."

"Yes. I couldn't be more proud of him," Rachel said. "Now, if I could just get him to agree on a wedding date..."

She looked up at Ian with wide eyes that were intended to convey innocence, but Ian suspected Rachel knew exactly what she was doing.

Rachel was as methodical about her personal life as she was about the senior partnership on which she had her sights set at the law firm of Brown, Brown and Fitzgerald. From the beginning, she'd made no secret of the fact that she thought a marriage between them would be mutually beneficial. She'd continued pressing her case for the past two years until she'd finally convinced him she was right.

Two weeks ago, when Ian had asked her to marry him, it had been with the understanding that there was no rush. They both had full lives, and a piece of paper wouldn't change things drastically. Or so he had told himself.

When Sherry had died right after Luke was born, he had never intended to marry again. Unexpectedly losing his wife at the age of twenty-three was the most painful thing he'd ever gone through. Something inside him had simply shut down. For the first five years after her death, he hadn't dated at all. And when he did start seeing someone here and there, he made sure it was never for any length of time, never long enough to let things get serious. But with Luke almost grown now, he didn't relish the idea of spending the rest of his life alone. His relationship with Rachel was a comfortable one. It made no demands on his heart or even hinted at happily-ever-after and white picket fences. At one point in his life, he'd believed in destiny and people who were meant for each other. A young man's dreams. He no longer believed in any of that. And if what he had with Rachel was more about compatibility than love, he still appreciated her. She was smart and beautiful, and he personally knew of a dozen men who envied the hell out of him.

"So what's the holdup, Ian?" Curtis asked with a punch to his left shoulder. "You need a reason to leave the office before midnight."

A waiter approached them and handed Ian a cordless phone. "There's a call for you, Mr. McKinley."

"Now, who could that be?" Curtis joked. "We're the only ones who ever bother you at this hour, and we're all here."

Ian shrugged and moved to the window, away from the noise of the party. "Hello."

"Mr. McKinley?"

"Yes?"

"This is Detective O'Neill with the New York

City Police Department. Is Luke McKinley your son?''

Alarm shot through Ian. "Yes, he is."

"He and some of his buddies were arrested tonight for possession of marijuana."

It took a moment for the words to sink in. Disbelief washed over him. "Is he all right?"

"He's fine, sir."

"There must be some mistake. Luke has never—"

"There's no mistake, Mr. McKinley. We need you to come and pick him up." The detective gave him the address of the station and told him where to find Luke. Ian hung up, feeling as if someone had just punched him in the gut. As quickly as possible, he told Rachel everything he knew. When she offered to go with him, he asked her to stay and explain to the others that he'd had an emergency.

It took exactly twelve minutes for the cab to get him to the police station. Ian tossed a twenty at the driver and sprinted for the front door, his stomach churning. Inside, he took the elevator to the third floor. Even at this hour, the place was busy, and he got his fair share of stares as he wound his way through a maze of desks littered with coffee cups and mounds of paper. Dressed in a tuxedo, Ian was definitely the one out of place.

Detective O'Neill was on the phone when Ian stopped in front of his desk. A thin man with graying hair and skin that could use a little sunshine, he had a smoker's voice and looked as if he, too, badly needed a vacation. He put his hand over the receiver and said, "Can I help you?"

"I'm Ian McKinley. You called about my son."

"He's in the room across the hall. Go on in. I'll be right with you."

"Thank you."

The detective went back to his call. Ian wound his way across the room again, still stunned to find himself here. At the door the detective had indicated, he stopped and drew in a deep breath before entering. Relief flooded through him at the sight of Luke standing by the window with his hands jammed in his pockets. His hair, which he wore in the current style, long in front and short in back, halfway covered his eyes. His stance was defensive, his mouth set in a straight line. "Guess I messed up your party, huh?" he asked, his tone belligerent. If the boy was scared, he wasn't showing it.

"Is that what you meant to do?" Ian asked quietly, not at all sure where to go with this.

"I didn't mean to do anything." Luke shrugged, a rebel with a cause, the origins of which Ian couldn't begin to guess.

"They said you were arrested for drug possession."

Another shrug. "Big deal."

"Big deal?" Ian repeated. "Do you have any idea how serious this is?"

"It must be if you could find the time to come down here."

The verbal slap had its intended sting. "Luke, I know things have been busy lately, but—"

"Lately?" Luke interrupted with a short laugh. "You've been saying 'lately' since I was six years old. Probably before then, but I just can't remember that far back. Face it, you don't have time for anything other than work. And Rachel, of course, now that she's going to be your wife.''

The declaration was layered with bitterness. The vehemence behind it shocked Ian. Luke wasn't a big talker. And for the past few years, getting information out of him took the finesse of a secret service agent. Ian had chalked it up to teenage rebellion. Now that he thought about it, the boy had been even less communicative since he'd told Luke about his engagement to Rachel. He looked at his son now and felt as though he were seeing him for the first time in a very long while. ''I think we need to talk about this.''

''So pencil me in before your nine-thirty and I'll tell you all about how I know you wish I'd never been born.''

The anger in the boy's voice hit Ian like a brick in the face. ''Why would you say a thing like that, Luke?''

''Because it's the truth.''

''No. It's not. Son—''

''If it hadn't been for me, she wouldn't have died,'' Luke yelled. ''Don't you think I know that?''

Ian grappled for composure. ''Nobody could have prevented what happened to your mother. She had a stroke. It was one of those things no one could have predicted. How could you possibly think I would—''

''I don't know,'' he interrupted. ''Maybe because you work all the time just so you don't have to be around me.''

''Luke!'' Ian stopped, stunned. He was at a complete loss for a response. Somehow, when he hadn't been looking, something had gone terribly wrong between the two of them. Looking across at his son, part boy, part man, Ian wondered how Luke could have felt this way without his knowing. How long had his son been trying to get his attention? "Does this have something to do with my marrying Rachel?"

"I don't care who you marry. I'm sure you'll make all the time in the world for her."

Ian felt as if someone had just held a mirror in front of him. He didn't like what he saw. He thought about the party held in his honor tonight and realized what the price for that had been. He'd spent the past seventeen years trying to make sure Luke had all the things he himself had never had as a kid. He'd sent the boy off to a camp in Wyoming every summer and to Austria in the winter with his ski team. In fact, he'd given him everything he could possibly want except one thing. Time.

Maybe if he had, none of this would be happening.

Maybe if he had, he wouldn't have needed this kind of wake-up call to see what a mess he'd made of things.

Ian sank down onto the chair behind him. He raked a hand through his hair and wondered how he could have gone from such heights to such depths in one night. Luke was in trouble. And he was largely to blame. He hadn't been there for him. He had to find a way to fix this, to make up for it. He simply had to find a way.

# CHAPTER ONE

IT WAS A MONDAY morning like every other Monday morning this past month. God help her, Colby Williams did not understand the adolescent mind-set. She shot a glance at her watch, then looked at her daughter. "Baby, why can't you just wear the first outfit you had on? We're late. I've got to get to the clinic."

"Don't call me that, Mom." Lena frowned. "I'm not a baby. And the first outfit looked like dogsh—"

"Lena!" Surprised, Colby stared at her daughter. Lena didn't talk that way. At least not until recently.

Lena rolled her eyes and stomped up the steps to change for the third time that morning. "Dog poop," she called out as she went. "The first outfit looked like dog poop."

Critter, Lena's one-eared cat, pounced up the stairs behind her. From the oriental rug on the living room floor, the two dogs, Petey and Lulu, eyed Lena's ascent as if they knew it wouldn't be her last.

"You're probably right," Colby said to the pedigree-free duo, then dropped onto the oversize sage green chair next to the fireplace. She surveyed the small but cozy room with some measure of satisfaction. At least there was order in this part of her life. Bookcases lined the wall to the right of the couch, shelves filled with hardbacks she had collected since childhood. She had everything from *Beezus and Ramona,* which she had read in the fourth grade, to *Gone With The Wind,* which she had read four times and still pulled out on rainy days.

The home she and Lena had furnished and decorated together with casual, country touches was more than comfortable, but someday, Colby hoped to buy them a house big enough to have a room for her books and a bigger bedroom for Lena. She had hoped that house would be Oak Hill, an old farm outside of town, but it had sold recently, and that hope was no longer a realistic one.

From the radio on the kitchen counter, a singer twanged an appropriate tune about not dwelling on things you couldn't change. Following her advice, Colby got up and went into the kitchen, where she began putting things away, her thoughts turning to Lena. She didn't know whether to laugh or cry these days. She was a thirty-four-year-old woman. A mother. A veterinarian with a thriving practice. And she was losing control of her fifteen-year-old daughter. The worst part was, she had no idea why.

In the past several weeks, Lena's grades had dropped from almost straight As to nearly all Cs. The kid was smart. Colby knew that wasn't the problem. Lena had always been a good child. Maybe too good. Maybe Colby had been spoiled. But her relationship with her daughter had been the most fulfilling aspect of her life for so long that she couldn't imagine it any other way.

The change in Lena had seemingly happened overnight. It was as if aliens had swooped down and stolen her beautiful, fun-loving daughter, replacing her with a surlier version of herself. The kid who lived in her house looked just like Lena, sounded like Lena. But she wasn't Lena.

More than once, Colby had started to drive over to her parents' house and ask their advice on how to deal with this new side to her daughter. But she'd stopped herself each time. Samuel and Emma Williams had always been there for Lena and her. They'd helped put Colby through college and then vet school, lending a hand when Lena was a baby and Colby had been determined to stay in school. They'd been the best of parents, and she'd called on them far too often. She'd find a way to work this out on her own.

The phone rang. Tucking her shoulder-length hair behind one ear, she picked it up with a distracted "Hello."

"I know you're on your way out the door, but I've got a proposition for you."

"Does it involve convincing whoever stole my daughter to bring her back?"

Phoebe Walker laughed. "Hormones raging, huh?"

"I don't know what it is, but isn't there some kind of pill I can give her until it goes away?" Colby stretched the cord across the kitchen and picked up Lena's plate of uneaten French toast.

"You're the doctor. You ought to know."

Colby dumped the toast in the disposal and stuck the plate under the faucet, watching the syrup slide down the sink. "My expertise is in cows. They don't turn on their mothers."

Phoebe chuckled. "If it's any consolation, I think this is normal."

"It's not," Colby muttered, swiping at a water

spot on her blue cotton shirt. "So what's the proposition?"

"Well...it's an invitation. To dinner."

Colby tucked the phone under her chin and grabbed a paper towel to rectify the damage. "What kind of dinner?"

"The kind where you put on a dress, a spritz or two of perfume and leave your calf-birthing clothes at home in the closet."

"You want me to do all that just for you and Frank?" she asked, deliberately misunderstanding.

"Well—"

"That's what I thought. Thanks, but no thanks."

"Colby—"

"Don't Colby me." She slipped the plate into the dishwasher. "Have you forgotten what I told you the last time you tried to fix me up?"

"Are you going to hold that against me forever?" Phoebe asked.

"I should. You certainly deserve it."

"He wasn't that bad."

"Yeah, if your idea of a hot date is an octopus pickled in Brut."

"Oh, for Pete's sake, Colby, you're too picky!"

"And you've got too much time on your hands." As Colby's best friend, Phoebe refused to stay out of her love life, saying she had known her since the beginning of time and therefore had a vested interest in her happiness. Personally, Colby thought she should join the garden club or take up knitting, anything to relieve Phoebe's self-appointed burden of finding Colby a husband.

No matter how often they went over it, Phoebe just didn't get it. She refused to believe that a woman could be happy living her life without a man—maybe because she happened to be married to one of the last good men on earth. But Colby was walking proof that she was wrong. Colby had done the dating scene off and on over the years, thinking Lena needed a father figure. Once in a while, she'd even dated out of a true desire for companionship. But at some point, it had stopped seeming worth the trouble. The only men she ever seemed to meet were either newly divorced and neurotic or looking for a housekeeper instead of a wife.

She'd long ago decided that love rarely turned out to be anything like Hollywood depicted it. But then, she'd learned that when she'd been eighteen and too green to know better than to fall for a great-looking guy with a great-looking car who came from a different world from the one in which she'd been raised.

"Exactly who are you going to meet," Phoebe continued, "tromping around in dairy barns in waist-high rubber boots?"

"The bulls I run into there are a lot more interesting than most of the men I know."

Phoebe let out an inelegant snort.

Just then, Lena tromped back down the stairs in black military boots, her purple bombshell replaced by a tie-dyed explosion of orange, red and green that made the first outfit look tame by comparison. The streaks of purple hair, in tribute to the discarded outfit, remained. "It looks as if Lena's finally decided on the ensemble of the day," Colby said, lowering her voice. "I've got to get going. We're already late."

"Wait! You didn't answer my question. Dinner this Friday. My house. Be here."

"Phoebe—"

"I promise you won't regret it." Phoebe added a hasty goodbye and hung up before Colby could argue further. If she'd had the time, she would have called her back and given her a definite no on the spot, but Lena was already late for school and Colby had an appointment in less than twenty minutes. Turning down Phoebe's invitation would just have to wait.

TEN MINUTES LATER, Colby pulled up in front of Jefferson County High School. Built on a small rise, it was brick with classic lines, the kind of building that would never look outdated. A football stadium—impressive for a town the size of Keeling Creek—sat to the right of it.

The engine of her old Ford truck shook a bit as she put it into park. Out of habit, she leaned across the seat to give Lena a goodbye kiss on the forehead.

"Mom!" Lena strained against her door as if Colby had just come after her with a hot branding iron.

Colby sat back in her seat, her hands resting on the steering wheel. The kiss had been a reflex action, one of those things that was hard to stop when she'd been doing it for so many years. It had only been in the past several weeks that Lena had rebuffed her affection. A ridiculous lump of emotion lodged in Colby's throat. How she hated to see her daughter grow up. If this was how the young made themselves independent from their parents, then she could only wish the process was over. It was too painful to watch her daughter pull away from her day by day. "Are you coming by the clinic after school?" she asked, keeping her voice light.

Lena shook her head. "A bunch of us are going to the Dairy Queen."

It had been weeks since Lena had come by the office. Ever since she'd started school, Lena had been hightailing it to the clinic as soon as the bell rang, helping out with dog dippings and feedings, anything to be around the animals. Now, she seemed to have lost interest. Colby forced herself not to say anything, but it hurt, nonetheless. "What time will you be home, then?"

"The usual."

Colby refrained from mentioning that "the usual" had recently stretched its boundaries to anywhere between four and six o'clock. "Just be home by dinner."

A black Mercedes sedan rolled into the spot in front of them, its bumper barely missing the front end of Colby's truck.

"Oh, no!" Lena slid down in her seat.

"What is it?" Colby asked, startled.

"The new guy. Luke McKinley. Oh, my God, he's so awesome!"

Not once in fifteen-plus years had Colby ever heard such words from Lena. She'd always been a tomboy. As a child, she'd have chosen playing in the dirt over playing with dolls any day of the week. Not so long ago, boys had still been on the same level as fish bait. Colby had to admit she wished they'd stayed there. Nonetheless, she strained her neck for a glimpse of the paragon.

"I gotta go, Mom," Lena said, reserve creeping back into her voice as she opened the door and slid out of the truck.

From the back seat, Petey and Lulu barked in protest when Lena forgot to say goodbye.

Colby glanced over her shoulder at the wounded-looking pair. "So you've noticed, too, huh?" She put the truck in gear, stretching for another glimpse of the vehicle in front of her. The boy hadn't gotten out yet, and she could hardly sit here all day waiting for him. She wheeled around the Mercedes, glancing back to see her daughter lingering at the front door, no doubt waiting for Awesome Luke.

COLBY HEADED UP Main Street toward the clinic, frustrated by the twenty-five-mile-per-hour speed limit. Joe Dooley was in front of her in his farm-use pickup, an old Chevy that had seen its fortieth birthday and then some. A firm believer that laws were laws, Joe was known for keeping the needle of his speedometer safely on twenty-four.

Telling herself to stop fretting and enjoy the early September morning, Colby waved at Ruby Lynch, who was sweeping the sidewalk in front of Thurman's Hardware. Keeling Creek was one of the few towns that had so far been bypassed by the fast-food chains and super shopping stores. Small family-run businesses still comprised the chamber of commerce listing, and Colby had to admit she liked it that way.

Just past Thurman's was Tinker's Drug and Soda Fountain. Then the First Bank of Jefferson County. Across the street was Kirk's Department Store. Then Cutter's Grocery. And next to it was The Dippety-Do Hair Salon, where she went for a monthly trim and the current dose of gossip that came with it.

Just ahead sat the county courthouse, where Euell Clemens and Oat Henley, local farmers, stood talking, waving at her as she drove by. In two more blocks she reached the Dairy Queen, where Joe Dooley turned off, no doubt making a pit stop for his morning sausage biscuit. Colby waved and sped up a little, only to spot the town maintenance crew up ahead, doing some kind of repair work that had brought the morning traffic to a halt. She glanced at her watch and sighed. She was late. She was about to be later.

She rolled down her window and waved at Ellis Holbrook, who was holding the Stop sign at the front of the line of cars. He stepped back to her truck. "Mornin', Doc."

"Good morning, Ellis. Think this is going to take long?"

Ellis shook his head and pushed back his Jefferson County High Eagles cap, wiping the sweat from his forehead with the back of his hand. "Shouldn't be but a few more minutes. I'd tell you to back up, but you've got too many cars behind you now."

"I understand," she said. "How's Toby?"

Ellis reached through the window to pet Petey, then turned his attention to Lulu, who was impatiently waiting her turn. "He's fine. That was a nasty cut on his leg, but it seems to be healin' up real nice."

"He's lucky he didn't lose it, getting tangled up in that barbed wire."

"I wager he'll steer clear of it from now on. I'd better get back up there. We'll have you movin' in a few minutes, Doc."

"Thanks, Ellis." Colby rolled up her window, thumped her thumbs on the steering wheel, then flicked on the radio. WKKI announced the First Baptist Church's plans for a bake sale on Court Street this coming Saturday morning and then promised to be right back with a new tune from Reba McEntire after a few messages from its sponsors.

This was Colby's favorite time of year, when summer wound down and took the heat with it, leaving cool mornings and warm days in its place. Traditionally, it was a time of year that she and Lena had always enjoyed together, shopping for back-to-school clothes and supplies, registering for school and buying textbooks. But this year had been different. Lena had merely endured each of those outings, as if she couldn't wait for them to be over.

Reba came on, as promised, and Colby's fingers followed the rhythm on the center of the steering wheel while she wondered if she'd somehow taken a wrong turn in her efforts to make up for Lena's never having had a father. Being a good parent was the most important thing in her life. She'd always felt driven to make up for Doug's choice not to be there for Lena.

In most ways that counted, she hadn't let Doug be the stumbling block in her life that he could have been. She'd done exactly what she'd always planned to do. Gotten her college degree and gone to vet school. Opened the first female-owned practice in Keeling Creek. In fact, since Dr. Granger had retired two years ago, she was the only vet in town. All of that in spite of being a single mother at nineteen. All of that in spite of Doug Jamison's refusal to take any responsibility for the daughter they had created together.

Doug had, however, left singe marks on her soul where relationships were concerned. That was what

Phoebe didn't understand. Colby had given up trying to make her see that even if she ever met someone worth the effort, she wasn't sure she could put her heart on the chopping block again. She'd had it pulverized once in her life, and that was quite enough for her.

SOME TWENTY MINUTES later, Colby pulled into the parking lot of the Jefferson County Animal Clinic. She pulled the truck into her usual spot and hopped out. Petey and Lulu, used to the routine, waited for her to raise the seat so they could get out. She had found them three years ago at a gas station in Grayson County, where someone had apparently dropped them off. Viewing her as their savior, they wanted to go everywhere she went and hated to be left at home.

She hurried across the full parking lot toward the brick building enclosed by a white rail fence with red-and-white impatiens circling each post. She rushed through the front door with Petey and Lulu at her heels, all three of them nearly tripping over Don Juan, who lay stretched out like a welcome mat at the clinic entrance. Don Juan was one of several animals who actually lived at the clinic, pets with problems that made people decide they no longer wanted them. Colby didn't have the heart to take them to the animal shelter, so they ended up making the clinic their home. She and Lena had christened him Don Juan because all the female dogs loved him and followed him around like lovesick señoritas. Even the cats adored him.

For the past two years, Colby had been trying to raise enough private funds to build a noneuthanasia shelter where pets could stay until someone adopted them. Unfortunately, she was still a long way from her goal, and, meanwhile, her collection of animal dependents was growing. Which was just how it would have to be for a while. She gave Don Juan a quick rub behind the ears. "We're going to have to find you another spot, lover boy."

The waiting room was full to overflowing with pets and their owners, several of whom gave Colby and her entourage welcoming smiles. The others simply looked annoyed at her tardiness. She didn't blame them. "Sorry, everybody. I'll try to make up for lost time here."

Luckily, her two assistants, Laura and Ruth-Ann, already had the examining rooms ready, a petrified-looking dachshund in one, a bored-looking Saint Bernard in the other. "We took it as far as we could without you, Dr. Williams," Laura said, smiling. "I've checked little Slim Jim for worms, and Ruth-Ann is in the back cleaning up. George there had decided not to go to the bathroom since his surgery last Friday, but when she pressed on his bladder, he changed his mind."

"Just another day at the office," Colby said, shaking her head and smiling. Laura chuckled and handed her the white jacket hanging on the coatrack behind the door.

It was almost one o'clock before she finally got a breather. Her last patient had just left when Stacey Renick came through the examining room door with a can of Coke held out in front of her. At twenty, Stacey had worked at the clinic since graduating from high school, and hers was the smiling face customers were always assured of seeing when they walked through the front door. Colby had often wished she could clone her. Stacey's only character flaw was that, she, too, had the matchmaking bug and was always reporting in on recent "hunk sightings."

"A receptionist's job is never done," Stacey said. "Here. You look like you could use this."

Colby took the soda from her. "Thanks. I could."

Petey padded in and plopped down on the floor beside Stacey. Laura and Ruth-Ann had gone to lunch, and the clinic was empty except for the two of them and a couple of part-time girls in the back who did dippings and clippings.

"You've barely looked up since you got here." Stacey leaned against the doorjamb, taking a sip of her own Coke.

"I can't seem to get Lena out the door these days."

"I take it you two are still at odds?"

Shaking her head, Colby ran her thumb across the condensation on the side of the can. "It's as if she's become a different child or something."

Stacey tilted her head. "Maybe that's just it. She's not a child anymore. Could there be a guy in the picture?"

"She did mention someone this morning. Some new boy at school. But that's the first time I've heard her say anything. I don't know what to do."

"Kids go through a stage a week at that age," Stacey said, waving a hand.

Colby grinned. "I'm surprised you can remember that far back."

The doorbell dinged outside the examining room. Stacey stuck her head around the corner and said,

"Be right with you." She turned back to Colby and mouthed a whistle, followed by a silent "Wow!"

"What is it?"

"*Major* hunk sighting!" Stacey stage-whispered before heading back to the front desk. Petey followed, tail wagging. Colby heard her greeting someone in a far more welcoming tone than even good-natured Stacey usually managed.

Colby put the Coke on the counter behind her and began cleaning up the instruments she'd used that morning.

"Dr. Williams?"

She swung around, finding herself face-to-face with the hunk in question. The man nearly filled the doorway in both height and breadth. He was dressed in faded blue jeans, a crisp-looking cotton shirt and leather loafers. His hair was dark and thick with a few flecks of gray at the sides. His eyes, in startling contrast, were blue. And his face...

He had the kind of striking good looks that made women stop and stare and turned their voices to squeaks.

"May I help you?" she asked, a little shaken by how much he reminded her of Doug.

"Your sign out front said you don't take appointments again until three o'clock, but she's got a thorn in her paw," the man said in an accent so neutral she knew he wasn't from around here. "Could you take a look?"

It was only then that Colby noticed the black Lab standing by his side, her right front paw suspended in midair. Uncharacteristically rattled, Colby cleared her throat and knelt down in front of the dog, smoothing a hand across its head. "What's her name?"

"U-2."

She looked up at him, trying not to smile. "U-2?"

The man nodded. "Like the rock group. She's my son's dog, but he's in school, so I went ahead and brought her in."

Colby nodded, gently picking up the dog's paw. She carefully turned it over and pulled the pads back to see where the thorn had lodged. It was stuck in the middle, fairly deep. U-2 whimpered and pulled her paw back.

"Sorry, girl. Let's get that out for you." She stood up and added in a calming voice, "I'm going to put you up on the table now. Easy, girl."

She bent over to pick up the dog just as the man leaned forward and said, "I'll get her." Their heads collided with a *thwunk*. Colby saw a few stars. They both stood up and began to apologize at the same time.

"It's all right." Colby held up one hand and rubbed her forehead with the other, amused. "I'll get her. I'm used to it. Really."

The man stepped back, nodding in surrender. She picked up the dog and placed her on the table.

"Sit, U-2," he said in a kind but authoritative voice.

U-2 sat, still dangling her right paw in front of her and keeping her sorrowful gaze on her owner.

"She's a little wary of being here," he said. "She got beaten up by a boxer once and had to stay at the hospital for a few nights."

"It's all right, U-2. I'll fix you up and send you right back home."

U-2's pink tongue lolled to one side, and the look on her face could have been one of gratitude.

"She thanks you," the man said.

"I think you're right." Colby smiled. She had a habit of judging people by the way they treated their animals. She had to admit he was making the A-list so far. When he'd first entered the room, her guard had gone up. Which was ridiculous. He really wasn't anything like Doug. It was just the confident way he carried himself, the way his clothes proclaimed him comfortable with status, the fact that he obviously came from a very different place than Keeling Creek. Maybe it was the situation with Lena that had her making comparisons.

Focusing on the task at hand, she went to the cabinet behind the table and pulled out a pair of tweezers and an antibiotic dressing. Holding U-2's paw with one hand, she extracted the thorn while the man rubbed the dog's head and kept her calm.

Colby doused the wound with peroxide. "There," she said. "I'll wrap it up and give you an antibiotic for her. She'll need to take the entire course. We don't want to let an infection set in."

"You're very good with animals," the man said, still rubbing the dog's head. "But then, why wouldn't you be? You're a vet."

She smiled and put the tweezers in a jar of disinfectant, saying over her shoulder, "Comes with the territory. She seems to like you pretty well, too."

"I can't do any wrong with U-2."

"That's the great thing about pets." Colby unrolled a package of gauze and snipped off a strip. She began wrapping it around the still-tender paw, her touch light.

"Wish the same were true of kids," the man said.

"You and me both." She looked up. "You must have a teenager in your house, too."

"As a matter of fact, I do. Don't tell me you're old enough to have one yourself."

She wrapped the tape around the gauze and made sure U-2 couldn't work it lose too easily. "I've been told she's probably just in a stage, but if it doesn't pass soon, I'll look plenty old enough."

"I know what you mean."

"There." Colby stepped back. "That should take care of it. Keep an eye on it. Change the gauze daily. And if you notice any redness, swelling or heat in the paw, bring her back in immediately."

"I'll do that." He lifted the dog down from the table, setting her gently on the floor and patting her head. "Good girl."

U-2 looked up at her owner, her tail thumping on the floor.

"She should be fine." Colby wiped her hands on her jacket, annoyed with herself for not letting her gaze quite meet his. She'd been off-kilter since the moment he'd walked in the door.

"I'm Ian McKinley, by the way." He stuck out his right hand. "We've only been in town for a couple of weeks."

"Welcome to Keeling Creek, Mr. McKinley," she said, gripping his hand with her own and wondering why that name sounded familiar. "I hope you and your family will like it here."

"I hope so, too." He let go of her hand, though his gaze stayed fixed on her for a second longer than was comfortable. He glanced away, then backed toward the door. "Come on, U-2. Let's get you home so you can put your paw up for a while."

Colby smiled and followed them through the doorway. "Don't forget to make sure she takes the full seven days' worth of medicine."

"I won't." He raised his hand in a wave before stopping at the front desk to pay Stacey, who beamed a thousand-watt smile his way. He pulled out his wallet and smiled back at her, apparently oblivious to the admiration in the young woman's eyes.

Colby went back into the examining room, wondering about the man and what he was doing in Keeling Creek. She heard Stacey tell him goodbye, the familiarity of his name still nagging at her.

The front door dinged. She waited another second or two to make sure he was gone before she went back out front.

"Was he incredible or what?" Stacey asked from behind the computer.

Colby ignored her dreamy-eyed receptionist and went to the door, where she saw Ian McKinley getting into the same black Mercedes she had seen at the high school that morning.

And then it came to her. Ian McKinley was Awesome Luke's father.

## CHAPTER TWO

COLBY WILLIAMS WAS the first person Ian McKinley had met in Keeling Creek who hadn't looked at him as if he'd just stepped out of a flying saucer. She'd been polite but hadn't asked him the questions he'd been getting from almost everyone he met. He supposed it was natural for people to be curious. He was the outsider, after all. And this was a small place. Very small. He still hadn't gotten used to that, or to the quietness. Police sirens were background noise in New York City. He couldn't remember hearing one since he and Luke had moved here two weeks ago.

Flicking on his blinker, Ian turned off Main Street onto 152 and headed out of town.

So far, U-2 was the only one who had happily adjusted to the move. She loved it here. Her tail had barely stopped wagging since they'd first let her out of the car.

Luke was another matter altogether. He hated it here and made no secret of the fact.

There were times when Ian still had trouble believing he'd actually packed up everything and left the city. It was difficult to put into words what had happened to him the night Luke had been arrested. But he'd had his eyes opened in a big way. Luke had always been an exemplary student, had never gotten into any trouble. Seeing him in the police station had shaken Ian to the core. But Luke's accusations of his deliberately not spending time with him had been the biggest curve of all. It sickened him to think his son had been suffering those kinds of feelings and he hadn't realized it. After that night, Ian had known only that he wanted to make up for not being the father he had always intended to be.

Judge Watley Townsend had taken Luke's case under advisement, putting him on one year's probation with the admonition that if he got into similar trouble again, the incident would go on his record. After the hearing, Ian had met with the judge in his chambers. Not sure how his request would be received, he had said, "Your Honor, with your permission, I'd like to move Luke out of the city for his senior year in high school. I've bought a home in a small town in Virginia where I think he'll be exposed to a different way of life."

The judge had peered at him over the rims of his tortoiseshell glasses and said, "With all due respect, sir, what makes you think Luke's surroundings will have any effect on his behavior?"

Ian cleared his throat before saying, "I grew up in one of the roughest parts of this city, but when I was about Luke's age, I spent some time in Virginia at a football camp. Needless to say, things were a little different in that part of the country. It made an impression on me I've never forgotten. I realize that temptation exists everywhere, but I believe a change of scenery would be good for my son. And I've realized recently that I've let my work get in the way of spending as much time with Luke as I should have. I've decided to take a one-year leave of absence so we can spend some time together.''

The judge's eyebrows rose above his glasses. ''I take it you're a single parent, Mr. McKinley?''

''Yes, I am.''

The judge sat for several long moments, thrumming his fingers on the top of his desk. ''If you think your time and attention can make a difference in your son's life and where he goes from here, then I'm not going to stand in your way. I'll grant permission for him to leave the state under the terms of his probation. But I'll want him to report to an officer there on a regular basis.''

If Ian had been pleased by the judge's response, no one else had been. His partners at CCI were less than thrilled at the prospect of his taking a leave of absence. Rachel had been even less so. Since they had only been engaged for a few weeks, she had been understandably upset at putting things on hold for a year. He'd explained to her how important it was to him to try to get his relationship with Luke back on track, but she'd accused him of overreacting, telling him that the situation wasn't as dire as he perceived it to be. Nevertheless, Ian saw it as a turning point— and he had to believe it had happened for a reason. Luke was almost a grown man, and Ian felt as if this might be his only chance to right some of his wrongs before the boy moved out on his own.

When Rachel had realized that he wasn't going to change his mind, she had reluctantly agreed to postpone their wedding plans. He had reassured her that nothing was going to change between them. Once school was over, he would come back to New York and pick up his life where he'd left off. And if he was lucky, maybe by then he would have mended the rift between him and his son.

MABEL ATKINS WAS waiting at the back door when Ian parked his car at the rear of the house a few minutes later. "Did they get you all fixed up, Miss U-2?" she asked, wiping her hands on her apron.

"She'll be fine." Ian followed Mabel into the kitchen and smiled at the way U-2's name rolled off the tongue of his plump, flour-dusted housekeeper.

"Well, that's certainly good news," she said, giving the dog an affectionate pat on the head.

Ian had known Mabel little more than a week, but he already felt as if he'd known her forever. She was one of those people who made no attempt to hide herself from the world. She was blunt and to the point and took great pride in her work. Although she claimed to have once been more than five feet tall, she now stood an inch or two under that height and frequently complained that she would soon need a step stool to wash the dishes. She wore her hair in a kinky perm and had a penchant for chocolate malt balls, which she kept in the cabinet above the stove, high enough to make her think twice about pulling them out.

Ian had spent his first few days in Keeling Creek thinking he could do everything on his own. He and Luke could manage. But when the laundry had started to pile up and the dishes in the kitchen sink multiplied exponentially, he'd given up and gone in search of a housekeeper. They'd been in town less than a week when he'd asked Maude Cutter at Cutter's Grocery if she knew of anyone who would be interested in the job. She'd said Mabel was just the

woman he was looking for. And she'd been right.
Mabel fit in as if she'd always been here. She'd taken
a firm hand with Luke, too, informing him of kitchen
rules on her first day in the house. Luke needed that
kind of structure. It was something Ian hadn't been
around enough to give him.

U-2 managed an exaggerated limp over to her
bowl where Mabel had a dish full of leftover chicken
waiting for her. No dog could be a bigger ham when
a little sympathy could be conjured up.

"Now if she'll just stay out of the blackberry
bushes," Ian said.

"She's lived in the city all her life," Mabel replied
in the dog's defense. "Been running around like a
wild thing set free since you got here. She'll learn
soon enough."

"Let's hope so," Ian said doubtfully. Only a few
days before, they'd found her in the creek behind the
house, hip deep in mud and howling like a hyena.

"Did you get to meet Colby?" Mabel asked.

"Dr. Williams?"

"Funny as that sounds to me, yes." The older
woman chuckled, stirring the contents of the pot simmering on top of the stove. "Known her since she
was knee-high to a grasshopper. Still can't believe
she's old enough to be called doctor."

"She seemed very good." Ian opened the refrigerator and pulled out the pitcher of lemonade Mabel
had just made that morning. Colby Williams wasn't
what he would have envisioned in a small-town veterinarian. She was attractive. Very attractive. She
was different from the women he knew in New York.
Her style was casual, a blue cotton shirt tucked into
slim-fitting Levi's, her straight blond hair pulled back

in a ponytail, emphasizing a face with nice cheekbones and expressive green eyes.

"Even as a little girl, she wanted to be the first female vet in town," Mabel said. "And she was. We're lucky to have her."

Intrigued, Ian said, "She mentioned having a daughter. How old is she?"

Mabel ladled out a bowl of soup from the pot on the stove and set it in front of him. "A little younger than Luke, I believe. Colby raised her by herself. Nice kid, so she must have done a good job."

"She's not married?" The question was out before he even realized he was going to ask it.

Mabel turned to look at him, both eyebrows disappearing beneath gray bangs. "As a matter of fact, she's not."

Ian swallowed a spoonful of soup and burned his mouth in the process.

"Careful there." Mabel eyed him with a thoughtful look on her face. "It's hot."

"You're right, it is." He washed away the sting with the lemonade and wondered at the glint in his housekeeper's eye. "Good, though."

"Glad you like it. After my Thomas was gone, there was just me, and food doesn't taste nearly as good if you're not cooking it with someone other than yourself in mind. It's a real pleasure to have you and Luke to cook for."

"Thomas was a lucky man. You'll spoil us if we're not careful," Ian said with a smile. He knew what she meant about eating alone. When Sherry had first died, he thought he, too, would die of loneliness. Knowing that the small, helpless infant who was his son had needed him had been the one thing that kept him going. Despite what Luke thought, Ian didn't know what he would have done without him.

Mabel dropped the soup ladle into the sink and turned to give him an assessing look. "That's all right by me. I know you said you and Luke would only be here until he finished high school, but if you and Colby happened to hit it off, you might not want to go back to the big city."

He nearly choked on his soup. Mabel scurried across the kitchen floor, whacking him on the back. "You all right, Mr. McKinley?"

Once he'd gotten his coughing under control, he nodded and sat back, wiping his eyes with his napkin. Not wanting her to get any ideas, he said, "If you remember, Mabel, I mentioned that I recently got engaged."

"Oh, yes, you did, didn't you?" the older woman said with a deadpan expression.

"She's coming down this weekend for a visit. On Saturday."

"I didn't mean to be making any untoward suggestions, Mr. McKinley," Mabel said hastily. "And if your intended is planning a visit, then I'd better quit yakking and get this house in tip-top order, hadn't I?" She left him in the kitchen to finish his soup alone.

Ian put his dishes in the sink and went out on the front porch of the two-story brick house. U-2 followed him, sprawling on the floor beside him. With his glass of lemonade in one hand, Ian leaned against a porch column that was noticeably in need of paint and stared out at the oak trees lining the driveway as far as the eye could see. Oak Hill was a beautiful place. There was no denying that. But a lot like Tara must have looked to Scarlett after the war.

The farm had been built in the late 1800s. It had been used to raise both cattle and horses. But that had been a couple of decades ago, and the place had become run-down in the past few years.

Ian had asked his Manhattan real estate agent to find Luke and him a place that might need some work. The thought of that had appealed to him, even though he didn't own a toolbox and had next to zero experience in carpentry work. Coming here had been his decision, but going from a sixteen-hour workday to a one-year leave of absence was like being forced to a halt halfway through a marathon. He'd consoled himself with the thought that he might spend part of his time making improvements to the house. And he'd also hoped that might be something he and Luke could do together. A common ground.

The agent had found him what he'd been looking for. But photographs of the place hadn't revealed just how much work the farm needed. The barn was in dire need of paint, and a good number of boards needed replacing, not to mention the roof. The fields beside and behind the house looked as if they hadn't been mowed in years. But the house itself was the most daunting of all, with peeling wallpaper, floors in need of refinishing and bathtubs that needed re-sealing. There wasn't a room that didn't need something done to it. He definitely had his work cut out for him.

In the distance, he heard the school bus roll to a stop and then move on down the road. A few minutes later, Luke appeared at the top of the driveway, his book bag slung over one shoulder, his baseball cap and loose, baggy clothes marking him as the city kid he was. His expression was set and unsmiling until he spotted U-2 wobbling across the yard toward him, limping on her bandaged paw.

Luke looked up at Ian, a worried frown on his face. "What happened to her?"

"She had a thorn in her paw. I took her to see the vet. She got it out and gave her something for infection."

Luke plopped down on the ground and wrestled with the ecstatic dog for a couple of minutes while Ian watched them with a catch in his heart. The boy's love for the dog was obvious, and he had to admit he wished Luke exhibited as much affection for him. The boy had been even less communicative than usual since they'd arrived here at the end of August, and Ian could only hope patience would eventually pay off. He knew the changes weren't easy for Luke. A new school. New kids. But schoolwork had always come easily to him. He was smart and, if anything, often bored by his classes. He had been one of the top soccer players at his school in the city, but Jefferson County High didn't have a soccer team, and so far, he'd shown no interest in any other sports.

Luke got up and bounded up the porch steps past Ian without saying a word.

"How was school today?" Ian asked.

Luke turned around at the screen door, his gaze on U-2. "Great," he said, his tone less than convincing.

"It can't be that bad. Surely, there are some kids there that you like."

"They're all too wild for me."

Despite his intelligence and athletic ability, Luke

had a shy side that made it difficult for him to make new friends. Ian ignored his sarcasm. "I started chipping away the old paint on the back porch this morning. I thought maybe you'd like to help this weekend."

Luke kicked at a twig on the wood floor. "You're the one who wanted to come out here and play farmer. I didn't want any part of this. Believe me, if I'd known you were going to bring me to this no-action town, I'd have asked that judge for jail time instead. There wouldn't have been much difference, anyway." He disappeared inside the house, the screen door slapping closed behind him.

"Luke!" Ian called, starting after him, then deciding against it. He dropped down on the top step of the porch. He had known that nothing about this was going to be easy. So far, he'd been right. He would just have to take things one step at a time. His relationship with Luke hadn't fallen apart overnight, and it was certainly going to take longer than that to fix it.

AT FIVE MINUTES past five that afternoon, Colby stepped through the front door of the Dippety-Do Salon for her monthly trim. Her basic, shoulder-length cut required little more effort than a nip off the ends.

A bell dinged, announcing her arrival. A waiting area held several chairs and a couple of couches. Magazines littered the coffee table, *GQ* and *International Male* among them. Louise Mason, the owner of the salon, theorized that her customers didn't come here to read about the latest tuna casserole recipe or how to paint their kitchen in less than five hours. Here, women were free to gossip, ogle men's magazines and generally let their hair down, so to speak. Judging from the fact that the place rarely had an empty chair, Louise apparently had the right idea.

"Hey, Colby. You're right on time as usual," Louise said, approaching the desk. At five feet ten inches tall, Louise often joked that the only thing that kept her from being a professional model was her looks.

"Hi, Louise. Looks like you're keeping busy."

The woman threw a glance at the shop behind her, where hair dryers buzzed and the smell of permanent solution hung in the air. "If it weren't for vanity, I'd be in the poorhouse."

Colby smiled and followed the heavyset woman to the back, where she shampooed her hair and applied an apple-scented conditioner. When she was finished, Louise wrapped a towel around Colby's head and led her back to her station at the front of the shop.

"So what are we gonna do today, honey?" Louise asked after Colby had settled in the chair.

Colby met her hopeful gaze in the mirror. "Just the usual."

"How'd I know you were gonna say that?"

Louise had been trying to talk her into going the way of big hair for years. "Men like a lotta hair," she'd said more times than Colby could count. "You walk into a nightclub and you gotta compete with all those Dolly Parton types. You can't just let yourself blend into the woodwork."

Like Phoebe, Louise ranked Colby's lack of interest in the dating scene right up there with self-administered haircuts and chipped nail polish. It simply wasn't acceptable. Smiling, Colby said, "I have to give you credit for trying, Louise."

"Now, Colby, you know I think you're one of the prettiest gals around. I'd just like to give you a little pizzazz, that's all."

Pizzazz, as Louise defined it, meant frosting and a perm. "Thank you, Louise, but—"

"I know. I know. You like it the way it is. I just thought with that new man in town, you might have changed your mind. Let's see, what's his name? McKlellan, Mc—" Louise snapped her fingers, searching for the name.

"McKinley," Ellen Ann Edwards offered up from the next station. "Ian McKinley."

There was that name again.

"I shoulda known you'd have it down pat," Louise said to the other woman with a chuckle.

"Well, why not? It's not as if someone like that moves to Keeling Creek every day of the week," Ellen Ann declared.

"You're right about that," Louise agreed. "I saw him at the DMV last week. I was gettin' my county sticker and he was in front of me. Didn't even mind spendin' my lunch hour standing in line. That is one fine-looking man."

Ellen Ann's nod of agreement carried with it a look of wistfulness. She added another permanent rod to her customer's hair. "I saw him out jogging on the way to work yesterday. It was all I could do to keep my eyes on the road."

"Oh, that's good, Ellen Ann. All we need is for you to run over him."

Ellen Ann rolled her eyes at Louise. "Somebody said he's from New York."

"City?" Louise asked.

Ellen Ann nodded again.

"So what's he doin' here, you think?"

"Beats me, but I'm not complaining."

"Me, neither. If I didn't already have me a fella, I'd go knock on his door and introduce myself. He's got a boy at the high school, but nobody's seen hide nor hair of a wife."

"Now what would you do with a city slicker like him, Louise?" the customer in Ellen Ann's chair asked with a giggle.

"I could think of one or two things," Louise replied with a wink and a nod.

The remark brought on a fit of giggles from the women around them, all of whom had been listening to the conversation.

The woman in Ellen Ann's chair waved the copy of the *National Tattler* she had been reading. "He might find himself a wife here. I just read a story about a prince from some small country on the other side of the world. He came over here on a visit and met some little gal from Kentucky. Married her and took her back to his kingdom."

"Sounds like paradise," Colby said, deciding then and there that the women of Keeling Creek had been seriously deprived for too long. All this fuss over one man moving to town. Okay, so he was good-looking. He'd seemed nice enough at the clinic earlier, but from all appearances, he'd fit in here like the proverbial square peg in a round hole.

"What I want to know," Louise went on, "is what

Colby here thinks of him. After all, she's the one who's free and single.''

"And not likely to forget it," Colby chimed in.

"I can see why you're choosy, hon," Louise sympathized. "The bachelor pickin's are pretty slim around here. That's why you better get in on this one. Cindy Stoneway was in this morning trying to figure out a way to meet him. Last I heard, she'd decided on a flat tire in front of his house."

"Tell her I said good luck next time she's in," Colby said.

Louise brushed the loose hair off Colby's plastic cape. "Just don't hold your breath waitin' for another one like this to land in Keeling Creek. Might as well be holdin' out for aliens."

"I won't, Louise." Colby shook her head and smiled. "I won't."

BY THE TIME Friday arrived, Colby was feeling a little shopworn. The last thing she wanted to do was go to Phoebe and Frank's for dinner. But Phoebe had called that afternoon for a confirmation. The clinic had been swamped, and Colby, having no time to argue, had given her a hasty, "I guess so." She would have looked forward to having dinner alone with the two of them. It would have given her a chance to talk to them about Lena. But she knew Phoebe, and she'd bet her last dollar there would be another man sitting across the dinner table from her. A new lawyer from Frank's firm, or someone Frank had met playing golf, or the brother of someone Phoebe did aerobics with. Going to Phoebe's house had become a lot like facing a firing squad. The only bright spot in the evening was that once she'd given the man the thumbs-down, she'd have a couple of months' reprieve before Phoebe got brave enough to try it again.

With two children and a farm which she practically ran herself, Phoebe should have better things to do, anyway.

Going into the bathroom, Colby ran herself a bath, then sank into the bubbles with a sigh, rationalizing that if her first love had been a man like Frank, she wouldn't be such a cynic on the subject. But he hadn't. Doug had been nothing like Frank.

She had met him during her first week at the University of Virginia. He'd been the complete opposite of the boys she'd dated in high school and competed with at local 4-H fairs. City-smooth, he had grown up in Philadelphia, where his family name was written in blue ink on the social register.

They'd met one afternoon when he had nearly run over her in his red Porsche at a crosswalk in front of her dorm. He'd been speeding and barely able to avoid plowing right into her. Angered by his carelessness, she'd been prepared to give him an earful. But he'd gotten out of the car, apologizing profusely. His dark good looks and polished manners had caught her off guard, and she had reluctantly forgiven him.

The obvious differences between the two of them had made her both wary of him and attracted to him at the same time. He'd asked her out to dinner to prove that he was really sorry, but she turned him down, telling herself she'd be better off staying away from him. He was persistent, though, and one night when he nearly knocked a hole in her dorm window trying to get her attention, she pushed aside her doubts and went downstairs to meet him.

From that night on, they spent all their time together. He treated her well, took her to dinner at fancy places and met her at the library every afternoon. When they had ended up making love in his room one night after a party where they had both had a little too much to drink, it had seemed a natural, if unplanned, extension of where they were headed. Vowing not to let it happen again without protection, Colby had convinced herself there was nothing to worry about.

She attributed her first missed period to stress. She took her studies seriously, and she'd been whacked out over a couple of classes in which she was determined to make As in spite of the teachers' tough reputations. Doug had been moody with her lately, accusing her of caring more about school than she did him. He didn't look at school the same way she did, but then, regardless of what kind of grades he made, he would still have a whopper of a trust fund waiting for him when he turned twenty-five. It was flattering to have one of the most sought-after guys on campus wanting to spend all his time with her, but she was determined to make the grades she needed to keep her scholarship and get her into the well-known vet school at Virginia Tech.

When the second month went by and there was still no sign of her period, Colby panicked. With a sick feeling inside her, she made a doctor's appointment without telling Doug. Maybe she'd known deep down what his reaction would be.

The test came back positive. She spent three days agonizing over what to do, still keeping the secret to herself. She had finally told Doug one night in her room. He'd gotten up from the bed and gone to the window, staring out at the campus for several long minutes before turning to her and saying, "There's only one thing to do. It's not too late."

She'd already thought about that, but it wasn't a solution she was comfortable with. "I don't know if I want to do that."

"We don't have a choice," he said, his voice rising. "My parents would cut me off flat if they found out."

She'd asked him to leave then, needing to be by herself. Somehow, he hadn't said the things she had hoped he would say, even though she wasn't sure what they were. The decision tore at her for days. In the end, she decided that Doug was right. She would only be nineteen when the baby was born. How could she possibly finish school? What would her parents say? She could only imagine their disappointment.

She got as far as the clinic's examining-room table before the reality of what she was about to do hit her. Although she couldn't yet feel the baby's physical presence, something had changed within her the moment she'd learned of its existence. How could she do away with something so precious and fragile? Her reasons suddenly seemed selfish and shallow.

Doug was outside in the waiting room when she ran from the office. He sprinted after her, calling out for her to wait. She stopped at the corner of the street, her breath coming fast and uneven.

"What happened?" he asked, taking her by the shoulders.

"I couldn't do it."

"You can't back out now," he said, looking incredulous.

"I was only thinking about myself. About my life. Not about the baby. Lots of people have children and still get through school."

Doug stepped back, his expression closed. "We agreed."

"No. I won't do it, Doug. I'm sorry. I just can't."

They drove back to the dorm in silence. He dropped her off without saying goodbye. She didn't hear from him for the rest of the week. When she went back to the dorm on Friday after class, there was a note from him on the door.

From that moment on, she'd been on her own. Looking back, she supposed she'd thought he would come around, own up to his share of the responsibility. But he hadn't. And she'd eventually realized that it would have been a mistake for the two of them to try to make a go of it for the baby's sake. After the initial shock, her parents had been anxious to do whatever they could to help. She got an apartment off campus, determined to be as independent as she could. She had run into Doug a few times during her pregnancy. Their meetings were awkward, and it was obvious he couldn't wait to get away. Colby wondered what she had ever seen in him. She hoped he would be very happy with his Porsche and his trust fund.

The following year, he had transferred to another college, closer to Philadelphia, without ever trying to see Lena. For the first few years of her daughter's life, Colby had agonized over what to tell her about her father when she asked, as she inevitably would. And she had. Colby had never intended to lie to her, but when Lena had taken her initial answers of "Your daddy went away" to mean he had gone to heaven, she had never corrected that impression. Somehow, it seemed a lot more palatable than the truth.

That was something she hoped Lena would never have to know.

Glancing at the watch she had left on the side of the tub, Colby got out and dried off. She'd lingered in the bath too long, and now she would have to rush to be on time. But then, that was what she got for dwelling on things better left in the past.

## CHAPTER THREE

AFTER FIXING LENA a hurried dinner and leaving it on the kitchen table, Colby went to the bottom of the stairs and called her name.

No answer. The bass from her stereo beat a tattoo on the floor beneath Colby's feet. She ran up the steps and stopped in her daughter's doorway. "Lena, honey, I'm late. Are you sure you have a ride to the game?"

Lena leaned over and turned down the volume. "Yeah. Millie Mitchell's mom is taking us," she said in the same sullen tone that had been there for the past month.

"You'll be home by eleven-thirty?"

Lena nodded without raising her gaze from the magazine in front of her.

It was getting to the point where Lena spent more time at her best friend's house than she did her own. Trying to ignore her own bruised feelings, Colby said, "I'll see you tonight, then."

A few minutes later, she backed out of the driveway and headed toward Phoebe's place, some five miles outside of town. How long would this go on? She'd asked Lena over and over what was wrong, only to be given a hostile-sounding, "Nothing, Mom."

Colby missed her daughter, the child she'd loved.

She felt as though someone had stolen her best friend. And she didn't know how to get her back.

At the Walkers' turnoff, she put on her blinker and swung onto the road that led to their farm. She loved it out here. Most of Jefferson County lay in a bowl of land beneath a ring of the Blue Ridge Mountains. Now, just before sunset, they really did look blue. Colby's eventual goal was to buy a place outside of town with plenty of land. She'd been interested in Oak Hill, the farm that bordered the Walkers' place, for years. When she'd learned that it had been sold a few weeks ago, she'd been more than a little disappointed.

Pulling up in front of the house, Colby got out and knocked at the front door. A few seconds later, Phoebe opened it and greeted her with a hug.

"You're here," she said. "And on time, too. No last-minute calls to make?"

"I even left my calf-birthing clothes in the trunk."

"So you do own a dress." Phoebe gave her a long look and a whistle. "Is that new?"

"No."

"That shade of blue has always been your color. You look great."

"So do you," Colby said, nodding at Phoebe's coral-colored pantsuit and chunky gold jewelry. With her dark hair layered around the bottom so that it always seemed to be moving, Phoebe was an attractive woman. She had dark brown eyes that were incapable of hiding her thoughts.

"Thanks," she said. "Come on into the kitchen and help me check on things."

"Where's Frank?"

"He's getting ready. He'll be down in a few minutes."

"And where's Mr. Right?"

Phoebe shot her a look of innocent surprise. "What makes you think there is one?"

"I'm fairly certain there isn't. But when was the last time you invited me to dinner without trying to convince me otherwise?"

"You're entirely too cynical for your age, Colby Williams."

"Hey, I earned my stripes in the trenches."

"So you've been out with a few duds. Big deal."

"A few?" Colby folded her arms across her chest and rolled her eyes. "Let's run through some of your more memorable setups. There was Harvey Matthison, who brought his mother on our first date. And then there was Tip LaPrade, who slipped a prenuptial agreement under my dessert plate while I was in the ladies' room. And, oh yes, there was Dr. Payne, who washed his hands nineteen times between the time he picked me up and dropped me off—"

"All right, all right," Phoebe grumbled. "Several. But that doesn't mean they're all like that."

"I wish you would just accept the fact that I'm not going to kiss a thousand toads on the minute chance that I might eventually find a prince."

"If you call this one a toad, I will officially resign from all matchmaking duties."

"Is that a promise?" Colby asked hopefully.

"Only if you give him a real chance. The problem is, you're looking for faults from the first moment you meet a man."

"I hate to disillusion you, but when they're as obvious as the San Andreas, they're not that hard to spot."

The doorbell sounded from the hallway. Colby heard Frank's voice and then another male voice that sounded somehow familiar.

"Oh good, he's here," Phoebe said, wiping her hands on a kitchen towel.

Biting back a resigned sigh, Colby leaned against the counter and yearned for the evening to be over.

Frank appeared in the doorway. "Hello, ladies," he said, stepping aside while the man behind him moved into the kitchen. Surprise and a tidal wave of embarrassment washed over Colby. Ian McKinley. What was he doing here? She glanced at her best friend, who was looking extraordinarily pleased with herself.

"Colby?"

She realized that Frank was speaking to her. "I— yes. I'm sorry," she said.

"This is our new neighbor, Ian McKinley. Ian, this is Colby Williams, our local veterinarian and Phoebe's best friend."

"Former best friend," Colby said in a voice only Phoebe could hear.

The new neighbor moved across the floor and shook Colby's hand. He smiled down at her, something in his expression indicating that he had been caught off guard by this as much as she had. "Hello again, Dr. Williams. We've already met," he said to Phoebe and Frank. "She fixed up my son's dog for me."

"Please, call me Colby."

"Only if you call me Ian."

"Ian it is. How is U-2?" she asked, forcing her

gaze to remain level with his and trying not to look as thrown by this as she felt.

"Playing it up for all it's worth."

She smiled in spite of her discomfort. "She deserves a little extra pampering."

"How about a drink?" Frank suggested. "We can all go into the den."

A few minutes later, Colby sat in a chair with a glass of red wine in her hand, plotting an appropriate payback for Phoebe. Nothing horrible enough came to mind. Of all people for her friend to have fixed her up with. To think she'd met him earlier today and hadn't known...Of course, he probably thought she *had* known. This was getting more amusing by the moment.

"Isn't that right, Colby?" Phoebe asked.

"I'm sorry?" Colby had no idea where the conversation had gone.

"I was just telling Ian that you'd been interested in Oak Hill for years."

"Oh. So you're the one who bought it? It's a beautiful farm, Ian."

"It is. Needs some work, but I hope to get it in shape. Virginia's a beautiful state. It's a full one-eighty from New York City."

"I'm sure. What are you planning to do with Oak Hill?"

"Right now my main objective is to get the place in presentable condition. I'm afraid I don't know very much about farming."

"Oh, that's too bad," she said, thinking it an injustice for some New York City tycoon who wouldn't know an alfalfa field from a turnip patch to get the farm she'd dreamed about buying herself someday.

"I need to check on dinner," Phoebe said, getting up and heading for the kitchen. "You stay put and enjoy your wine, Colby. I'll be right back."

Colby got up from her chair and forced a smile at the two men. "I'll go give her a hand. She's far too thoughtful to ask for help."

In the kitchen, Colby thumped her glass down on the counter. "Phoebe, I may have to kill you for this."

Phoebe looked up from the vegetable lasagna she was removing from the oven. "Now, Colby, don't tell me he's not drop-dead gorgeous."

"I was too embarrassed to notice."

"Why on earth are you embarrassed?"

"Because!" she said, throwing up her hands in exasperation.

Phoebe rolled her eyes. "Didn't I once hear you say that I'd found the last good man left on earth? I might have just found another one for you."

"Oh, Phoebe! He was in my office earlier this week. He probably thinks I knew about this then."

"We're all adults here. What difference does it make?"

"This is the last time, Phoebe Walker," Colby stated. "I'm not ever coming to your house for dinner again unless you sign a legally binding statement that there will be no potential husbands sitting on the other side of the table."

Phoebe placed the lasagna on the stove top with a frustrated look on her face. "Once the single women in this county get wind of this man, he's a goner. I was just trying to get you in the starting gate a little ahead of the others.''

"You make me sound like some kind of desperate old racehorse about to be put out to pasture.''

"I've never thought of you as desperate,'' Phoebe protested. "I just hate to see you alone.''

"I'm not alone. I have my daughter,'' she said.

"That's not the same.''

Frank appeared in the doorway, interrupting them. ''Dinner about ready?''

"We were just about to bring the food into the dining room,'' Phoebe said with a bright smile.

Colby grabbed a couple of bowls and followed Frank out of the kitchen, feeling every bit like an old racehorse.

COLBY ENDED UP seated beside Ian at dinner, with Phoebe and Frank directly across from them. Once they had all filled their plates, Phoebe dimmed the chandelier above the dining room table. And although the ambience hinted a little too strongly at romance, Colby was grateful that she didn't have to look directly at Ian for the entire night.

By this point, she had accepted the humor in the situation. Maybe it was kind of funny that she'd met the man on Monday without any idea that he was the main ingredient in Phoebe's matchmaker soup.

Their seats were close enough that they kept bumping elbows. Every time his jacket sleeve brushed her bare arm, she felt as though she'd encountered a force field of electricity. She ended up sitting poker straight in her chair, keeping her elbows tucked tightly at her side.

Phoebe smiled at her every now and then, imploring her with her eyes to loosen up.

If it had been anyone else sitting beside her, maybe she would have after a few sips of wine. But there had been something about meeting Ian McKinley the first time that had stayed with her, brought up thoughts of Doug and the past. He was handsome in the same too-good-to-be-true way. He drove an expensive car, and he obviously had enough money to buy the farm she had hoped to eventually buy. He simply wasn't her type, and she was surprised at Phoebe for not realizing that.

To his credit, he made every attempt to make the meal as painless as possible, asking about her practice, mentioning that Mabel Atkins had told him she was the first female vet the town had ever had.

"From first grade on," Phoebe chimed in, "Colby was the one with career aspirations. I was the one who didn't understand what was so wrong with Betty Crocker."

They all laughed.

"Frank has already told me that you're the one who keeps this place running while he practices law. With two children, I would think that takes quite a bit of effort," Ian said graciously.

"Well, I don't have much time for bonbons," Phoebe admitted, obviously pleased by the compliment.

"How do you know Mabel?" Colby asked Ian, taking a sip of her wine.

"She came to my rescue when I mistakenly thought I could do my own housekeeping. Luke and I were nearly drowning in laundry when she agreed to take over."

Colby smiled, doubting that a man like him would be able to locate the On button of a washing machine, much less wash his own clothes. "You're in good hands with Mabel."

"I've already gained five pounds since we moved here," he said, patting his stomach. "She claims the two of us need fattening up. I'm trying to outsmart her by adding another mile or two to my run every day, but I think she's on to me."

"Mabel's known for her fried chicken at church dinners, so you're right. You are in trouble," Colby said.

Again, they all laughed, and Colby found herself reluctantly wanting to know more about him. "Are you a big runner?"

"I try to do six miles a day."

"You must be in good shape," she said.

"I'm not sure I could run six yards right now," Frank said with a chagrined smile.

"I'm not that fast," Ian said modestly. "But I enjoy it. I started running as a stress reliever during the day. It was a good way to clear my head."

"What kind of work do you do?" Colby asked.

"I'm a stockbroker for a company called CCI in Manhattan."

Phoebe looked impressed. "From Wall Street to Keeling Creek. That's quite a leap. So how did you end up—"

Colby's beeper went off, interrupting Phoebe's question.

"Oops. Sorry about that. I'd better call and see what's up." Colby slid back her chair and stood up. Ian stood, too. She headed for the kitchen phone, telling herself that just because a man had the good manners to stand when a woman left the room in an age when most men had forgotten how didn't mean his character was without flaw.

She called her answering service, then came back into the dining room and said, "There's a problem with one of the cows at Pasley's Dairy. I have to go. I'm sorry to leave so early. It was nice to see you again, Ian. Say hello to U-2 and Mabel for me."

"I'll do that," he said.

"If you don't mind, I'll change clothes in the bath off your garage."

"Sure," Phoebe said, looking positively stricken by the interruption.

"Thanks for the dinner," Colby said, before letting herself out the front door, feeling strangely regretful that she had to leave.

THE HORRIBLE NOISE coming from the driveway told Ian that as glad as she must have been to leave, Dr. Colby Williams wasn't going anywhere anytime soon. They'd heard her engine grind for the third time when he stood up and said, "I'll go see if I can give her a hand."

Frank started to get up as well. "I'll go with—"

"That's all right, Frank," Phoebe said. "Ian probably knows all about cars. You can help me with the dishes."

Frank sat back down, while Ian tried to appear oblivious to Phoebe's not-so-subtle tactics.

It had been apparent to him from the moment he arrived tonight what was going on. When the Walkers had called a few days ago and invited him for dinner, he'd accepted, thinking he should make an effort to get to know his neighbors. If he'd known

what they'd had in mind, he'd have saved both Dr.
Williams and himself the discomfort of their matchmaking. Once he'd arrived, he hadn't wanted to embarrass them or their friend by telling them that he
was engaged. He knew Phoebe had talked to Mabel
earlier in the week about inviting him to dinner, and
he had a feeling his not-so-innocent housekeeper had
conveniently neglected to mention that he had a fiancée.

He stepped out into the Indian summer night, the
air warm and fresh smelling. He still hadn't gotten
used to the simple pleasure to be found in breathing
in air that hadn't been tainted with carbon monoxide.

From the driveway came the sound of the engine
grinding again. He crossed the driveway, and at the
truck door, bent down and tapped on the window.

Colby's head shot up, sheer frustration etched on
her face. He didn't think he'd ever seen a woman
look that desperate. The window lowered with a
slight squeak. "I know that was awkward, but was I
that bad?"

She sat back in her seat, failing in her attempt to
look surprised by the question. "No. I just—" she
began, then stopped, looking chagrined.

"Their intentions were good. They obviously
think the world of you."

She shook her head. "What's that old saying?
'With friends like that, who needs enemies?'"

He laughed then. She did, too, and he found he
liked the sound of it. The awkwardness hanging between them eased, and it was then that he realized
how good laughter felt. Laughing wasn't something
he did too often. "If you'll pop the hood, I'll take a

look. I don't know much about engines, but it sounds like your starter's bad. Got a flashlight?''

She rummaged through the glove compartment, then handed him the light. She popped the latch, and he said, "Give it another try.''

She did, and he spotted the problem. "You're going to need a new one,'' he called out from around the hood.

"Great,'' he heard her say. She got out of the truck and came around to the front.

He straightened and lowered the hood, pressing it closed. He noticed then that a pair of blue coveralls had replaced her dress. "I'll be glad to give you a ride.''

"I can't ask that of you,'' she said, not quite meeting his eyes.

"I don't mind. Let me just go thank the Walkers. I'll be right back.''

Ian went inside and explained what had happened to Phoebe and Frank. Phoebe was anything but disappointed by his departure. She looked so clearly happy that he wondered if she'd ruined the starter herself. He said good-night and went back outside, where the other victim of Phoebe's matchmaking was unloading some things from the back of her truck.

"Would you like to put that stuff in the trunk?''

"Yes, please.'' He stuck the key in the lock and opened the lid. She dropped her bag inside. He started to close it just as she reached inside again. He grabbed her arm and jerked it back, barely in time to prevent the lid from slamming on it.

They both stood in shock for a second or two while his hand still gripped her arm. She took a hasty step back. "Thanks. I forgot to put my keys in the bag."

"No problem. But I'd hate to be the person responsible for putting the town's only vet out of commission."

She smiled, rubbing her arm where his fingers had just been.

He opened her door, and she slid inside the car. To his surprise, he found himself noticing that she had a very nice shape beneath the faded coveralls. Wondering if it had been a mistake to offer his taxi services, he went around and got in on his side. "You'll have to tell me where to go."

"Take a right out of the driveway. It's about ten miles from here."

Ian backed up and headed away from the house. They'd just reached the main road when she said, "I'm really sorry about Phoebe's lack of tact."

"It's all right." From the sound of it, Phoebe Walker was in a lot of trouble with her friend. Strangely enough, he hadn't minded the evening, setup or not. The Walkers were nice people. "If it makes you feel any better, I won't be pestering you. I knew as soon as I saw your face tonight that you had nothing to do with it."

"I didn't mean to be rude," she said quickly. "Now I'm really embarrassed."

"There's no reason to be," he said, glancing at her with another unexpected jolt of appreciation. She was an undeniably pretty woman. He started to tell her that he was engaged. The moment was right, but the words somehow wouldn't come and he wasn't sure why. Except that he didn't remember ever meeting a woman quite like Colby Williams. "It was a nice dinner. And I'm glad to have the chance to get to know my neighbors better.''

Silence lingered between them for a few moments before she said, ''What made you move here from New York?''

''My son needed a change of pace. We'll just be here for his senior year,'' he said, not wanting to elaborate further. The last thing he wanted to do was put a black mark on the boy in the eyes of the community before he'd had a chance to prove himself.

''Oh,'' she said. ''My daughter mentioned him. He's made quite an impression on the girls at Jefferson High.''

Glad to hear that maybe things weren't as awful as Luke wanted him to believe, Ian said, ''How old is your daughter?''

''Fifteen going on thirty.''

Ian smiled.

''She's a sophomore, but she was young for her class. It seems like yesterday that she was just learning how to walk and—'' She stopped, her expression troubled.

Wondering if her relationship with her daughter might have problems of its own, he said, ''It's a tough age. They grow up before we know it.''

''Yes, they do,'' she said, sounding resigned. ''I'm just not ready to admit it.''

He drove for a few minutes, then flipped on his signal light when she directed him to take the next left-hand turnoff. ''Go on down to the barn. The lights should be on.''

He stopped just outside the open barn door. A man in blue overalls and a red-checkered flannel shirt trotted out to greet them. "Hurry, Doc. She's having a lot of trouble."

Colby got out of the car, grabbed her bag and ran after the man who had disappeared inside the barn. Ian sat there for a minute, thinking about her. She was a nice woman, easy to talk to, intelligent. And apparently able to handle with grace and good humor what was an uncomfortable situation for both of them.

He couldn't believe he'd nearly slammed her arm in the trunk. That would have topped the evening off nicely. He thought about those few moments when his fingers had encircled her wrist. The contact had shocked him every bit as much as it apparently had her. He recalled now that she had very small wrists and hands. She was a petite woman. Probably not more than five-three. But somehow it wasn't something he'd noticed about her initially. Maybe because there was something about her that exuded strength and self-sufficiency.

He got out of the Mercedes and made his way toward the barn. There was only one light on outside, making it hard to see where he was going. Farm smells permeated the air, a combination of hay and manure and a fresh country breeze. Cows mooed in the fields beyond the barn. A stretch of mud lay between the gravel-covered driveway and the entrance to the barn. With no way to go around it, he waded through, his leather shoes squishing in the mire. He knew then how the city mouse must have felt visiting the country mouse.

Inside the barn, he stopped outside the stall. A black-and-white cow lay stretched out on the straw-covered floor. She was straining heavily, and her eyes looked wild and pained. Sympathy for her plight stabbed through him.

Colby looked up from where she was pulling supplies from her bag and spotted him standing there. "Ian, this is Harry Pasley. Harry, Ian McKinley. He's new in town. My truck broke down, so he gave me a ride out here."

"Nice to meet you, Mr. McKinley," Harry said, his hands tucked inside bib overalls, his weathered face concerned.

"It's nice to meet you, too," Ian said.

"Would you like a pair of coveralls to put on over those clothes?"

Ian looked down at his pants, the bottoms of which were now rimmed in mud. "Oh, no, that's all right. It'll come out in the wash."

Ian watched while Colby pulled on two plastic gloves that reached all the way to her shoulder.

The cow's straining ceased, and she lay still. "Is she all right?" he asked.

"She's taking a breather. Let's see what we have here," she said, reaching her right arm inside the cow. A few seconds passed before she said, "There's the tail. Definitely a breech, Harry."

Ian watched as a frown crossed her face. "Uh-oh. There's a nose," she said. "We've got a second one on board."

Just then, the cow began straining again. Colby went still. She looked up at him and said, "When she's working, I rest. When I'm working, she rests."

"Oh. I see."

"Have you ever seen a delivery before?" she asked.

He'd never even been around a cow before, and

certainly not one in this condition. The closest he'd gotten was a city petting zoo, and that had been years ago, when Luke was five or six. "Ah, no, I haven't. Is there anything I can do to help?"

"If she tries to get up," Harry said, "I might need your help getting her back down."

"Sure," Ian said, wanting to ask how they could possibly get what looked like an eight-hundred-pound cow to lie down if she wanted to get up. But he didn't, not wanting to sound like any more of a greenhorn than he felt.

When the cow stopped straining again, Colby said, "Okay, my turn."

She wedged her left hand inside the cow and began to push forward. Without looking up, she said, "What I'll try to do is push this little guy up enough that I can straighten his hind legs out. In a normal birth he would have come out front hooves first."

Ian watched in amazement as she slowly pushed the calf forward. When the cow began to strain again, she stopped and held the position. It was a long, slow process. He couldn't take his eyes off the scene. He'd never witnessed anything like it in his life.

Here was this petite woman up to her shoulders in work that he couldn't imagine too many men having the fortitude to do. Watching her, Ian marveled at how at ease she was, approaching the situation matter-of-factly. But when she spoke, her voice was low and easy, soothing, and he could see that she, too, sympathized with the cow's pain.

The front of her coveralls was now splattered with blood, and a strand of her hair clung to the side of her face. He subdued an unexpected urge to smooth it back for her.

After what seemed like forever, she said, "Okay. I've got the back hooves out. We're on the right track now."

Ian stood to the side of the cow, his arms folded across his chest, the drama of the situation making him tense. The process went on for a good while longer, with the cow pushing and Colby helping to pull the calf forward until it finally slid onto the straw in a heap.

"There you go," Colby said, smiling. "You were doing your best not to join us out here, weren't you?"

Harry picked up the calf and moved it to the side of its mother, placing it back on the straw. Wonder assaulted Ian. He thought about his own son's birth and how incredible it had been to hold the tiny body in his arms. He recalled the instantaneous love he'd felt for him, and his chest ached with the memory of it and a yearning for things to be right with Luke again.

"Let's get the other one," Colby said, reaching back inside the cow.

When the second calf emerged onto the straw with Colby's help, the same sense of wonder washed over him. This one was noticeably smaller, its eyes round and startled. Ian's heart contracted.

"That's it, girl. We're almost there," Colby said to the mother cow, looking up at Ian and adding, "I just need to make sure there's not a third."

"She could have another one?" he asked, incredulous.

"Oh, yes. I've had it happen."

Amazed, Ian hoped for the cow's sake that it didn't happen now.

A minute or so later, Colby said, "Looks like that's it." She sat back on her heels and patted the cow's side, her face alight with satisfaction and what looked like the same kind of relief he felt for the animal. "You're all finished."

Ian bent down and stroked the cow's head. He'd never really thought about it, but he would have imagined this sort of thing became routine for a veterinarian. But the look on Colby's face suggested it was just as gratifying to her now as it would have been the first time she'd helped with a delivery.

The second calf raised its head and let out a half-hearted bleat. Colby laughed. "Looks like she arrived with an appetite."

Harry Pasley bent over to give the cow a pat on the side. "You did good, girl. You, too, Doc. But then you always do."

The cow weakly reached around to swipe the closest calf with her tongue. If the birth of the first one had amazed Ian, the second seemed like a miracle.

"These three have some bonding to do." Colby wiped her damp forehead on her shoulder, then looked up at Ian and smiled. "Thanks for being so patient."

Ian didn't remember a smile ever affecting him quite the way hers did in that moment. It made him feel as if he'd witnessed something incredibly special. He thought of the business he'd put his life into over the past seventeen years and couldn't remember one incident during that time that had made him feel this way.

It was crazy but true.

And he had no idea what to make of that.

# CHAPTER FOUR

COLBY FINISHED CLEANING Tilly up and gave her a shot to fight infection. "Let me know if they have any problems, Harry."

"I'll do that, Doc. Thank you for coming out so late. I really appreciate it."

"No problem." She pulled a fresh pair of coveralls from her bag and said, "Could I use your office to change into these?"

"Sure thing," Harry said.

Alone, Colby wondered what Ian had thought of being here. She was certain this wasn't his cup of tea, but throughout the past few hours, she'd been surprised by the range of emotions she'd seen on his face: sympathy, interest, amazement. After she'd changed, she left the office and returned to the stall, where Harry was still standing. "Good night," she said. "Call me if you need me."

"'Night, Doc Williams," Harry said. "Thanks again."

Outside, Colby found Ian staring up at the night sky. "Sorry to keep you waiting," she said, coming up behind him and glancing at her watch. "It's after midnight. I didn't realize it was that late."

He turned around, his gaze finding hers. "I'm in no hurry. How did you do that?" he asked, pointing at the coveralls.

"I keep an extra pair in my bag. I don't think you'd want me riding in your car with the other ones on," she said.

"It wouldn't have mattered," he said, shrugging.

"Are you sure you don't mind taking me home? I could ask Harry—"

"Of course not," Ian said. "Come on, get in. You're probably tired after all that work."

Giving in, she got inside the car and gave him directions to her house.

He put the car in reverse and backed up, cutting the wheel to the right.

"I wouldn't turn around in the driveway if I were—" Before she could finish, the two back tires of the car dropped off the gravel driveway. "Uh-oh. I should have mentioned that there's mud back there. You can't see it in the dark."

"Shouldn't be any problem." He put the car in drive and gave it some gas. The back wheels made a whirr-hissing sound, spinning uselessly.

"I could go get Harry," Colby offered. "He could give us a pull with his tractor."

"That's okay," Ian said, opening the car door.

"Watch out!" she warned just as he slid out of the car and was mired up to his shins in mud.

Silhouetted in the light shining from the car's interior, he looked at the ground where his two feet were currently held prisoner. He pulled one free, then the other. They made a loud, sucking noise.

Laughter bubbled up in Colby's throat. She clapped her hand over her mouth to stop it, but failed miserably.

Ian ducked his head back inside, a chagrined look

on his face. "Guess I should have taken Mr. Pasley up on those coveralls, huh?"

She did her best to keep a straight face, but the tears leaking from the corners of her eyes gave her away.

"Can you slip across and get behind the wheel? I don't recommend getting out of the car."

"Sure." Colby's cheeks hurt with the effort of trying not to laugh.

He made his way to the back of the car, mud slurping at his shoes with each step. "I'll let you know when I start to push," he called out. "Give it the gas when I say go."

"Okay."

She adjusted the seat so her feet could reach the pedals. A few seconds later, he said, "All right. Hit it."

She pushed the pedal. The car groaned and protested, the back tires whirring again.

She stopped, and he called out, "One more time."

They repeated the process, only this time the tires spun once, then the car shot out of the mud like a launched rocket.

Back on the gravel, Colby put the car in park and got out.

Harry came out of the barn. "What happened?"

"We got stuck," she said.

"I could have pulled you out."

"It only took two pushes," she began, and then stopped when Ian stepped back into the light shining from the barn.

She stared at him in disbelief. "Oh, no!"

"It splattered," he said, wiping a hand across the side of his mud-covered face.

Harry chuckled. "I'll say."

Colby couldn't hold back her laughter any longer. The sophisticated New Yorker beside whom she'd sat at dinner earlier that evening was now covered in mud, head to toe. "I'm sorry," she said, trying to stop. "It's not funny. Really. It isn't."

"No. Go right ahead. I deserve it," he said, his smile broader now.

"How about those coveralls?" Harry offered. "I've got a hose inside the barn if you'd like to rinse off."

"I think I'll take you up on them this time," Ian said, disappearing inside the barn with a grinning Harry.

Colby waited outside, drying her eyes with the back of her hand. At least the man had a sense of humor. She thought about Doug and the comparisons she had made between the two. When she and Doug had started dating, she'd brought him home one weekend to meet her parents. She'd taken him out to the Bower farm, where she'd worked part time in high school, doing odd jobs. She had tried to teach Doug how to milk one of the cows, and when he'd been less than gentle at the task, the cow had planted a hind hoof beneath his chin. From then on, Doug had done a poor job of hiding his eagerness to leave Keeling Creek. She'd often thought that was the point at which she should have seen there was no future for the two of them. The Doug she had known would not have laughed about what had happened here tonight.

Harry and Ian reappeared. Ian was wearing a pair of old blue coveralls that would have sold *Progres-*

*sive Farmer* a record number of copies had he been wearing them on one of their covers.

He had apparently taken Harry up on the use of his hose, too. His hair was wet, and the mud was no longer evident on his face and hands.

"Sure you trust me to drive you home?" he asked with a sheepish grin.

"Of course," she said with a straight face.

Shaking his head, Harry waved good-night and went back inside the barn.

Ian threw his discarded clothes in the trunk, and they both got into the car. Their gazes caught and held for a second before they both started laughing again.

When she finally stopped, Colby wiped her eyes and said, "I'm really sorry about all this."

"Hey, it's not your fault. I'm the one who backed into the mud and then insisted on playing Superman."

She chuckled again. "Yeah, but I should have warned you."

"I'm a little bit like U-2. I might have to bumble my way through a few mishaps before I get the hang of country life."

"That could have happened to anyone."

"Right," he said, looking skeptical. "Thanks for trying to save my pride, but I already left it in tatters back there in the barnyard."

Colby smiled. "You've been a good sport to-night."

"You're the one who did all the work," he said as they headed down the driveway. "That was pretty amazing in there. Are twins uncommon?"

"Not really. With the hormones they're giving the

cows these days, the odds are increased. Unfortunately, the little girl will probably be sterile. She won't be of much use to Harry.''

Ian frowned. "Meaning?''

"He'll sell her to the stockyard.''

"Oh. That's too bad,'' he said, sounding more than a little bothered by the thought.

"That's one part of my job I don't think I'll ever get used to. Farming is a business. Feed costs money. Farmers like Harry value their animals, but they can't afford to be sentimental.''

"I guess not.'' He paused and said, "You were great in there.''

The offhand compliment pleased her. "Thanks. So, you'd never seen anything like that?''

He shot her a sideways smile. "I'm city born and bred. We don't have too many cows in Manhattan.''

"So how did you end up in Keeling Creek?''

"I had a Realtor looking in this part of the state.''

"It's a long way from New York. In more ways than one.''

"I think I pretty much found that out tonight.''

She watched him for a moment, and then, realizing she was staring, quickly turned her gaze back to the road. It had been a strange night, yet she felt more relaxed than she had in ages. She couldn't remember the last time she had laughed so much. Even if it had been at Ian's expense, she had the impression he really hadn't minded. Although she wouldn't admit it to Phoebe in a million years, she had actually enjoyed his company.

Ian turned the vehicle into her driveway, braking to a stop just beyond the porch light. Colby reached into the back seat for her bag, then turned and said,

"Well, thank you for the ride. And for waiting around for me. I'm really sorry about the mud."

"No problem. I actually learned a few things tonight. If you need any help getting your truck—"

"Oh, no. Thanks. I'll get a tow truck out there tomorrow. You've already gone way beyond the call of duty for someone duped by the local matchmakers."

Ian smiled, and Colby couldn't help noticing that he had a memorable one. The kind that reaches the eyes and transforms them.

They studied each other for a second too long, saying nothing in a moment of unexpected awareness. Colby looked away first, climbing out of the car and ducking back to say, "Well, thanks again. Good night."

"Good night," he said, then waved and drove away.

Colby watched his taillights disappear down the street, surprised to find herself sorry that the night was over.

IAN HAD BEEN on the phone with Curtis Morgan for a full two hours on Saturday morning when the other man finally said, "Well, that should bring you up to date on the past few days, anyway."

"Thanks, Curtis. Sounds like things are pretty crazy around there."

"Are they ever any other way?" the other man asked, a smile in his voice. "I still can't believe you walked away from all this. Aren't you missing the hell out of this place?"

"It's only till the end of the school year," Ian said, strangely unable to say that he was missing it. So far, he didn't at all. But then that was probably because he'd been overdue for a vacation. He'd be missing it before long.

"A year must seem like forever in a place like that. Not a whole lot going on, I'll bet. Not when you're used to the life you led here."

"It's different, that's for sure."

"You deserve a father-of-the-year award for what you're doing."

Ian couldn't have disagreed with his friend more. Judging from his success with Luke so far, that was the last thing he would qualify for. The two of them talked on for a while longer before Ian hung up.

Even though he was on leave, he felt obligated to keep himself apprised of what was going on. He turned his attention to the computer screen in front of him and worked for a while, checking stock prices through his modem. With fax machines, telephones and electronic mail, he could do practically everything he would have done in his office on Wall Street.

He glanced out the window to the side of his desk, where the huge old maple tree had begun to take on the tint of fall. The view here was a lot better. And it was a hell of a lot more peaceful. For now, at least, he would let himself enjoy that. Soon enough, he'd be back in the city where the trees were rare and the noise omnipresent.

The sun had stretched full tilt across his desk when he glanced at his watch. Almost noon. Rachel would be here any minute. Even though the trip had been planned since before he'd moved here, he almost wished she wasn't coming now. Which was ridiculous because he hadn't seen her in almost three weeks.

Ian turned his chair toward the window again and thought about Colby Williams. No doubt she'd thought him a first-class buffoon last night. He couldn't have looked any more convincing as an outsider had he been trying for an Academy Award.

After he'd dropped her off, he'd driven home, wondering why he had never gotten around to telling her he was engaged. Maybe because some part of him had been intrigued by her. And he had enjoyed himself more than he had in a long time. The realization shook him more than a little.

The doorbell rang, interrupting his thoughts. Ian left his study and went out into the front hall. Rachel stood on the porch, dressed in a black pantsuit and a red silk blouse, looking as out of place in the countryside as a polar bear in Arizona.

"Ian." She stepped forward and put her arms around his neck. "God, I've missed you."

She pressed her lips against his. He wrapped his arms around her waist and pulled her to him, seeking a connection that would put him back on track. Her perfume was familiar, as was the feel of her, and he told himself he had done the right thing in asking her to marry him. Rachel was part of his real life. The life he had created here was just temporary. Rachel represented all the things he would go back to when the year was over. And go back, he would.

COLBY SPENT SATURDAY morning at the clinic. Things were busy, and she didn't see her last patient until after two o'clock that afternoon. She'd called Granger's Tow Service and asked them to pick up her truck and take it to the service shop to have the starter repaired. They'd done so, and someone had dropped it back off shortly after noon.

On Sunday morning, she and Lena went to church, a weekly ritual. Growing up, Colby had been part of the youth group of Keeling Creek First Baptist, going on youth retreats to other churches and summer bus trips to Busch Gardens in Williamsburg. Now, Lena was doing the same things. It was the kind of small, close-knit church where everyone knew everyone else, and there was a sense of family among the members.

She and Lena sat in the second row with Colby's parents, both of whom were actively involved in the church's social life, organizing such events as summer Bible school and monthly breakfasts in the fellowship hall where the men cooked for the women. They were good people with strong roots in the community, well liked and respected. The only rough points in her relationship with them had come when she was trying to get through school with Lena. They had wanted to help, and out of guilt or pride, she had been determined to do as much as she could on her own. They had let her flounder even though, as a parent herself, she knew it had hurt them to do so.

After the services, she lingered at the door with her mother while her father and Lena chatted with the preacher. The sight of her purple-haired daughter nestled in the crook of her grandfather's arm warmed Colby inside, and at the same time, brought forth a surge of regret for the closeness with Lena she seemed to have lost.

"Things aren't any better with you two, I take it?"

Emma Williams asked, placing a sympathetic hand on Colby's shoulder.

She turned her gaze back to her mother and tried not to look worried. "I've tried to talk to her, but she won't open up. I keep telling myself it will blow over."

"More than likely it will. You had a rebellious streak of your own, you know," Emma said with a smile.

"I remember," Colby confessed. "But I don't think it ever really affected my relationship with you or Daddy."

"No. Thankfully, it didn't," Emma admitted. "But all children are different."

Colby shook her head. "I'm beginning to wonder if I'm doing something wrong, if maybe I'm just not a very good mother."

"Now you stop that, dear," Emma admonished her. "You're a wonderful mother. You know how proud your father and I are of you for the way you've handled things."

"Thank you, Mom," Colby said, somehow needing to hear the words today.

Emma squeezed Colby's shoulder. "You made a mistake at a very young age," she said, her voice softening. "And you didn't take the easy way out. You made a life for yourself and that child. I know there were times when you must have wondered what it would be like not to have all that responsibility. To be free to do what you wanted to do."

Colby gave her mother a grateful smile. "You know I could never have done it without you and Dad."

"Oh, yes, you would have. I know you well

enough to be sure of that," her mother said with pride in her voice. "Maybe Lena could spend the afternoon with us. You go be good to yourself."

Colby sent a glance at her daughter, who was laughing at something the preacher had said. "I'm sure she'd like that."

Samuel and Lena waved goodbye to the preacher and moved across the lawn toward Colby and Emma. "What do you say I take my three favorite ladies over to Libbie's for some lunch?" Samuel called out when they were a few yards away.

Lena's relaxed demeanor disappeared behind the sullen facade she'd been wearing for the past few weeks. As much as Colby would have liked to go, it would be good for Lena to spend some time alone with her grandparents. "You three go on. I've got a few things to do at home, Daddy."

"You sure, honey?"

She nodded and smiled her most convincing smile.

"All right, then. We'll bring the punkin home later," he said, ruffling Lena's hair.

"We'll have her home by dinner," Emma promised.

"Have a good time, honey." Colby waved as the three of them headed to her parents' car. But Lena didn't answer. She merely tucked herself closer inside the curve of her grandfather's arm while Colby watched them drive away, a dull ache deep inside her.

BACK AT THE HOUSE, Colby straightened up, then put in a load of laundry. She rarely went to the clinic on Sunday, since she had part-time help who came in to feed the animals on the weekend. After turning on the washing machine, she made her way into the kitchen and stared at the items lining the pantry shelves. Macaroni. Tomato soup. Black olives. Fat-free cookies.

Critter sidled against the back of her legs, letting out a soft meow.

Colby looked down at her and sighed. "I know. Kind of lonely around here, isn't it?"

Critter answered with another meow.

She reached down and picked her up, tucking the animal under her chin. The cat purred like a lawn mower. Petey and Lulu lay under the kitchen table, looking across at her with sleepy eyes. "I guess in a few years, it'll be just the four of us, huh?"

Petey groaned in protest and rolled over on his back, his paws in the air.

"I know how you feel." She considered her own question for a moment. In the past, she hadn't allowed herself to dwell on what life would be like after Lena grew up and left home. She'd meant it when she'd told Phoebe that she was happy with the way things were. Her life was full. She didn't need a man to make it complete.

But would the house always be this quiet once Lena moved away?

She thought about Ian McKinley and wondered if he felt the same way about his son leaving home. But then, a man like that probably had enough female companionship to ensure that he never got lonely.

She was being silly. Lena wouldn't be going to college for another two years. That was a long time away.

The phone rang, mercifully diverting Colby's

thoughts. She picked up the receiver with her free hand and managed a hello just as the cat swatted it with her paw.

"I want all the details. Every single one," Phoebe demanded, not bothering with a greeting.

"You're just now getting around to it?" Colby asked in mock surprise.

"We left at the crack of dawn yesterday to take Frank's mother to see her sister. We didn't get back until an hour ago, or you can bet I'd already have called."

"No doubt," Colby said while Critter continued to torture the phone cord.

"Well?"

"Well, nothing. If I were smart, I'd disown you as a friend."

"You're not still mad at me, are you?" Phoebe cajoled.

"I should be."

"I'll admit that, but can't you just give me the details anyway?"

"You're impossible." Colby had never been able to stay mad at Phoebe for long. Not even in the fifth grade, when she had told Ricky Peters that Colby stuffed her bra. "Besides, he's only going to be here for a year. You forgot to figure that into your perfect-for-Colby equation."

"A year!" Phoebe said, sounding as if she couldn't believe it. "Well, maybe you could change his mind," she added, rallying.

"Phoebe—"

"So, what happened after you left here?"

"He watched me deliver twin calves and then took me home," she said, leaving out the part about the mud bath. Even now, the thought of it made her smile.

"That's all?" Phoebe asked, her disappointment evident.

"That's all," she said, not about to give her friend more bait than that.

"You've been out of commission for too long—" Phoebe broke off and shouted her son's name. "Oh, shoot, Colby. I'll have to call you back. Jacob's hanging by his knees on top of the swing set. Gotta run."

Glad to be spared Phoebe's inquisition, she untangled Critter's paw from the phone cord and set her on the floor.

Throughout the church service that morning, she had thought about Friday night. Despite Phoebe's meddling, the night had been full of surprises. Ian had been more than gracious about the whole thing, considering that he'd been set up and all but forced into driving her out to Pasley's when her truck had broken down. On top of that, he'd ended up ruining what she was sure had been some very expensive clothes. Maybe she would bake him a pie as a thank-you. Baking was something she enjoyed when she had the time. There was a certain pleasure to be had in creating something from scratch, and over the years, she'd gotten pretty good at it. Imagining the gleeful look on Phoebe's face if she found out, she almost nixed the idea. But deciding she would go crazy if she didn't occupy her mind and hands with something this afternoon, she went to the pantry and began pulling flour and sugar from the shelves. From the back porch, she retrieved some of the red Delicious apples she'd bought yesterday afternoon, and for the next hour, she busied herself putting together two homemade pies. While they baked, she sat at the table and leafed through the newspaper, telling herself that there was nothing wrong with doing a little something for someone who'd done her a favor. She was just being a good neighbor.

COLBY TOOK THE left-hand turnoff onto the road that led to Oak Hill. The driveway stretched ahead for a good mile. It was lined with enormous oak trees, most of which were nearly a hundred years old.

Oak Hill had always been one of her favorite places. It had once been one of Virginia's most prosperous farms—tobacco and wheat its mainstays—before becoming a well-known horse farm in the mid-1950s. In the past twenty years, the place had deteriorated, since the house had sat empty for so long. She could hardly hate Ian for beating her to it, but nevertheless, she wished he hadn't.

She stopped her truck in the circular driveway behind a car with New York license plates. He had company. Maybe she should forget delivering the pie. She didn't want to interrupt. But it would be silly not to leave it now that she was already here. There was no way she and Lena could eat two pies, even if they were Lena's favorite.

She knocked at the front door, then stepped back, holding the dish in front of her.

The large oak door opened, and a tall, very beautiful woman stood in the entryway. She was dressed in navy pants and a white silk blouse that somehow managed to look elegant and casual all at the same time. She smiled, her expression expectant. "May I help you with something?"

Colby glanced down at the pie, suddenly too conscious of her own khakis and UVA sweatshirt. "I just wanted to leave this for the McKinleys."

The woman stared at her for a moment, before smiling again and extending her right hand. "How nice. I'm Rachel Montgomery. Ian's fiancée."

"Oh!" Startled, Colby shifted the pie to her left hand, returning the woman's firm handshake, noticing that the proffered hand was smooth and manicured against her own work-roughened skin and short, unpolished nails. She took another step back, still holding the pie out in front of her. "I'm Colby Williams."

"Ian says the people here are very nice. It seems he was right."

"My truck broke down the other night, and he was kind enough to help me out. This is just a little thank-you. I hope you all enjoy it."

"Would you like to speak to Ian?" Rachel asked. "He's in the shower, but he should be out anytime."

Colby backed down the steps, raising a hand and wishing she could grab the darn pie and run without Ian ever knowing she'd been here. "No. Really. That's all right. Nice to meet you, Miss Montgomery."

A mile or so down the road, Colby pulled over and glanced in the rearview mirror. Her face was flushed and hot with embarrassment. Way to go, Williams. Why had she ever given in to the impulse to do such a stupid thing?

She sat back in the seat and shoved a hand through her hair, feeling more than a little foolish. It wasn't at all like her to have gone to Ian's home. She, the same woman who had told Phoebe she wasn't willing to do the song and dance that came with the dating scene.

And yet, she'd baked the man a pie.

A pie, of all things! A pie she had ended up presenting to the man's fiancée.

Anger with Ian edged its way past her own embarrassment. How could he have sat through dinner at Phoebe's and never bothered to mention that he was engaged? And what about the rest of the evening? He'd had more than ample opportunity to do so. But he hadn't.

And then there was Phoebe. Her own best friend, who supposedly had her best interests at heart. Phoebe, who had neglected to mention that one small but vital detail about Ian McKinley.

## CHAPTER FIVE

"I DIDN'T KNOW. I swear."

"How could you not have known?" Colby asked in disbelief.

"Mabel never mentioned it when I called her to ask if she thought he would like to come to dinner. I even told her that you would be there and that I wanted to introduce you two."

"Don't tell me she's in on this, too!"

"She said she'd been hoping you two would get a chance to meet. How could I have known he was engaged?" Phoebe wailed. "What was I supposed to do? Ask for a full personal history before inviting him to dinner?"

"Yes."

"Next time, I will."

"There won't be a next time."

They were sitting in the wooden swing attached to two old maples in Phoebe's backyard. The day was Indian-summer warm, and the shade surrounding them hadn't done much to cool the heat in Colby's cheeks.

"I can't believe he's engaged," Phoebe said, still looking shell-shocked.

"Believe it. I met her. What more proof do you want?"

"Well, he never said anything about—"

"No, he didn't. He probably thought it was some grand joke. He's probably still laughing about it."

"Oh, Colby, I don't think so. He seems like a nice guy—"

"Then how do you explain his not bothering to mention having a fiancée?"

"I don't know."

Colby dropped her head back against the swing and stared up at the cloudless sky. "I can't believe I actually made him a pie. What is it about attractive men that turns normally intelligent women into noodle brains?"

"Now, Colby, that was a perfectly nice gesture. If I'd thought of it, I would have suggested it myself."

Colby gave Phoebe a look out of the corner of her eye. "And that's supposed to make it intelligent?"

"Legitimate. It makes it legitimate."

"Right. I'm giving you fair warning, Phoebs. No more setups. That's the last one. My life is complicated enough right now."

Phoebe let out a long-suffering sigh and gave the swing a push. They swung in silence for a few minutes before she said, "Everybody has complications, Colby. Including me. I think Frank's having a midlife crisis."

Colby looked up, surprised. "He's not old enough to have a midlife crisis."

"How old do you have to be? I've known the man since I was fifteen. He's never had an ounce of interest in clothes, and all of a sudden, he goes out and buys two new suits. *Armani* suits. Do you know how many mortgage payments you can make on two *Armani* suits?"

Colby had to admit it didn't sound like Frank.

She'd known him almost as long as Phoebe had, and he'd never shown a penchant for high fashion. "Maybe he's trying to impress you."

"Impress me? He came downstairs wearing one of the darn things Friday morning and was almost...I don't know, embarrassed, when I questioned him about it."

"I wouldn't make too much of it, Phoebe. It's probably just a phase."

Phoebe chewed her lower lip. "A phase is what teenagers go through. Adult men don't have phases."

"Says who?"

"Dr. Green. That lady psychologist who's on the radio every morning."

"You called her?" Colby asked, staring at her friend in disbelief.

"After Frank left Friday morning. I call her a lot," she said a little defensively. "She's very smart. She said there's always a reason for the things people do. A change in behavior means something is different."

"Oh, Phoebe, for heaven's sake. The man bought a couple of new suits. You'll let this woman convince you he's having an affair. Frank, of all people."

"Why not Frank of all people?" Phoebe asked, sounding offended.

"Because you've been together since Adam and Eve. And besides that, he's nuts about you."

Phoebe slumped back in the swing. "*Used* to be nuts about me. He's been so distracted lately, we've done nothing but sleep in the same bed."

Getting the point, Colby said, "Maybe the two of you need to talk."

"I've tried. He thinks I'm being silly."

Colby didn't know what to say. For as long as she could remember, Phoebe had been the one with the rock-solid relationship. The thought that it might not be as stable as she'd assumed was unthinkable. But then, maybe lasting relationships really weren't possible for people of her generation.

Colby stopped the swing with her foot and got up, shoving her hands inside her jeans pockets. "I'm going home, Phoebs. Go inside and seduce your husband. You probably just need some time alone together. Since the kids are at your mom's house, you have the perfect opportunity." She headed across the yard, waving over her shoulder.

"Hey, Colby."

She turned around just short of the truck. "Yeah?"

"He'll come along."

"Who?"

"The one good man you've been waiting for."

Colby rolled her eyes. "I'm not waiting for anyone."

"I'm still not convinced it isn't Ian McKinley," Phoebe said, ignoring her. "Engaged isn't married, after all."

Deceit was deceit, though, Colby told herself as she drove away.

It was really none of her business whether the man was engaged or not. She was angry at him for not mentioning it, but beneath the anger was a ridiculous sense of hurt. She had actually let her guard down for a little while Friday night. Something she didn't do very often.

Back on the main road, she told herself to forget about it. She certainly had better things to do with her time than stew over an unavailable man who had trouble with the truth.

COLBY'S FATHER DROPPED Lena off just before six that night. Colby met them outside. Lena gave her grandfather a hug and then went inside the house without so much as a hello. Trying to keep the hurt from her expression, Colby said, "How about some dinner, Dad?"

"I'd better get on home." His gaze followed Lena and then rested on Colby, his dismay evident. "Emma'll have dinner ready. Don't want to make her wait."

"She's a better cook, anyway."

Samuel put his arm around her shoulders, then pulled her close for a hug. "Don't be too hard on yourself over this thing with Lena."

An unexpected surge of emotion swelled in Colby's chest. "Oh, Dad, I wish I could just wave a magic wand and make everything like it used to be."

"That's both the beauty and the sorrow of life, honey. Nothing ever stays the same. But she'll come around with whatever's bothering her soon enough. Take my word for it."

Colby hugged her father, grateful for his steady reassurance. She wanted to believe him. More than anything, she wanted to believe him.

UPSTAIRS, LENA TURNED on her stereo, putting on the heavy metal group she knew her mother liked least. She turned up the volume and flopped down on the bed, telling herself that she *did* like it. Staring up at the ceiling, she forced herself not to think about the hurt look on her mother's face when she'd ignored her. She didn't want to be so mean to her, but she just couldn't help it. It was as if some ugly person had gotten inside her and she was no longer in control.

Flipping over on her side, she reached in her nightstand drawer and pulled out the wrinkled envelope she'd found in the top of her mother's old closet at Grandma's house. The letter had been written on notebook paper, the kind with blue lines. It had been read so many times that it was now thin and lifeless.

Lena unfolded it and let her eyes scan the page, even though she'd long since memorized the words.

Dear Colby,
I wish I didn't have to say this, but things aren't working out. There are too many differences between us for it ever to last. As for the baby, the decision was yours. I can't be a part of it.

Doug

Unwanted tears stung Lena's eyes. She refolded the letter and carefully tucked it back inside the envelope. All these years, she'd believed her mother when she'd said her father had died. She remembered asking her mom why they had the same last name as Grandma and Grandpa Williams. Her mom had explained that she'd just decided to keep her own when she and Lena's father had married. And after Lena's father had "gone away," as she had always put it, she'd wanted them both to have the same last name. At the time, she'd been too young to question the story. Looking back on it, she remembered the guilty look on her mother's face and knew now that it was because she'd been lying.

Lena's father had never married her. Lena had been born out of wedlock. That was why she'd been given her mother's maiden name.

A knock sounded at the door, followed by her mother's voice. Lena shoved the envelope back in her nightstand drawer and sat up on the bed, clutching a pillow to her chest. "Yeah?"

The door opened. "I've got dinner ready," her mother said, sticking her head around the corner. "Why don't you come on down?"

"I'm not hungry." Lena studied the bedspread, hearing the sullen note in her own voice. "I've got homework to do."

"I made your favorite. Macaroni and cheese."

The desire to hurt her mother as she'd hurt her was too strong to resist. She glanced up at her and said, "No thanks."

"You're sure?"

Ignoring the look of surprise in her mother's eyes, Lena reached for the book on the nightstand and turned to the marked page. "Yeah, I'm sure."

After a second or two, her mother stepped back and closed the door behind her. Lena almost called her back but quashed the desire before the words were out.

She lay there for a few moments, regretting her actions, but she pushed away her remorse and turned her thoughts to Luke McKinley, instead. She thought about him all the time now. The problem was, he didn't know she was alive.

She'd been trying to find a way to introduce herself to him since the first day of school. But what did a girl say to a guy like that? He was gorgeous. No, more than gorgeous. He had coal black hair and moody blue eyes that looked as if he'd seen things most of the kids around here hadn't even thought of yet.

She'd had her chance one afternoon after school when she and Millie had gone to the Dairy Queen. Lena had just placed her order at the register when she turned around to find him standing behind her in line. At first, she couldn't think of a thing to say, but realizing this was her chance, she forced herself to smile and said, "Hi. I'm Lena Williams. You're new here, aren't you?"

"Yeah," he said, looking surprised. "I'm Luke McKinley."

"I know. I mean, someone mentioned your name."

He didn't say anything for several seconds. He just stared down at her with those incredible eyes of his while her cheeks caught fire, and she longed for enough sophistication to say something cute and flirty, but nothing came to mind. He finally said, "I'd better place my order."

She stepped back and lifted a hand. "Okay. See you around."

"Yeah. See you around."

Lena had gone back to her table, where Millie had demanded all the details.

At home that night, Lena had longed to talk to her mother about Luke. Ask her how she could get him to notice her. She and her mom had been best friends for as long as she could remember. She'd always asked her advice on everything. But all that had changed when she'd found the letter. Her mother had lied to her. And now that Lena knew that, how could she ever believe another word her mother said?

MONDAY MORNING WAS a busy one at the clinic. After things slowed down, Colby told Stacey to go to lunch with Laura and Ruth-Ann. Cecil Maynard had just brought in his German shepherd, Wally, for his yearly shots, but she could manage that on her own.

"The old lady was supposed to bring him in during her lunch hour," Cecil said when Colby lifted the dog up on the table. "She had to work though, so I just brought him in myself."

Colby opened the cabinet beside her and pulled out the supplies she needed. She'd never considered herself a bra-burning feminist, but there were times when she understood how the whole movement got started. "Exactly how old is Myrna, Cecil?"

"I don't know, Doc." His eyebrows rose in surprise. "I reckon she's past forty."

"I see her car at the Exercise Hut on Tuesdays and Thursdays. I'd say she's a pretty well-maintained forty."

"I reckon she is."

"Then why do you call her your 'old lady'?"

A few seconds of puzzled silence followed the question. "Heck, I don't know, Doc. It's just a figure of speech. What difference does it make?"

"Let's put it this way, Cecil," Colby said, aware that part of her outrage for Myrna was based in her own recent experience with the lack of sensitivity on the part of the male gender. "She doesn't go to the Exercise Hut twice a week to keep herself looking good just so her husband can go around calling her his old lady."

Another pause was followed by a chagrined, "I expect you're right."

"Hello."

Colby looked up to find Ian standing in the doorway of the examining room. The sight of him caught her by surprise. She struggled for a professional smile and said, "I'm with someone at the moment. If you'll have a seat in the waiting room, I'll be with you when I'm finished."

"Sure," he said, looking a little taken aback by her tone.

So much for tact today. First, she'd attacked Cecil on behalf of womankind and now she was giving Ian the deep freeze. After giving Wally his shot, she put the dog back on the floor and said, "Stacey's at lunch, so we'll send you a bill."

"Sure thing, Doc. I'll be sure and tell *Myrna* you said hello," he said with a grin.

She smiled and shook her head. "You do that."

Once Cecil had left, Colby took a moment to gather her composure. Cool, calm, poised. That was the picture she would present. She didn't want to provide Ian with another reason to think she'd given a second thought to his surprise fiancée. Tucking her hair behind her ears, she stepped into the waiting room and found Ian sitting on one of the benches with Don Juan stretched out beside him, the dog's head in his lap. He stood up and smiled at her. "That was very diplomatic. I'm surprised Myrna didn't hit him over the head with the frying pan a long time ago."

Colby shrugged and met his gaze head-on. "I guess some men don't realize how their words or actions might be perceived by others."

Ian shoved his hands in the pockets of his jeans and looked more than a little uncomfortable. "Including me, right? Look, Colby, I should have said something about my being engaged Friday night. I started to, but once I figured out what Phoebe and Frank had in mind, I didn't want to embarrass them or you. As it turns out, Mabel had a little part to play in all this. I threatened to hide her kitchen step stool if she ever did it again.''

As hard as she tried not to, Colby smiled. He was making it difficult to stay angry with him. After all, he'd been under no obligation to tell her anything about himself.

"I didn't mean to deceive you, Colby," he said. "Everything about that night caught me off guard. I guess I was just enjoying myself and…''

They stood for a moment looking at each other, and she found herself wishing he would finish the sentence.

But he didn't. "Well," he said, running a hand around the back of his neck. "I'd better be going. I just wanted to stop and thank you for the pie. It was all gone by last night. I couldn't keep Luke out of the refrigerator.''

"You're welcome. It was the least I could do to repay you for carting me around. Not to mention getting your car stuck in the mud.''

"That was my fault," he said, his smile self-deprecating. He stood there for a few moments, watching her, before saying, "Okay. I should go.''

"Yeah. I've got things to do.''

Still, neither of them moved. They just stared at one another until he finally backed away, then turned and pushed through the door. Colby heard him pull away and told herself that it made no difference that he had semiredeemed himself by apologizing as if he really meant it. The man was engaged. And even if he hadn't been, she wasn't the kind of woman to let her head be turned by some too-handsome, too well-off, out-of-towner who was nothing but a surefire prescription for heartbreak.

ON THE WAY home, Ian stopped by Thurman's Hardware to pick up some paint. He was in the back, leafing through sample chips when he overheard a conversation with his name in it.

He stretched his head around the corner and saw two older men in bib overalls standing by the cash register. He recognized them as the Nolen twins, Dillard and Willard. The two other times he'd been in the store, he'd seen them sitting out front on the wooden bench where locals gathered to talk. Willard had just reached into his back pocket for a pack of tobacco when Dillard said, "It's a shame to see the place go to weeds like that. I'd hoped whoever bought it would get it back in shape."

"Yeah, that's some of the best farmland around," Willard agreed.

"That McKinley seems like a nice enough fella, but I doubt if he'd know the front end of a tractor from the back. He's a city slicker if I ever saw one."

They both chuckled. Ian stayed where he was, feeling inadequate in ways he'd never imagined would bother him. He'd gone to college on scholarship and built a career that had earned him more money than he was ever likely to spend, and yet he felt like less than a man because two old geezers had labeled him as the city boy he was.

When he got home, he put the paint inside the storage building behind the house and looked out at the grounds. As much as he hated to admit it, the

Nolen brothers were right. The weeds were taking over. It was up to him to do something about it.

The tractor was parked at the back of the barn, full of gas, the mowing blade attached. Piece of cake. If he could drive a car, he could certainly drive this thing. He'd show those two old-timers city slicker.

Luke was in school, and Mabel had taken the day to visit her brother two towns up the Interstate. Rachel had returned to New York. At least if he messed up, there would be no one here to witness it.

He found the ignition and turned the key. The tractor sputtered and lurched forward, coming dangerously close to rolling through the wall in front of him. He slammed his foot on the brake, realizing he'd forgotten to press in the clutch.

Honest enough mistake. Could have happened to anyone.

He gave it another try. The old tractor labored to life, black smoke billowing out the back. He fumbled with the gears until he hit reverse. The tractor torpedoed backward out of the barn at a speed that would have flattened anyone unlucky enough to be standing in its path. Ian sent a frantic glance over his shoulder to make sure it hadn't done exactly that.

Saying a quick prayer of thanks, he worked the transmission into first with a grinding of metal against metal, then lurched toward the gate that led to the south pasture. He arrived there in a frenzy of jerks and starts that gave serious pause to the thought that the engine might be on its last leg. He stopped at the gate, got out and opened it, then rolled through, the sputtering tractor bouncing him around like a basketball at center court.

Inside the field, he worked with a few levers until

he figured out how to raise and lower the mean-looking blade attached to the back. That took no time at all, and with a ridiculous feeling of pride, he set off across the pasture, the tall grass falling in his wake.

Despite feeling as if he were in the middle of a "Green Acres" episode, he decided this wasn't so bad, after all. He could do this. Over the years, he'd grown so used to financial success that it was simply a part of what he did. As a reward, it had lost some of its gratification. But this, crazy as it was, made him feel as if he'd accomplished something. He considered driving into town just so he could roll past Thurman's Hardware and see the look of shock on the faces of Dillard and Willard Nolen.

He had too much time on his hands. That's what this was about. Either that or he was losing his mind.

He worked on for a half hour or more. There was something almost peaceful about jostling along on the old tractor with the warm September breeze tugging at the collar of his shirt. He was on a slope now, the tractor at an angle. A little too steep. He probably shouldn't go any higher....

Suddenly, the machine tilted. For a moment, it held there, then tipped and teetered drunkenly. He tried to hold on, thinking it would right itself. No way. It was going over, and he was going with it. In the next instant, he was airborne, projecting himself as far from the tractor as he could manage. He landed on his back with a crack that ripped the air from his lungs. The blade hung above him, swaying like a guillotine about to drop.

Ian rolled, tumbling down the hill, his head slamming against the ground. And then he didn't know whether he'd outrun the blade or not. The blue sky above him went black.

# CHAPTER SIX

HE WOULD HAVE come back for them sooner or later.

Colby eyed the set of keys bouncing on her dashboard. She wouldn't have bothered to drop them off if she hadn't needed to deliver some medicine to the Carter farm anyway. When she'd gotten back from lunch, Stacey had found the keys on the bench where Ian had been sitting next to Don Juan. Realizing they must have been for something other than his car, Colby had told Stacey she would take care of them, not mentioning that she thought they were Ian's. That way there would be no probing questions.

She could have mailed the keys to him. Asked Stacey to run them by his house. Left them outside the clinic for him to pick up. But here she was. Delivering them in person when common sense told her she shouldn't be.

Pulling into the driveway, she cut the engine and sat for a moment, the keys in her hand. The front yard was newly mowed. The pasture gate was open. She went to the back door of the house and knocked, but there was no answer. Ian's car was here. She peered out across the yard, then toward the field behind the barn.

Wait. What was that noise?

It sounded like an engine running. Faint, but a definite *chug, chug, chug.* A tractor engine.

She stepped down from the porch and called out, "Ian?"

Silence except for the still-idling machine.

She ventured toward the open gate. He wouldn't be out on the tractor. Would he? Someone was. She'd walk out a little way to see if she could spot him.

She'd gone no more than fifty yards past the gate when she saw the tractor sitting at a crazy angle on the hill. And then she saw Ian. Her heart flip-flopped, then lodged in her throat. She took off at a dead run for the ravine at the bottom of the hill.

He was lying flat on his back, his face turned to one side. Her first thought was that he was dead. Her heart was pounding against the wall of her chest, and sweat beaded across her forehead.

Dropping to the ground beside him, she checked his pulse, relieved to find it steady.

"Ian?" She put her hand against his cheek and repeated his name several times.

His eyes opened finally, slowly, his pupils dilated and unfocused. "What happened?"

"You must have had an accident. Can you move? Where do you hurt?"

"I'm not sure." He tried to struggle up on one elbow, then sank back onto the ground, one hand going to his head. "Ouch. That answers that."

"Don't move," she said. "You could have a concussion. Wait here and I'll go call the rescue squad."

"No. Don't. There's no need for that."

"We won't know until we get you checked out. I'll be right back, okay?"

He nodded, wincing again as if the action made his head hurt.

"I'm going to turn off the tractor first," she said, heading up the hill at a run.

Part of the blade lay on the slope, as if it had been broken off. A few yards from the machine, she thought she noticed one tire roll back slightly. Probably just her imagination. She kept her gaze on the back tires. The right one slipped a notch. Oh God, it *was* moving. She sent a frantic look over her left shoulder. Ian was in the direct path of the now-rolling tractor.

There was no time to try to stop it. Without thinking, Colby sprinted toward Ian, reacting on pure adrenaline. A glance over her shoulder told her the tractor was gaining on her. A few feet from where he lay, she tackled him, and rolled, pulling him with her. Over and over they went. She groaned with each turn.

They came to a stop at the edge of the creek, Ian lying on top of her. Neither of them moved.

"Do you want to tell me what that was—" he began, then glanced up the hill and spotted the tractor, which was now sitting where he had just been lying, the engine stalled. He looked back down at her, a stunned expression on his face.

Colby tried to find her voice, but she was too aware of the muscular length of the man whose body was intimately pressing into hers. His chest was crushing her breasts. One of his arms was wedged between his belly and hers. Her right arm was pinned behind her back. And his—

She scooted out from under him as if someone had just set a match to the seat of her pants. She tried to sit up, moaned and sank back down on the grass, feeling as if the tractor had actually run over her.

Ian slumped beside her. One hand braced his fore-head. "You just saved my life," he said in a shaken voice.

She slipped a hand inside her jacket, pulled out his keys and dropped them in his lap. "Now I remember why I charge extra for house calls."

He picked up the keys and dropped them in his shirt pocket. Despite his pained expression, a hint of a smile played about his lips. "Are you all right?"

"A little flatter than a few minutes ago, but I've been meaning to do some ab work," she said, glad she could still joke about it.

He stared at her for a few seconds, shaking his head. A half smile spread across his face. "Just send me your bill. I'll expect it to be a big one."

Colby stared at the blue sky above them. They could joke about it now, but she didn't want to think about what might have happened if she hadn't found him in time.

Ian sobered, too, and she wondered if he was also thinking about the close call he'd just had.

"I can't believe I did that," he said finally.

"Accidents happen."

"But I endangered your life, too."

"Oh, hey, the life of a veterinarian is a risky one."

That prompted another smile.

"What happened?" she asked.

"It just started tipping, and over it went. Serves me right. The only reason I got on the blasted thing was because I overheard Dillard and Willard Nolen talking about how unfortunate it was that Oak Hill had been bought by a city slicker who would never do anything with it."

She heard the chagrin in his voice and realized that

what they'd said had mattered to him. He cared what they thought. And he'd gotten on that tractor in an attempt to prove them wrong. The realization touched her somehow, made him more human to her, vulnerable in a way that only increased his appeal. She glanced out at the field where rows of fallen hay now lay. Despite resenting the fact that he'd been the one to buy Oak Hill, she had to admit he seemed determined to give new life to the place. She had to admire him for that. "It looks like you were doing a fine job."

"There's no reason for you to be so kind. I make a lousy farmer, but thanks for what you just did. I don't know too many people who would have done that," he said.

"If I'd taken the time to think about it, I doubt I'd have done it myself."

"Yes, you would have," he said quietly. "You're not the type to stand around waiting for someone else to do things for you, are you?"

Colby knew his comment was a compliment, and yet something inside her wanted him to say something altogether different. What, though? That she was feminine and beautiful? That she made Rachel look like last year's prom queen? Right.

Maybe *she* was the one with the concussion.

She tried to get up, pushing off with her left hand, and letting out a pained yelp.

"What's wrong?" Ian asked, sitting up and looking a little gray himself.

She tried to rotate her left wrist and barely suppressed another moan of pain. "I think I've sprained it."

"Damn," he said, looking sick with guilt. He got

to his feet, swaying with the willow tree just behind him. "Come on. I'm taking you to the emergency room."

Before she'd realized his intent, he bent over and scooped her off the ground. Her protest was delayed for a few seconds because of the absolutely satisfying way she fit in his arms. His chest felt exactly as it should have. Broad and firm. Masculine in a way that made her feel protected, something she would have sworn she couldn't care less about.

His arms felt just right, too. Tight and secure around her. The only thing wrong with the picture was that he was about as steady on his feet as a seasick sailor. "Ian, this is ridiculous. Put me down. I sprained my wrist, not my leg."

"Are you sure you can walk?" he asked, sounding as if he hoped she would say yes.

"I'm fine. You're the one with the possible concussion."

Once he'd lowered her to her feet, she said, "You wait here and I'll call an ambulance."

He shook his head. "We tried that once and almost turned into pancakes."

She smiled. "Are you sure you can make it?"

He nodded, and with one hand at her elbow, set off up the hill, his expression determined. She suspected that he felt much worse than he was letting on.

At the house, a short altercation ensued over who was getting behind the wheel. Colby came out the winner since she could manage to keep them on the road with one wrist incapacitated. Ian's ability to stay upright was still in question.

She got them to the hospital's emergency room

door without incident. She knew most of the doctors and nurses there, and of course, all ears were perked when she relayed the story of the near-fatal tractor incident. It would be all over town within an hour or two. And since she didn't have enough money to pay everyone for their silence, she would just have to live with it.

Two separate nurses wheeled them into individual examining rooms. Molly Cramer was in charge of Ian. A sweet girl with big, blue eyes and a perky smile, she was a member of Colby's church. Unfortunately, Colby could hear everything the young woman was saying to Ian. The conversation centered around Molly's awareness that Ian was the recently relocated bachelor the single women in town had been talking about since he'd arrived.

Colby tried not to wince while the nurse took an X ray of her wrist. And while she waited for the results, she had to endure Molly's all-too-audible giggles and admonishments to Ian. Little did Molly know that she was wasting her time with all the flirting.

A young resident returned a few minutes later to tell Colby what she already knew. Her wrist wasn't fractured but she did have a bad sprain.

They put her arm in a sling, which she would need to wear for a week or so. Once they'd finished with her, she was released and free to go. She went back to the emergency room to check on Ian and found him waiting by the door.

"How's the wrist?" he asked.

She held up her bandaged arm. "It'll live. Just a sprain. How about you?"

"Just a knot the size of an egg. I'm a free man."

"Come on, then. I'll drive you home."

This time, he got into the truck without arguing.

NEITHER OF THEM said much during the drive back to Oak Hill. Ian's head was pounding, and he was subdued by the reality of what had nearly happened that afternoon. Apparently, Colby was as well. She was quiet, too, concentrating on the road in front of her.

She stopped the truck in the driveway and left the engine idling. "Would you like some help getting inside?"

"No, I'll be fine. I think you've done quite enough for me today."

"It was nothing."

He cocked a brow at her and shook his head. "Right."

He opened the door but didn't move. "Sure that wrist is all right?"

She gave him a stiff wave. "Be good as new soon."

"You really did save my life, you know. I won't forget that."

"I'll be sure to send you the bill," she said, her voice light, a smile on her lips.

It was after six, and the light had begun to fade, casting shadows across her face. He sat there in the twilight, knowing he should go and yet not wanting to. The wrongness of that did not escape him. "Would you like to come in?" he asked before he realized he was going to. "I could fix us some dinner."

She looked down at her wrist, toyed with the bandage and then shook her head. "I'd better not."

She was right to turn him down. Since the moment

he'd found himself lying at the edge of the creek with her pinned beneath him, things had somehow felt different between them. The urge to kiss her right now was nearly overpowering. Before he could figure out where the devil that thought had come from, the screen door at the side of the house wheezed open. Luke stepped out. Ian waved him over, glad for the diversion.

"What happened?" Luke asked, eyeing the scrapes on the side of Ian's face.

"I kind of had a run-in with the tractor," Ian explained. "Dr. Williams happened by and saved me from myself."

"Are you all right?"

Ian wondered if he'd imagined the note of worry in his son's voice. "I'm fine. Thanks to me, Dr. Williams has a sprained wrist, though. Luke, this is Colby Williams. Colby, my son Luke."

"Hello, Luke," she said. "It's nice to meet you. You might know my daughter, Lena."

Luke scuffed a tennis shoe against the pavement. "Yeah, we've met."

Nodding, Colby said, "Well, I've got to get going."

"I owe you one," Ian said, then waved as he watched her drive off, telling himself it was just gratitude he was feeling.

COLBY HAD BEEN home for less than an hour when Phoebe called, wanting to know everything. A tennis buddy of hers who worked with a nurse at the hospital had told her that Colby had saved Ian McKinley's life.

"The town grapevine is up to the speed of light now, I see," Colby said, shaking her head.

"And you didn't tell me?" Phoebe asked indignantly.

"Phoebe, I just got home. It was no big deal, anyway."

"No big deal? Did you really push him out of the way of a rolling tractor?"

"Sort of."

Phoebe's whoop of laughter was less than ladylike. "Incredible! How could a man resist a woman who saved his life?"

"Phoebe—"

"Well, really, Colby. I couldn't have planned it better myself."

"The man is engaged. What is it about that word you don't understand?" Colby asked, exasperated.

"Things change. You never know."

"My dinner's burning. I'll talk to you later." She hung up, feeling only slightly guilty for the exaggeration. The pot on the stove did need stirring. She removed the lid and checked the boiling potatoes. It was way past time Phoebe gave up on this particular venture. Colby thought about those last few moments before Luke had appeared. The tension between Ian and her could be easily explained. People who went through traumas together often felt a temporary sense of closeness.

That night, Lena joined Colby at the dinner table without being prodded to do so for the first time in weeks. Colby hid her surprise and sat down with her daughter as if her presence were nothing out of the ordinary.

"What happened to your wrist?" Lena asked.

Any concern that might have prompted the question was adequately concealed. With the way things had been going between them, Colby was surprised she'd asked at all. "I had a little accident at the McKinley farm. It's nothing major. Just a sprain," she said, not wanting to elaborate.

Lena looked as if she wanted to know more, but didn't ask. Colby asked her about her day, how school was, all the things she would automatically have asked her not so long ago.

Lena answered each of her questions in monosyllables.

Colby had nearly given up hope of a two-sided conversation when Lena said, "There's a camp-out two weeks from this Friday. The Fellowship of Christian Athletes is sponsoring it. Is it all right if I go?"

She realized then what Lena's sudden appearance at the dinner table had been about. Disappointment stabbed at her, and she wished for the first time since her daughter's birth that the child didn't have such power over her heart. "Sure."

Lena dropped her fork, obviously startled by the unexpected response. Judging from her defensive posture earlier, Lena had expected an argument. Colby wasn't going to give her one. She didn't have the energy. She got up from the table and dumped the remains of her dinner into the garbage.

With her back to the table, she heard Lena get up and leave the room. Sighing, she began gathering up the bowls of vegetables they'd barely touched. For the first time in fifteen years, she disliked being a single parent. It had never been like this before. Always, she and Lena had been able to work out whatever minor difficulties they might have had. How small they seemed in comparison to this. Lena wanting her ears pierced. Lena wanting to meet Chuck Bailey at the ninth-grade sock hop. Lena wanting to learn how to drive out in her grandparents' pasture. Those decisions seemed so simple now.

She put the frying pan in the sink. With her good hand, she scrubbed it for all she was worth. She resented this sudden yearning for a partner with whom she could share these decisions. She was single by choice. And she couldn't just pull a father for Lena out of a hat. There wasn't anyone she'd ever wanted to marry enough to give up her own independence.

Unbidden, Ian McKinley popped into her thoughts. Her hand stilled, and she stared out the kitchen window at the stars dotting the September sky. She remembered what it had felt like to find herself stretched flat out on the ground with Ian on top of her, the unexpected surge of desire that had swept through her....

She cut the memory off. Dangerous territory.

He was engaged. Taken. Spoken for.

Ian McKinley was trouble with a capital *T*. Walking potential for heartbreak. And she had enough experience to know heartbreak when she saw it. So stop thinking about him, Colby, she told herself. Just stop thinking about him.

SHE STUCK TO her own mental guns for the next week, keeping busy at work and spending her nights making one-sided conversation with Lena.

On Thursday morning she stopped at the bank before dropping Lena off at school. They were sitting in the drive-through line at the bank when she spotted Ian coming out of the post office across the street. Her first uncensored thought was that it should have been illegal for anybody to look that good in a pair of blue jeans. He was wearing a worn-looking leather jacket, a Nike T-shirt and running shoes. Dark sunglasses hid his eyes, and his black hair was slicked back and wet, as if he'd just gotten out of the shower.

Warmth assaulted her midsection.

The car behind her tooted its horn, reminding her that it was her turn to pull forward. Ian looked up just then, catching sight of her. He waved. She waved back. Casually. Smiling as if she'd just seen him, too.

He crossed the street and stopped at the truck door. Colby lowered the window and said, "Hello."

"Hi. How's the wrist?"

"Fine. I already got rid of the sling. How's your head?"

"Hard as ever, I'm afraid." He smiled, and something inside Colby shifted. Despite what Dillard and Willard Nolen thought, there was nothing slick about this man. His crooked smile crinkled the corners of his eyes and hinted at possibilities. As weapons went, it was particularly deadly.

"Good," she said, hating the breathlessness in her voice.

He ducked down and peered across at Lena. "Hi. I'm Ian McKinley."

"Sorry," Colby said. "Ian, this is my daughter, Lena."

Lena looked at both of them curiously. "Hello."

"I can see beauty runs in the Williams family. Nice to meet you, Lena."

Lena was actually blushing! But then, Colby's own face felt warm, too.

The car in front of them pulled away, and it was their turn to move forward.

Ian stepped back. "I'm holding things up. See you later," he said, his gaze lingering on hers a second too long.

She waved goodbye, and pretending intense concentration on her banking business, ignored her daughter's scrutiny.

AT SEVEN-THIRTY the following Sunday morning, Colby and Lena arrived at church for the monthly women's breakfast prepared in the fellowship hall by the men of the congregation.

The hall was a big, open room in the basement of the church, used for dinners and get-togethers of this sort. The aroma of sizzling bacon and fried apples greeted them as they entered the room already abuzz with conversation. Lena waved at her grandparents and went over to join them.

"I just want to make it clear that I'm not the one who invited him."

Colby turned around to find Phoebe standing in defense mode with one hand on her hip. "Who?" she asked, knowing full well there was only one person her friend could be talking about.

"It was all Frank's doing. He invited Ian to go fishing at our pond the other morning, and then he asked Luke and him to come to the breakfast."

"As a deacon of the church, that was a nice thing for Frank to do," Colby said, trying to sound unconcerned.

With a suspicious look on her face, Phoebe said, "You mean you don't mind?"

"Why would I mind?"

"I just figured you would accuse me of trying to fix you two up again."

"Now that you know he's engaged to someone else, I know you would never do that," Colby said deliberately.

"Of course not," Phoebe said with angelic innocence.

"How are things with Frank and you?"

"I don't know." Phoebe sighed. "He's just so distracted all the time now. He barely hears what I'm saying to him. It's as if he's in another world or something."

"Maybe it's a case at work."

Phoebe shook her head. "He says everything there is fine."

Josephine Robertson approached them, saying, "There you are, Phoebe. Reverend Thomas asked me to get together with you on the quarterly fund-raiser. Do you have a minute?"

"You two go right ahead. I'll talk to you later, Phoebe." Colby hung up her jacket and made her way toward the front of the room, stopping to chat with several people along the way.

Just as she was headed over to say hello to her parents, Davis Fralin stopped her with a tentative smile. "Morning, Colby."

"I see they've got you on table-setting duty."

"You know what they say about too many cooks in the kitchen," he said.

"Especially when they're all men," she said, smiling.

He laughed. "You might be right about that."

A dairy farmer, Davis was a nice man, tall and somehow stocky at the same time. He had dark

brown hair and shy eyes. His wife had left him a
year or so ago, and from what Colby knew about the
situation, he'd been badly hurt by it. He'd been asking her out for the past few months. She'd turned
down his invitations because she herself had no in-
tention of getting serious with anyone, and she
sensed that he was looking for someone to fill the
hole in his life left by his divorce.

Just as Davis began telling her about a problem
he'd been having with one of his heifers, Colby
glanced behind him and caught sight of Ian in the
kitchen with the other men, a smile on his face. He
was wearing a white shirt and tie, apparently having
taken off his suit jacket.

Lena and Luke were standing on the opposite side
of the counter from him, and it looked as if Lena was
trying to explain something to him. Surprised, she
watched as Lena went around to stand beside Ian.
She picked up an egg and cracked it on the side of
a measuring cup, showing him how to break it without getting any shells in the mixture, just as Colby
had shown her years ago. Since Lena had recently
made a point of rejecting all advice or parental guid-
ance from her, the sight did Colby's heart good.

Ian picked up an egg and tried it himself. Lena
reached for a fork and fished a piece of shell out of
the cup. There was something about watching the
two of them together that did strange things to Colby's insides. The only real male role models Lena
had ever had were her grandfather and Frank. Seeing
her with Ian brought on familiar feelings of guilt for
the things her life-style had caused Lena to miss out
on.

Ian looked up just then and caught her gaze. He

nodded at something Lena was saying, but he didn't look away. Colby's pulse quickened. The look couldn't have lasted more than a moment or two, but it seemed like much longer. She forced her attention back to Davis, her voice a little unsteady when she said, "I could come out Monday and take a look at her if you'd like."

"I'd appreciate that. Sometime after lunch?"

"Sure," she said. "I haven't said hello to my folks yet, so I'll see you later."

"Enjoy the breakfast, Colby," he said, a wistful look in his eyes.

She joined her parents on the other side of the room, where they were chatting with Mabel Atkins. She kissed her mother on the cheek and gave her father and Mabel a hug.

"You're looking awfully stylish today, Mabel." Colby tilted her head at the woman's green silk dress.

"When you get to be my age, you start hoping people notice the dress and not the way you look in it," Mabel said with a chuckle. "You're the one who gets prettier every time I see you."

"We'd have to agree with you there," Colby's father said with a smile.

"Aren't you supposed to be in the kitchen?" she chastised him.

"Just taking a little break for as long as I can get away with it."

She laughed. "That doesn't surprise me."

"Me, either," her mother agreed.

"Mabel introduced us to Mr. McKinley a little earlier," Colby's father said. "And she told us how you saved his life the other day."

"It was no big deal," she said, certain that Mabel had stretched the story into Paul Bunyan proportions.

"If you call nearly getting run over by a tractor no big deal," Mabel objected. "If a person believed in fate and that kind of thing, I'd say the two of you—"

Not willing to let Mabel get started on that particular tangent, Colby said, "You know, it looks as if they're asking everyone to be seated. We'd better find us a place before they're all taken."

Reverend Thomas called for the group's attention. Once everyone grew quiet, he said, "I'd like to thank you all for coming this morning. Our turnouts for this event keep getting better and better. I'd have to say it probably has something to do with the cooking skills of our volunteers in the kitchen."

The men sent up a round of applause for themselves, and everybody laughed.

"I'd like to introduce two new faces to you this morning." Reverend Thomas stepped back and summoned Ian and Luke forward. "We'd like to welcome Ian and Luke McKinley to our church. They came as guests of Frank and Phoebe Walker. We welcome both of you to Keeling Creek. We hope you'll feel at home here."

"Thank you," Ian said. Luke merely stood beside him looking uncomfortable.

All the women sat down while the men began serving the food. The women joked good-naturedly about whether or not it would be edible, even though the men had proved themselves in the past. The smells were mouth-watering—homemade biscuits with scrambled eggs and gravy and freshly brewed coffee.

Lena joined Colby and her mother at the far end of the table. Phoebe and her two boys sat across from them.

"Would you like to ask Luke to sit with us?" Colby asked Lena.

Lena shrugged, and looking as if it didn't matter, said, "I already did. He said he'd just hang out in the kitchen."

Colby knew her daughter well enough to recognize rejection on her face when she saw it.

Frank filed past with the gravy, ladling some over the biscuits on their plates. "This will no doubt be the best item on the menu," he said with a wink. "I made it myself."

Phoebe shook her head. "I might have to argue with that, since he barely knows the location of the frying pan at home."

"Now, now, honey. We'll just let the ladies judge for themselves."

Behind Frank came Ian with a big blue bowl in his hands, the image somehow incongruous. He gave her a sheepish smile. "They put me in charge of the grits, and since I didn't even know what they were until twenty minutes ago, I'm not making any promises on how they turned out."

"I'll take my chances," Colby said with a half smile, uncomfortable, because her mother and Phoebe were taking in every word of the conversation.

He put some on her plate. "If it hadn't been for Lena, they probably would have thrown me out of the kitchen."

Lena smiled up at him, looking for the moment

like her playful, lighthearted daughter of old, and Colby wondered if Ian had that effect on all the women with whom he crossed paths.

# CHAPTER SEVEN

THE NEXT DAY, Colby ran errands on her lunch hour.
She was on her way out of Tinker's Drug when she
looked up to find Ian on his way in.

"Hi." He reached out to right a box of tissues
threatening to slip out of one of her bags.

"Hi," she said, her heart suddenly beating too
fast.

"Here, let me help you with that."

"Oh, no, that's okay. I've got them. Really."

He ignored her protests and took the bags from
her. "Where are you parked?"

"Around the corner. But you don't have to—"

"That's the least I can do for someone who not
only saved my life, but ate my grits without any obvious ill effects." Smiling, Colby followed him, running a hand across her hair and wishing she'd
thought to put on some lipstick.

At the truck, she unlocked the door, and he stuck
the bags inside before turning to her and saying,
"How about letting me treat you to some lunch? I
still haven't paid you back for saving my life."

She should have said no. Any number of excuses
would have been plausible enough to send her on her
way. But she did have a little time before her next
appointment. Reluctant as she was to admit it, lunch

with Ian McKinley sounded appealing. "All right. I'll take you up on it."

Tinker's Drug and Soda Fountain had been around for fifty years or more. It hadn't changed to speak of during that time, and it was busy now at lunch hour. Inside the front door, they were greeted by the smell of grill food, hamburgers, french fries and onion rings. They made their way down an aisle of soaps and toothbrushes to the snack bar at the back of the store. A row of booths lined one wall. The seats were red vinyl and squeaky clean. A white Formica counter with red-topped bar stools offered a view of the grill.

This was one of Colby's favorite places in Keeling Creek. When she was growing up, her dad had brought her here every Saturday morning for a Coke float.

"Booth or counter?" Ian asked.

"Counter," she said, thinking the booth sounded more intimate. Sitting there in full view would be less private, more like they'd just run into each other. Which they had.

"Counter, it is." He waited for her to take a stool and then sat down beside her.

Thomas Tinker approached them with a smile and a menu. He ran the place with the same pride his father had taught him to have in the family establishment. "Hey, Colby. How're things out at the clinic?"

"Busy," she said.

"I believe it. Your waiting room stays busier than Doc Smiley's office. Who's your friend?"

"This is Ian McKinley. Ian, Thomas Tinker."

The two men exchanged small talk, with Ian explaining that he'd recently moved to town. Thomas's welcome was sincere.

"I can't get used to the friendliness," Ian said when Thomas had left them with their drinks. "I guess the city's made me a cynic, but I keep expecting to find out they're putting me on or something. In New York, most people aren't that nice unless you're paying them to be that way."

Colby smiled, fiddling with the edge of her menu. "I guess things are pretty different here."

Thomas came back to take their order. Ian ordered a burger, since it was the house specialty.

"I'll take my usual, Thomas."

The older man shook his head. "Lettuce, tomato and cheese on a bun, coming right up."

"Are you a vegetarian?" Ian asked when Thomas had left with their order.

Colby shrugged. "I don't call myself that. I just prefer not to eat meat. Most people around here are convinced there's something wrong with me because of it."

"You've never eaten it?"

"Oh, sure. When I was a kid, my mom didn't consider the table complete without a roast or a baked chicken. It's my work. I've never been able to view the animals as just livestock."

Ian appeared to think about that for a moment, then said, "Mr. Tinker?"

Thomas turned from his stance at the grill. "It's Thomas. What can I get you?"

"Cancel that burger. I'd like to try one of those veggies."

Thomas shook his head again. "She's getting to you, huh?"

"My doctor has been after me to make a few changes in my diet. No time like the present to start."

Colby was surprised, to say the least. "I hope you didn't do that because—"

"I didn't. A veggie sandwich sounds good."

The declaration was casual and easy, and it both surprised and pleased her. Too much so. Most of the men she knew thought vegetables were for sissies. "So, you're planning to fix up Oak Hill?"

Ian nodded. "I'd like to do most of the work myself, so it may take a while."

"I actually had a notebook of plans, things I'd like to do to the place if I ever bought it," she said on impulse, and then, feeling silly, added, "My dad and I used to drive by there about once a week when I was growing up. I always made him stop so I could look at it. It was empty then. I thought it looked lonely. Like it needed a family. And it has one now."

"I feel bad for messing up your plans," Ian said.

She waved his apology away. "First come, first serve."

"If it helps any, I don't know how long I'll hold on to it. I can't say anything definite, but there's a good possibility I'll be willing to sell it at some point down the road."

"Really? I mean, I guess that would make sense. When you move back to New York, you'll hardly have any reason to keep a big house like that."

"No, I guess not," he said. "I'll certainly give you first dibs on it."

It was a nice gesture. She should have been overjoyed. The house might still be hers, after all, but something about the thought of it fell flat now. "Thanks," she said. "I really appreciate that."

Ian took a sip of his iced tea. "At one time, I guess it was a grand old place."

"It could be again with the right person giving it what it needs. Sometimes things just need a little love and attention."

"That's something I've realized myself recently," Ian said.

She sensed there was more to his statement than was readily apparent. But Thomas brought their veggie burgers just then, and he didn't elaborate. They ate in silence for the first few bites while conversation hummed around them. She felt a few gazes on them and knew the gossip would start within the afternoon. No sooner had the thought crossed her mind than she caught a glimpse of Louise Mason and her twelve-year old daughter waiting for a booth. Louise spotted her and all but sprinted over.

Colby managed a smile. "Hello, Louise. How are you?"

"Oh, I'm fine," she said, patting Colby's shoulder. "Aren't you going to introduce me to your friend?"

Grace won out over reluctance. "Ian, this is Louise Mason. She owns the hair salon in town. Louise, this is Ian McKinley. I don't have to tell you who he is."

Louise grasped Ian's hand in a handshake that Colby knew from personal experience could rival any sumo wrestler's. "Well, I've just heard so much about you, Mr. McKinley. And I'm so glad to see you've managed to get our Colby out and about.

We'd just about given up hope of her finding a good man."

"Nice to meet you, Miss Mason," he said, looking more than a little amused.

"Oh, it's Louise," she said, all but preening. If the woman hadn't had a wedding ring on her finger, Colby had no doubt she would have knocked her right off the stool and bowled Ian over with her charm. She said a prayer of thanks when Louise's daughter called out to her from their table. "I'd better be getting back. You two enjoy your lunch," she said, winking at Colby.

Colby lowered her forehead onto one hand and stared at the counter in mortification. "I can't believe she said that."

"She's harmless," he said, chuckling. "There's no reason to be embarrassed. Really."

"Easy for you to say." The humor in the situation hit her, and she smiled in spite of herself. "There are days when I wonder what it would be like to live in a place where people actually have a little privacy."

"Lonely, sometimes."

"It might be worth it once in a while," she said. "Being the eligible carrot on the end of the stick does get a little old. Fortunately, the positives of living in a place like this outweigh the negatives. The people who can't keep their nose out of your business are the same ones who would be there for you in a flash if you ever needed their help. Maybe this wasn't a good idea, though. There will be talk, you know."

"About what?"

"The two of us having lunch together. Louise will

have everybody in the Dippety-Do informed within thirty seconds of getting back to the shop.''

Ian toyed with a french fry. ''I've never cared too much about what other people think.''

Colby tilted her head and said in a low voice, ''With your being engaged, I didn't think you'd want anyone to get the wrong impression.''

He held her gaze for a moment too long while something inside her flared to life. The feeling was inappropriate, and she knew it. But she couldn't deny that it was there.

''To be honest, I could use a friend here,'' he said. ''Does my engagement have to stand in the way of that?''

His question brought with it a surge of disappointment. From an adult standpoint, there was absolutely nothing wrong with the two of them being friends. They had two difficult teenagers in common. She found him easy to talk to, as, apparently, he did her. Friends. What was wrong with the two of them being friends?

''No, it doesn't.'' She pushed her half-eaten sandwich away. ''As a matter of fact, I'm going to a meeting on Thursday night you might be interested in attending. The hospital hosts a lecture series each month. This month's topic is 'Understanding Your Teenager.' I thought I'd go just to see if they can convince me there *is* any understanding them. You're welcome to come if you'd like.''

''Fiction or nonfiction?'' he asked with a half grin.

''Non, supposedly,'' she said, smiling. ''We'll see.''

''Are you serious? About my going?''

"Sure, if you think it might help things with Luke."

"It certainly couldn't hurt."

She glanced at her watch, ignoring the voice inside her that questioned what she'd just done. "I'd better be getting back. I have a full afternoon ahead."

Ian reached for the ticket. "Yeah, I've got to go, too." He looked up and caught her gaze. The increasingly familiar awareness resurfaced. She resisted its pull. They'd established the boundaries of their relationship. They had something in common as far as their teenagers were concerned. He could use a friend. She could use a friend. That was all.

But sitting beside him, staring into those too blue, too appealing eyes, she wondered if she was kidding herself. Friends? Friends.

Colby twisted her stool around and slid to the floor. "Thanks for the lunch. The meeting is at the Kramer building on Sycamore Street. Room 212. It starts at six."

"I'll be there," he said, and her traitorous heart fluttered in gladness.

MAYBE HE WOULDN'T COME.

Colby had arrived a few minutes early for the lecture, but it was almost 6:00, and there was no sign of Ian yet.

Maybe he'd changed his mind.

Maybe it would be for the best if he had.

A hand touched her shoulder. She looked up to find the source of her thoughts looking down at her with an apologetic smile on his face.

"Sorry I'm late," he said.

"They're just getting ready to start." She turned

to the side so he could take the chair next to hers. Before they had time to say anything more, the lecturer stepped to the podium and tapped the microphone to get the room's attention. "Good evening, everyone. Thank you so much for coming. I'm Dr. Betsy Watson, and I hope to say a few things this evening that will convince you there is light at the end of the tunnel for you and your teenager."

Laughter rippled across the room, indicating that everyone there knew what she was talking about. For the next hour and a half, they listened while Dr. Watson discussed some of the ways in which they, as parents, could make the teenage years of their children's lives more bearable for all concerned. The most important thing, she stressed at the beginning of the talk, was to keep the lines of communication open. Easier said than done.

Colby made an attempt to listen intently. With things the way they were with Lena, she needed every morsel of intelligence she could garner. But awareness of the man seated beside her eroded her concentration until it was all she could do to focus on the speaker's words. She was far too disturbed by the proximity of Ian's shoulder, the knowledge that a fraction of an inch lay between them. Minute details assaulted her senses. The fresh, clean smell of his cologne, the starched crispness of his white shirt and the contrast it made with the sun-browned skin on his well-shaped hands.

At one point, he dropped his program and bent to pick it up. His left shoulder brushed her right thigh. Colby jumped.

Ian sat back up and whispered, "Sorry."

She shook her head and waved his apology away.

Feeling ridiculously self-conscious, she forced her attention back to the speaker. That lasted for all of thirty seconds, before her senses took over again, and she was grateful when the meeting finally drew to a close. For the past hour and a half, she'd felt as if she were on sensory overload. Standing, she introduced Ian to some of the people she knew. After a few minutes, they moved about the room, separately, until a half hour or so later, they both ended up near the door.

"Ready to call it a night now that we've learned how to deal with our kids?" he asked.

"I'd stay until morning if I thought I could go home and make things the way they were when she was ten."

"If I got anything out of what our speaker said, that's so much wishful thinking."

"Unfortunately, I think you're right," she said.

A few people called out good-night as they left the room.

"Nice people," Ian said in the hallway.

"Yes, they are." They took the stairs to the first floor, then hung back in the hallway.

"How about a cup of coffee somewhere?" he suggested.

It was a tempting invitation, but something told her it would be better to end the evening here. He looked entirely too good in a patterned blazer and black wool pants, both of which had *Italy* written all over them. Definitely not the kind of clothes that inspired women to think about friendship. She glanced at her watch. "It's late. I should get home."

"Sure. I understand."

But she didn't think he understood at all. She wasn't sure she did herself.

Despite her declaration, they made no move toward the door.

He leaned up against a locker, one foot propped against the door, his arms folded across his chest. "She was a good speaker."

"Yes. I got the feeling she'd definitely been through it," Colby agreed, hoping he wouldn't ask her opinion on something that had been said when she'd been paying more attention to him than to the lecturer.

"I think that's the only way anyone could understand it. Firsthand experience."

"It's hard to know what being a soldier is all about until you've been on the battlefield."

"Some days I definitely feel that way." His expression grew solemn. "I just wish I could go back and do some things differently."

She heard the regret in his voice and knew there was more to his situation than he'd let on. Sensing that he wanted to talk about it, she said, "Why did you move here, Ian?"

He looked down at the floor for a long while, his hands shoved deep in his pants pockets. "Luke got arrested on a drug charge," he finally said, his voice low. "I wanted to get him away from the city."

The revelation took her totally by surprise. She'd never imagined anything like that. She thought of her own problems with Lena and felt lucky. "Oh. I'm sorry, Ian. Lord, it's not easy being a parent these days."

"I wasn't doing a very good job of it, I'm afraid.

I spent too much time working and not enough time knowing where my son was and what he was doing.''

"You can't blame yourself for—"

"Oh, but I do," he interrupted firmly enough to indicate that he'd spent a great deal of time thinking about exactly that. "I do."

Again, Colby felt fortunate not to have had that kind of trouble with Lena.

"Don't short yourself, Ian. Putting your life on hold is pretty generous, even for a parent."

"Thanks. I appreciate that."

"Have things improved since you've been here?"

"Between the two of us, no. He's going to school and doing the things he's supposed to be doing. He swore to me that the drugs had never been a problem and wouldn't be in the future. I have to believe him."

He was appealingly vulnerable in this moment of admission. She knew it hadn't been an easy thing for him to talk about. "Well, as for Luke getting used to being here, give him time. He'll adjust." No sooner were the words out than she realized that she was offering him the same platitudes people had been giving her about Lena for the past two months.

"So, now that I've pulled all my skeletons out of the closet, what's the problem between you and Lena?" he asked, looking down at her.

"Hah. Now there's a question. It seems like she just woke up one day and decided she didn't like me anymore. I've reached the point where I don't think I can do anything more than take my own clichéd advice and wait for things to change again."

"Pretty sad, aren't we?" he asked with a wry smile.

"At least we're trying. All you have to do is open

the paper to see what happens to children who don't have parents who care enough to stick with them." She sighed and ran a hand through her hair. "I don't know. The older I get, the more I realize that being a good parent, a good human being, is just plain hard work. I'm human enough to wish I could be selfish and say the heck with it sometimes. But that's not what I want to teach Lena. And from what I can tell, it isn't what you want to teach Luke."

Ian watched her silently, his gaze lingering on her face. In that moment, she felt the forging of a bond that had been developing between them since the moment they'd met. And it scared the devil out of her. She stepped back and motioned toward the door. "I'm sorry. I didn't mean to get on my soapbox. It's late. I'd better get going."

"You didn't. I've enjoyed the evening. Might have actually learned something," he said, his gaze direct, warming her in a multitude of places. Clearing her throat, she made her way toward the door. He followed her outside to her truck.

"Good luck with Luke," she said, stopping at the driver's side door. "Maybe things will work out for us both soon. With the kids, I mean," she added hastily, and then felt like an idiot.

"I hope you're right," he said in that steady, even way of his.

She made a valiant effort not to look at him again as she started the truck, backed out of the parking space and headed toward the exit. But as she pulled out onto the street, she couldn't resist one last glimpse in the rearview mirror. He was still standing beneath the lamppost, staring after her.

# CHAPTER EIGHT

THROUGHOUT THE NEXT week, Ian attempted to put some of the information he'd gained at the parent-teenager lecture to use.

*Teenagers are no longer children. Consult with them. Ask their opinions. Suggest. Don't order.*

While Ian felt sure Dr. Watson's advice was all valid, he wondered if things were too far gone for any of it to make a difference with Luke and him. He thought about what Colby had said about parenting being plain old hard work. She was right. Rebuilding his relationship with Luke meant working at it each and every day, chipping away at the boy's anger, hoping he could move a little closer to his goal with each attempt.

One afternoon when Luke got off the school bus, Ian was outside with a ladder and a bucket of paint, giving the trim on the house the face-lift it needed. He spotted Luke coming up the driveway, his stride long and relaxed until he looked up and saw Ian watching him. Insolence made him slow his walk and frown.

Ian dipped his brush into the bucket on the tray at the top of the ladder, then carefully stroked the paint across the chipped trim beneath the roofline. The boy's aloofness stabbed deep, but Ian refused to let him see it. When Luke reached the top of the drive,

Ian waved and said, "I've got an extra brush handy if you're interested."

Luke didn't answer for several seconds. "What are you trying to prove, Dad?" he finally asked, his voice filled with condescension. "Do you really think moving me out to the country and pretending to be something you're not is going to change anything?"

The anger in Luke's voice sent a wave of despair through Ian. Did his son's resentment run so deep that he might never get past it? The thought scared him more than anything in his life ever had. What if it was too late to make up for his mistakes? He couldn't let himself believe that. They just needed time. And that was something Ian had plenty of right now.

Refusing to let Luke see that he'd rattled him, he said, "If you change your mind, the extra brushes are at the foot of the ladder."

Luke swung around and stomped inside without answering.

HE WAS UNBELIEVABLE.

Unbelievable!

Luke dropped his book bag at the foot of the stairs and stomped down the hallway toward the kitchen. That couldn't really be his dad out there on that ladder. It had to be someone impersonating him. His father never had time for things like house painting. He had other people do that kind of stuff. For as far back as he could remember, Luke could count on two hands the number of times he'd seen his father in anything other than a suit. Since they'd been here, he practically lived in blue jeans and running shoes.

He looked like a different person. And he acted different, asking him to help with things, wanting to spend time with him. Luke couldn't get used to it. He didn't want to, because it wouldn't last. He knew it wouldn't. It never had before. He thought about the times his dad had promised to come to a soccer match, only to be sidetracked by a last-minute meeting. Or the surprise birthday party he'd arranged for him and then been two hours late getting to. From the moment he'd been born, he'd been nothing but a burden to his father. He just wished his dad would stop pretending otherwise.

Inside the kitchen, the smell of Mabel's homemade chocolate chip cookies still hung in the air. A note on the table said:

Luke,
I've gone to the grocery store. Four cookies before dinner and no more. Back soon.

Mabel

Luke rolled his eyes and grabbed a handful of cookies from the glass jar she kept on the kitchen counter. Why was it that someone was always telling him what to do? His dad, who'd never cared enough to tell him anything until he'd decided it was his duty to reform him. Mabel, who acted like she was his mother or something. And his teachers, who said he was capable of far more than he was doing in school. What did they know?

Pulling a glass from the cabinet, Luke poured himself some milk and sat at the kitchen table. No one here really knew him. And if he had anything to do with it, they wouldn't be here long enough for it to matter.

He hated it here. He'd met a couple of okay kids. Football players who were actually more concerned about getting college scholarships than getting high. And a couple of cheerleaders who'd made it clear they'd like to get to know him better.

But they were all boring compared to the kids he'd hung around with in the city.

And then there was that Williams girl. Lena. She was cute. But she looked at him as if she had no idea what to say to him. As if they were from different planets—and they might as well have been. He'd passed her in the hall several times. He'd wanted to stop and talk to her, but he'd had no idea what to say. She wasn't his type, anyway. He liked girls who knew the score. Girls who didn't expect to wear his class ring after the second date.

All the kids at Jefferson High were just too straight for him. He wanted to go back to the city, where he knew how things worked. He belonged there, not here in this stuck-in-the-fifties town.

If he played his cards right, it wouldn't be too much longer before his dad gave up on him. He knew his father's interest in him was nothing more than the result of a guilt trip. Until he'd gotten into trouble, they'd merely lived in the same house. His father had left for work before he got up and usually didn't come home until he'd gone to bed.

And now he was acting like Ward Cleaver. Painting the house. Fixing up the barn. He'd get tired of it before long.

He finished his fourth cookie, reached for a fifth, then glanced at Mabel's note and put it back in the jar. For the briefest of seconds, he wished that this whole fake life his father had created could be true.

That he really had grown up in a house like this, that he and his father had the kind of relationship where he could go out and climb up on a ladder beside him, where he could tell him about the play they'd read in English class that day.

But they didn't. And they never would.

ON THE FOLLOWING Friday afternoon, Colby made an emergency call out to the Bowers farm. A horse had gotten into a half-full grain bin and had almost eaten enough of the sweet feed to kill her. Luckily, Lou Ann Bowers had caught the mare before she finished it off. As good as the grain might have tasted, Colby doubted the horse had enjoyed the dose of mineral oil that had followed it.

It was almost six o'clock by the time Colby unenthusiastically headed back toward town. With the end of September, the leaves were beginning to turn bright red and gold on the mountains in the distance. But Colby was feeling too down to appreciate them. Lena's camp-out was tonight, so she had an empty house waiting for her. She passed the Walkers's driveway without stopping. Normally, she would have stopped to visit, but Phoebe had called the night before, needing to talk to her about Frank. Things still weren't normal between them. She'd stayed on the phone with Phoebe for more than an hour, and although she had tried to sound optimistic, Colby was beginning to think that maybe her friend had cause for concern. She had suggested that Phoebe try to get a sitter tonight so that she and Frank could have some time alone.

Just past Phoebe's house, Colby spotted a large black dog in her lane, barking as if it had just cornered a T-bone steak. She caught a glimpse of a smaller animal disappearing into the brush. Slowing to a stop, she recognized the dog as U-2. The McKinleys' dog.

She pulled over and got out of the truck. "Here, girl."

The dog looked up, then trotted toward Colby, her tongue lolling to one side of her mouth.

"What are you doing way out here by yourself, U-2?" From ten feet away, Colby realized that the T-bone had been a skunk. And U-2 had come out the loser in the confrontation.

"I have a feeling you're going to be in big trouble, girl," she said, holding her nose. "Come on. In the back. As much as I like you, I don't think I'm up to sharing the front seat with you."

Colby let down the tailgate. U-2 jumped up and sat with her head over the side, panting. Pulling back onto the road, Colby considered taking U-2 home with her and calling Ian to come and get her. The entrance to Oak Hill loomed just ahead on the right. It was Friday night, and she didn't relish the idea of running into his fiancée again if she happened to be visiting. But that was ridiculous. So what if the woman was there? All she'd done was pick the dog up off the road, and now she was taking her home. She would have done the same for anyone in Keeling Creek.

Nonetheless, she swung the truck onto the drive with the hope that she could drop U-2 off and leave unnoticed. No such luck. At the top of the driveway, she spotted Ian on a ladder at the side of the house. He turned around at the sound of her truck, looking surprised to see her. Reluctantly, she got out while he climbed down and came to meet her. He was wearing a paint-splattered shirt with jeans. His hair was appealingly disheveled, and when he ran his right hand through it, she experienced the urge to do the same.

"I'm returning your wayward dog," she called out. "Although I'm not sure you're going to want her anytime soon."

U-2 bounded out of the back and greeted Ian in typical dog-love fashion. Tail wagging, she lunged and planted her paws on his chest, her tongue swiping at his jaw.

"Wait! U-2, don't—" Colby tried to stop her, but it was too late.

"Good grief," Ian exclaimed, leaping back. "What on earth did you get into?"

Colby shouldn't have laughed, but she couldn't help herself. The look on Ian's face was just too comical. "She had a one-on-one with a skunk," she said, trying to cover up a smile. "As you can smell, the skunk won."

"You sure you don't want to take her home with you?"

Colby smiled again. "Not tonight, I don't think."

Ian shot a disgruntled look at U-2, who was looking offended by his less-than-enthusiastic reception. "How do you get rid of it?"

"It's mostly a wear-off thing."

Ian shook his head. "It looks as if you're going to be sleeping in the barn, girl."

U-2 whined and plopped down on the ground, still panting from her adventure.

Colby should have said goodbye then and left Ian

to his own devices. But she found herself lingering. "There is one thing that might help."

"Hey, I'm willing to try anything."

"Tomato juice."

Ian looked at her as if she'd just suggested the dog could fly to the moon. "I'd like to see you make that dog drink tomato juice."

Colby laughed. "You don't make her drink it. You bathe her in it."

"Bathe her in it? She weighs over a hundred pounds."

Colby shoved her hands into her pockets and rocked back on her heels. "Yep. It would take a lot of juice."

Ian eyed her skeptically. "Are you serious?"

"It won't get rid of it completely. But it might make her bearable."

The breeze threw a pungent whiff of skunk in their direction. "I guess I'm desperate enough to try that," he said. "If I offered a pizza as compensation, could I convince you to hang around and help me de-skunk my son's dog?"

If a couple of minutes ago had been the time to not involve herself further, now was definitely the point to say she had to go. The words formed but didn't make it past her lips. There was something about the way he looked so darned appealing in his paint-splattered shirt and the thought of the empty house waiting for her that made her say, "Sure. Why not?"

He looked pleased by her agreement. "Okay. Give me a minute to hook Her Smelliness to her doghouse, and we'll go in search of tomato juice. I don't have any. I sure hope the stores around here do."

He was back in less than a minute, car keys jangling in his hand. "I'll drive."

Colby slid into the passenger seat, and they were off down the driveway. He had the windows down, and the fall air teased the ends of her hair. She suggested they try Smitty's Market first. It was only a mile or so away. He took a right onto the highway, and there was something about rolling down a country road with this man on a late September evening that felt free and good. Too much so.

At Smitty's, they both hopped out and went inside. They searched an aisle or two before locating three quarts. They bought them all, then headed on toward town.

"How much do you think it will take?" Ian asked.

"A lot more than three quarts," she replied.

They hit five stores in all, cleaning each one out. They both laughed at the last stop when the cashier asked if they were having a Bloody Mary party. "I wish," Ian said.

Just outside the store, he added with a grin, "I hope there's not a run on tomato juice in the next couple of days. We've just depleted the town's supply."

She smiled. "We definitely created a shortage."

Back at the house, Ian followed Colby's instructions and procured a large tin tub from the barn. They placed it near the water hose at the back door of the house. One by one they opened the jars and filled the tub with the juice.

Ian rolled up his sleeves. "I'm glad I don't have to climb in there."

"Oh, this is probably a terribly expensive skin treatment at some swanky spa in California."

Ian shook his head. "I wouldn't doubt it."

Shoving up her own sleeves, she said, "All right. We're ready for her."

"But is she ready for us?"

"Probably not," Colby said, smiling.

Ian untied the dog and led her toward the tub. Halfway there, U-2 must have figured out what was going on. She promptly put on the brakes, her legs stretched out in front of her like a balking mule. "You asked for this, you know," Ian scolded. "Now quit being stubborn."

At the tub, Colby helped him lift the reluctant dog and place her in the washtub. She had never seen a more offended-looking animal. The dog stood with one paw in the air as if to say, "You don't really expect me to do this, do you?" While the skunk hadn't seemed to bother her at all, the tomato juice was apparently a grave indignity.

They used cups to douse her with the liquid. She stood there like a statue, turning her nose toward the rising moon and letting out a protesting howl every minute or two.

"Okay. She needs to soak for a while," Colby said once they'd thoroughly doused her. She pushed the dog's fanny down so that most of her skunk-scented fur was submerged.

"So, how'd you discover the tomato juice secret?" Ian asked. "Did they teach you that in vet school?"

"Nope. That came from my grandmother. Actually, I kind of had the same thing happen when I was seven. I was waiting for the school bus and spotted a mother skunk with three babies. I thought they were cute, and naturally I wanted to pet them, but mama skunk had different ideas.''

"So you know exactly what U-2 is going through?" he asked with a grin.

"I don't think she minded as much as I did."

Ian smiled again, and they stood there watching each other. The moon hung high over his left shoulder, throwing shadowed light on his well-defined face. It was 9:00 on a Friday night. She was helping Ian McKinley wash his dog and having more fun than she'd had in ages.

The moment was broken when U-2 decided she'd had enough. Standing in the tub, she shook, nose to tail, sending tomato juice flying in all directions. Colby yelped and jumped back. Ian sidestepped the onslaught, too, but not in time. They were both covered. Faces, shirts, arms, pants.

Colby looked at Ian and started laughing. She couldn't help it. Even his long, dark eyelashes were dripping with tomato juice.

Judging from his expression, she didn't look any better. His face broke into a grin, and then he started laughing, too.

While their attention was diverted, U-2 hopped out of the tub and took off across the grass, running circles around the scattered old oak trees, a reddish-black streak in the moonlit yard.

Colby collapsed onto the ground, still laughing, holding her stomach now.

It took them a minute or two to regain their composure. Ian tried calling U-2 back a couple of times, but he couldn't muster any sternness, and the dog definitely wasn't taking him seriously. She wanted to play. She raced forward, stopping just short of him, barking and then taking off in a flash, fanny tucked low to the ground.

"All right, have your fun," he finally said, "but you've got the rinse cycle to go yet."

Colby got up from the ground, wiping her eyes. She lifted one side of the tub and helped him pour out the juice. He turned on the water hose and refilled the tub. The water level rose slowly, and again, Colby found herself studying him as discreetly as she could. His hair was tousled and damp at the temples. His shirt was plastered to his chest, now polka-dotted with tomato juice, as well as paint. His blue jeans were in similar disrepair, damp and molded to his long legs in a way that did nothing for her peace of mind.

Realizing she was staring, she jerked her gaze upward and found him giving her a like perusal. Her hand went to her hair, smoothing it back. No doubt she looked a mess. But that wasn't the message she saw in his eyes. He was looking at her as if he liked what he saw. The realization did crazy things to her insides.

An unexpected feeling of longing swept through her, a longing for something she'd claimed not to need, not to want. But she realized in that instant what she had been missing out on. Companionship. Simple, basic companionship. Someone with whom she could do silly things. Someone with whom she could let down her guard. Be herself. She thought of all the awful dates she'd had in past years. The stiff dinners for two, the awkward silences at her front door. None of them had ever felt like this. Maybe if they had, she would have been able to put Doug behind her long ago.

Shocked by her own thoughts, she turned away and called U-2. The dog slunk toward them, her head bowed. They lifted her over the edge of the tub, silent now. They rinsed and rinsed until all traces of the juice were gone.

"I think it really helped," Ian said, sounding surprised.

"It's still there, but at least it's a little more subdued."

"The miracles of modern medicine," he said.

"Sometimes the simplest cures are the most effective."

Standing there in the moonlight with a giant, wet black Lab between them, Colby couldn't remember the last time she'd felt so good. The realization was unsettling and more than a little disturbing. Enough so that she stepped back and said, "I'd better get going."

"Hey, I promised you a pizza. That's the least I can do, considering how you just spent your Friday night."

"I won't hold you to that. It's late—"

"Don't tell me you didn't work up an appetite after all this. Come on. I'll call it in and you can get cleaned up."

To stay longer would be to invite something different from what they'd shared so far. If not on his part, then certainly in her own mind. But she really didn't want to go. Shirking common sense, she said, "Okay. Pizza, it is."

"Good," he said, looking pleased. He turned U-2 loose. The dog took off again, cutting circles around the house in obvious appreciation of her freedom. Colby followed Ian inside, where he said, "You'll have to pardon the construction. We've got a little more to do yet."

She had never seen the inside of the house. It did, indeed, need work, but the actual layout was every bit as magnificent as the outside had promised. The foyer was two stories high, and a mahogany staircase wound from the first floor to the second.

"Would you like a tour?" he asked.

"I'd love one."

He led her through the house, stopping at the living room first, a grand room of enormous proportions with a stone fireplace as large as a small room. The kitchen was equally big, with windows on two sides. A butcher block sat in the middle, copper pots hanging above it. And someone, probably Mabel, had placed potted herbs on the sill above the sink. A small greenhouse opened up off the kitchen, the perfect place to raise tomatoes and flowers year-round.

"As you can see," Ian said, "I don't have much of a green thumb. Mabel's been after me to buy some plants."

"I think even I could grow them in here," Colby said. "And I'm known for my brown thumb."

"Couldn't be browner than mine." He led her upstairs to what was apparently his bedroom. This room, too, was in need of redecoration. The paint on the walls was circa 1960, and the hardwood floor needed refinishing. But a beautiful cherry sleigh bed sat in the center of the room. Two matching nightstands graced the sides of it. A dresser in the same wood sat near the window. If his choice of furniture was any indication, he had excellent taste.

"The bathroom is through there." He tilted his head toward the open door on the other side of the room. He opened the closet and pulled out a rugby shirt. "This will be too big, but at least it's free of tomato juice. I'd offer you some pants, too, but I don't think they'd fit."

"This is fine," she said, taking the shirt from him, feeling suddenly uneasy with the thought of wearing his clothes. It seemed personal in a way that brought to mind things she shouldn't be thinking about.

Their gazes caught and held. Outwardly, they were guilty of nothing. She was standing in his bedroom, holding one of his newly laundered shirts. Nothing wrong with that. So why did it feel as if there was?

"Well, I'll clean up and meet you downstairs," she said, breaking the silence.

He stepped back as if jolted from a trance. "Sure. I'll just go order the pizza. What do you like on yours?"

"Mushrooms and black olives."

"You got it." He stopped at the door. "When you're finished, there's something I'd like to show you."

And he left her then to wonder what it was.

## CHAPTER NINE

HE WAS WAITING for her at the foot of the stairs when she finished showering and changing. His hair was wet, and a few drops of water still clung to his neck after his own shower. He'd found a fresh shirt and a pair of faded jeans somewhere, and there wasn't a spot of tomato juice in sight.

He waved her toward the back door off the kitchen. "The pizza's on its way."

More than a little curious, she followed him outside to the barn. He pulled open the large, faded red door and motioned her toward a stall a few yards away.

What she saw inside was the last thing she had expected. Standing before her was a black-and-white calf, which she immediately recognized as one of the twins she'd delivered at Harry Pasley's. She opened the stall and went in, dropping down on her knees to rub the calf's forehead. "Hey, little girl. How'd you get here?"

She heard Ian move in behind her and looked up to find him with one shoulder against the door frame. "You said she wouldn't be of much use to Harry. I kept thinking about how she almost hadn't made it and what you said that night after the lecture about how easy it is to ignore things that make our lives more complicated. I've been pretty good at that. I know it sounds crazy, but I couldn't stand the thought of her being sent to the stockyard. Harry brought her over in his truck for me."

Colby didn't know what to say. She was so touched by what he'd done that she couldn't speak. Finally finding her voice, she said, "Well, I guess you surprised the devil out of Harry."

"Luckily, he hadn't let her go yet, and when I told him I'd like to have her, he seemed pretty pleased. He's keeping the other little guy. He said the father was one of his good bulls."

"So what did you name her?"

"Mabel thought Matilda suited her. What do you think?"

"I think…Matilda is a lovely name," she said, swallowing the lump in her throat and stroking the calf's soft fur.

"I'm feeding her by bottle three times a day. Harry showed me how to mix up the formula. She seems to like it."

The calf let out a bleat and butted its nose against Ian's leg.

"She likes you, too," Colby said.

Looking a little embarrassed, he said, "She's just hoping I'll give her an extra bottle. Actually, she's won us all over. Mabel's down here every hour or so checking on her. Luke didn't say much about her at first, but I've noticed that he heads straight for the barn every day when he gets home from school."

"What will you do with her when you and Luke move back to the city?"

"I haven't gotten that far yet. But I fully intend for her to get old and fat."

A horn sounded from outside.

"That'll be the pizza." Ian hitched a thumb back toward the house and stepped out of the stall.

"I'll be right up." Once he'd left the barn, Colby turned and stroked Matilda's soft forehead with the backs of her fingers, thinking about what he had done. She felt strange, as if the room had tilted and she didn't quite have the balance to stand.

Matilda looked up at her with enormous round eyes, swiping her hand with her rough, pink tongue. Colby rubbed a thumb across the calf's moist nose and said, "If we're not careful, Miss Matilda, you and I are both going to be in a heap of trouble."

A FEW MINUTES later, Colby sat on the couch with her pizza-filled plate in front of her. She'd felt decidedly awkward after returning to the house. She sensed that he did as well. They said very little while he gathered their plates and silverware and carried it all to the living room. She watched him when she was sure he wasn't looking. Saving Matilda from the stockyard wasn't the kind of thing she would have expected from a man whom she had initially likened to Doug. More and more, she was beginning to realize just how wrong she had been. Not sure what to make of that, she said, "So tell me about your work in New York. I know it had to be more exciting than painting houses. Not that you aren't good with trim."

"Thanks." He smiled, wiping the corner of his mouth with a napkin. "I'm keeping my finger in the pie from here. The miracles of computers."

"Do you like what you do?"

He considered the question for a moment. "It's pretty consuming work. Or rather, I let it be. I think the answer to your question is yes. When this whole thing with Luke happened, I'd just brought in the biggest client the firm had ever had. It was a moment I'd spent a lot of years working pretty hard for. But somehow it wasn't everything I thought it would be.''

"What do you mean?''

"I don't know exactly. It just felt as if something was missing. That was the night I found out about Luke being in trouble. And that was when I realized what a lousy father I'd been, that I hadn't really been there for him any more than mine had been there for me.''

"I can't imagine that being true.''

Ian didn't say anything for a few moments. "I grew up pretty poor,'' he said at last. "Really poor, in fact. My father left my mother when I was six. She spent most of her adult life trying to make ends meet. For as long as I can remember, I wanted to make something of myself, to make her proud of me. She encouraged me even though I think it was hard for her to believe I could really do it.''

Astonished that his childhood had been nothing like his life now, Colby realized she'd once again jumped to conclusions where he was concerned. "Is she still alive?''

He shook his head. "I had just found out about my scholarship to Columbia when she died.''

"She must have been very proud of you,'' she said, saddened that his mother hadn't been able to see what he'd done with his life.

"I think she was. That's always given me comfort, even if it is selfish comfort.''

"It's not selfish at all,'' she said softly. "We all want our parents to be proud of us.'' Colby put her plate on the table and sat back on the couch. "Did you get married in college?"

Ian shook his head. "I met Sherry, Luke's mother, my freshman year. We got married right after graduation. We had Luke a little over a year later. She died a few days after he was born."

Colby didn't know what to say. "I'm sorry. I shouldn't have asked. I just assumed you were divorced or—"

"It's all right. Really."

"Those were some pretty tough blows to be dealt at such a young age."

"Yeah. Life has a big fist sometimes."

She had to agree with that. "You were a single parent from the beginning, too, then."

He nodded. "And I was so determined to be different from my own father, to give Luke the things mine had never given me, that I messed up my priorities."

"You're being hard on yourself."

"I don't think so. One thing I've realized since being here is that CCI hasn't fallen to pieces without me. I could have spent more time with Luke. Maybe if I had—"

"Don't do that," she said. "Those 'maybe' games can get you into trouble. Believe me, I know."

"So, why aren't you married? I know it can't be for lack of offers."

Not wanting to discuss her past, she said, "I guess I just never found the right man. Once the toads started outranking the princes ten to one, I decided it wasn't worth the trouble of looking."

Ian laughed. "That bad, huh?"

"That bad."

"What about Lena's father?"

Colby sobered. "That didn't work out."

"I'm sorry."

"Most men with a baby would have remarried," she said, turning the conversation back to him.

"It took me a long time to get over losing Sherry. I never wanted to make that kind of commitment to anyone again. The thought was too painful."

He had obviously loved his wife very much. She heard it in his voice. And she respected him for that. "Rachel must be a very special woman."

He hesitated. "It's not the same kind of marriage. But our lives complement each other's."

"I see," she said, not sure she really did. Didn't he love Rachel? Would their marriage be based on compatibility rather than passion?

He watched her, not saying anything. Colby again felt somehow off balance, unsure of her footing. How long they sat there, she wasn't sure. But she did know that it was getting more and more difficult to pretend indifference to this man. The more time she spent with him, the more dimensional he became, the more she identified with him. "I should go," she said, breaking the silence. "I can help clean up before I leave."

"I can handle throwing away a pizza box and sticking a couple of plates in the dishwasher."

She smiled. "Okay, then. Thanks for the dinner."

"Thanks for the help."

"Let's just hope it worked."

He walked her outside. The moon hung high in the sky, throwing shadowed light across their faces. They stopped at the door to her truck and then stood there, uneasy with each other. Colby felt the electricity between them. She might not have been the most active member of the Keeling Creek dating circuit, but she could tell when a man was thinking about kissing her. And unless she was way off, that was exactly what Ian was thinking.

The scary part was that she wanted him to. Even though she knew it was wrong, unwise and highly unadvisable. She opened the door and got inside the truck. The sooner she left the better. "Good night, Ian. Thanks again."

"Good night, Colby."

She drove away then, her only consolation the note of regret she could have sworn she heard in his voice.

THROUGHOUT THE WEEK, Lena hadn't been able to muster much enthusiasm for the camp-out on Friday night. All of her friends were going. But the problem was, every one of them would be hooking up with a guy once they got there. Every one except her. She was beginning to think there was something wrong with her.

They'd just finished setting up the tents when Tim Anderson's Wagoneer rolled to a stop just above the pond where they were camping.

Millie tapped Lena on the shoulder. "Looks like it just might be your lucky night."

Lena's gaze followed her friend's to the Wagoneer at the top of the hill. Luke McKinley had just gotten out of the passenger side and made his way around to the back of the vehicle. He and Tim pulled out a couple of duffel bags, slung them over their shoulders and headed down the hill toward the campsite.

Jefferson County High had its share of good-looking guys. Football players with big muscles and broad shoulders. Luke McKinley was tall and lean and different from any boy she'd ever known. His walk was loose limbed and hinted at attitude. Her heart thudded in her chest. She couldn't find her voice. When she did, it came out much higher than normal. "I don't know what you're talking about."

"Oh, right, Lena. I've seen the way you look at him in the halls. You're crazy about him."

"I don't even know him," she said with what she hoped sounded like indifference.

"So? I didn't say you knew him. I said you were crazy about him."

Lena ignored Millie's baiting and went over to the campfire to help grill the burgers. So what if she thought he was cute? That didn't mean she was going to make a fool of herself.

For the next two hours, she did an admirable job of not looking at him. It had to be her overactive imagination that she felt his gaze on her, though. That or wishful thinking.

The Fellowship of Christian Athletes was one of the school's most popular organizations. Jim Bevson, the economics teacher who headed the group, was largely responsible for that. He was the coolest teacher at Jefferson County High, and all the kids loved him. His wife, Theresa, was just as cool as he was. She went with him on all the group field trips. Lena had often thought if she'd had a dad, she'd have liked him to be like Mr. Bevson. She was convinced the Bevsons had the best marriage she'd ever seen. Except for Aunt Phoebe and Uncle Frank, of course. Nobody had a better marriage than theirs.

Lena sat at the edge of the campfire and listened while Mr. Bevson told them a story about a boy who had been paralyzed from the neck down after diving off the high board at a swim meet. The boy had pretty much given up on life until, one day, someone had brought him a computer he could operate with his voice. He began to write stories with it and had gone on to write a prize-winning novel called *When All Is Black*.

Mr. Bevson's stories always had a point. "Every one of us has something in our lives that could hold us back if we let it," he said when he'd finished. "The key is to deal with it, then find a way around it."

Lena looked into the campfire flames and thought of the father she'd never met. Anger smoldered inside her when she thought of how her mother had lied to her. Could she ever find a way around that? Could she ever forgive her?

The group around the campfire began to break up, interrupting Lena's thoughts. They didn't have to be in their sleeping bags until midnight, so when someone suggested a walk, everyone agreed. For the couples in the group, it would be a perfect opportunity to sneak off and make out for an hour or so. Sure enough, ten minutes into the walk, both Millie and her date disappeared. Lena tagged along after the rest of the group, feeling like a fifth wheel. She might as well go back to the camp. She didn't want to end up one of the few geeks who didn't have a make-out partner.

Just as she turned to head back, she bumped into someone. She looked up and found herself staring into a pair of narrowed blue eyes. Luke McKinley's blue eyes.

"Hey," he said.

"Hey, Luke." The greeting came out sounding as if she'd just run five miles.

"You headed back?"

"Uh, I guess so."

"I'll go with you."

"Sure." She shrugged as though it didn't matter one way or the other.

They turned and headed back up the moonlit pavement. The rest of the group continued on, their laughter fading in the distance. They walked for a minute or two without saying anything. Finally unable to stand the silence any longer, Lena said, "I didn't expect to see you here. I mean—" She gave herself a mental *thwap* and then chastised herself. *Great, Lena. Now he thinks you were watching for him.*

"I didn't expect to come. Anderson said it would be a good time. So far, it's seemed pretty lame to me."

Lena immediately took offense. She stopped in the middle of the road. "I suppose there's a lot more action where you come from."

Luke stared down at her with his seen-it-all eyes. "Yeah, you could say that."

"So why'd you come here?"

He swung away from her and dropped his head back to stare up at the star-speckled sky, his hands in his pockets. "It wasn't my idea."

"Your dad made you?"

He shrugged.

"Why didn't you go live with your mother?"

"I don't have a mother."

"Oh." Lena considered that for a moment. "I don't have a father."

"Aren't we the pair of bookends?"

He had a smart mouth. But she had a feeling he did that to cover up something. What, though?

They continued up the hill, not saying anything for a couple of minutes. Lena stopped again halfway up. "So why *did* he make you come here?"

Luke hesitated, and then told her, "Because he thinks he can reform me."

The words were blunt and to the point, as if he wanted to shock her, or maybe scare her away. Determined not to let him, she kept her voice nonchalant when she said, "For what?"

He looked down at the ground and scuffed a sneakered toe in the dirt. "I got caught with some drugs at a party."

"Were you using them?" she asked, somehow unable to picture him as a druggie.

Luke looked at her for a long minute, as if trying to decide how to answer. "Would you believe me if I said it wasn't something I made a habit of?"

She held his intense gaze, considered the question and then said, "Yeah, I would."

"I don't know why I just told you that. I haven't told anybody else."

"Your secret's safe with me." She tilted her head back and said, "Do you believe in haunted houses?"

"No," he said, looking surprised.

"Wanna see one?"

He gave her a shrug that indicated he didn't have anything better to do. "Sure. Why not?"

Lena took off at a jog, cutting through the cornfield to their right. The moon slanted a path of light across the rows of corn stubs. She jumped each one with ease. She congratulated herself for not looking back to see if he was still following her.

At the edge of the field, she slowed to a stop.

"You run track or something?" he asked, coming up behind her.

"As a matter of fact, I do," she said, then took off again.

"Wait!"

She kept going until she reached the fence surrounding the property. Luke was right behind her. They leaned against the rickety fence, their breathing short and raspy.

"This is the old Hathaway place. Spooky, huh?"

"Looks like an old house to me."

The brick two-story house sat some one hundred yards away, eerie in the moonlight. One side of the front porch sagged like a lopsided smile. The roof had holes in it, and the breeze brushed a tree limb back and forth against a broken windowpane, the sound almost mournful.

Lena had a moment of doubt about going farther, but quashed it at the thought of Luke's earlier statement about the camp-out being so lame. She'd show him lame. "Come on. Let's go inside."

He looked at her as if he thought she'd lost it. "Why?"

"Why not?"

She hopped over the fence and bounded across the yard before she lost her nerve. She stopped at the front steps. They, too, were in terrible shape, partly rotted on one side. The moon shed little light on the front of the house. Lena tentatively touched a foot to the bottom step, then ventured up.

The front door moaned as she gave it a shove inward. Adrenaline shot through her veins. She was crazy to go inside, after what she'd heard about this

place. None of the kids she knew would come anywhere near it. But the desire to impress Luke prodded
her on. She glanced over her shoulder. He was still
behind her.

She stopped inside the enormous front hallway.
Moonlight shone in from the windows, but it was
hard to see. To their right was a winding staircase.
The banister at the top had come loose and hung
precariously above them.

Lena pointed at the room to their left. "That's
where they used to lay people out. It was called the
viewing room."

"What do you mean 'lay people out'?"

"They didn't have funeral homes in those days,
so people came to the house for the viewing."

Luke didn't say anything, but shifted from one
foot to the other. His uneasiness gave her courage.
She ventured forward. Boards creaked. From somewhere above, a bird flew out of its nesting place.

Lena stopped, hiding her own fright with words.
"This used to be an old plantation. One of the biggest around."

"What kind of plantation?"

Lena shrugged. "I dunno. Probably cotton or tobacco. Later on, it became a boardinghouse, but people eventually stopped staying here because of all the
things that kept happening."

"Like what?"

"Doors opening and closing in the middle of the
night. There was this one chair that no matter where
it was moved in the house, it always turned up in
front of the living room window. No one could ever
explain how it got moved. But it was rumored to be
Mrs. Hathaway's favorite spot to sit."

Luke gave a snort of disbelief. "There must have been some explanation."

Ignoring his skepticism, Lena said, "They say she locked him in the cellar."

"Locked who in the cellar?" Luke asked, his voice the slightest bit rattled.

"Mr. Hathaway," Lena said, enjoying herself. "The story goes that he was in love with a young woman who worked for them. They'd planned to run away together, but Mrs. Hathaway found out and put an end to it."

"She killed them?"

"That's what they say."

"What'd she do with the bodies?"

"Some people say she buried them in the cornfield. Others say she buried them in the cellar."

"Sounds like a tall tale."

"Maybe. I don't know." Lena shrugged and continued down the hallway. It led into the kitchen. Luke went over to the old dry basin and worked the pump handle. It squeaked in protest and shot out a puff of dust. At the back of the kitchen, a door stood ajar. Lena pointed at it. "That must be the cellar."

Luke went over and pulled it open farther. The bottom scraped against the floor. Lena jumped. Luke stuck his head through the doorway and peered down the steps. "It's pitch-black down there."

"I think this is as far as I'm going," she said.

He turned around and gave her a cocky grin, the tables suddenly turned. "Whatsa matter? You scared?"

"If I'd been scared, I wouldn't have come in here in the first place."

"No, I guess you wouldn't have. I don't know any girls who would have come this far," he admitted.

It was almost a compliment. Lena's courage reasserted itself. She moved to the door and peered down the steps. She couldn't see a thing. A board beneath her foot gave way, and she pitched forward. A pair of hands grabbed her shoulders and pulled her back to safety against a solid chest.

Lena's heart was beating so fast she thought it might actually explode. Luke turned her around and said, "You okay?"

"Yeah. Thanks." Her voice was all breathy again, and she ridiculed herself for not being a better actress.

They stood there for a few seconds, staring at each other while Lena tried to regain her bearings. Her fear was momentarily replaced by feelings of another sort. In the dimness, the planes and angles of his good-looking face were even more compelling. His hands were still on her shoulders. She didn't want him to let go.

How long they stood there, she didn't know. It was probably only a few seconds, but it seemed like forever. She didn't think forever would be long enough.

"We'd better get out of here," he said finally.

She nodded, not trusting her voice. He led the way this time, while she followed. They'd almost made it back to the front door when they heard a loud noise from upstairs. They turned around just as a piece of the banister railing fell from the stairway onto the hallway floor.

Lena looked at Luke. He looked at her. Without saying a word, they tore out of the house and ran for all they were worth. Across the porch. Down the steps. Flying through the yard. They didn't stop until they'd reached the edge of the cornfield, where they collapsed on the ground, their backs to the fence. They were both breathing as if they'd run a marathon.

They were silent for a minute or two, their rasping breaths the only sound in the stillness. They turned to look at each other at the same time. Smiles broke out on their faces.

"Chicken," Lena said.

"Like you weren't," Luke said, grinning.

"It's not so lame around here, after all, is it?" she asked, her own smile widening. If she had planned this night from the start, it never would have been as good as this. Never in her most outlandish imaginings could she have come up with the two of them ending up alone in a haunted house.

Silence hung between them again, but the air was full of unspoken things. Newfound attraction. A tension Lena had never before experienced. Luke turned then, his shoulder against the fence. His head lowered toward hers. Oh God, he was going to kiss her!

His lips brushed hers. He pulled back and said, "Your eyes are open."

"I know. I want to watch."

Luke smiled, cupped the side of her neck with his hand and kissed her again. She did watch for a second or two, but never-before-experienced feelings flooded her, and her eyes drifted closed. She savored every single sensation. There were so many. The smell of him, warm and overheated from their run across the field. The feel of him, big, broad, the very essence of him male and thoroughly intriguing.

His head tilted, and he deepened the kiss. Shock

waves of surprise and pleasure ricocheted through her. Somehow, they managed to get closer. His arms went around her waist, and she found herself pressed close against his chest. It felt so good. Better than she'd imagined. Better than she'd ever dreamed.

She'd been kissed a couple of times. But never like this. Not quite sure what to do, she let instinct guide her, hoping she wasn't opening her mouth too wide, following his lead when his tongue brushed against hers.

They kissed for long, heart-pounding minutes until Luke lifted his head. "When you set out to prove a guy wrong, you pull out all the stops."

Lena smiled. "I like to win."

"Yeah. I can see that." His thumb caressed her chin, lingering at her bottom lip. Lena was filled with a yearning for something she didn't quite understand but wanted more of nonetheless.

"I think we'd better get back," Luke said in a reluctant voice.

Disappointment tumbled through her. She straightened her clothes, feeling as if she'd done something wrong. "Yeah. Someone will have missed us by now."

"Hey." He reached for her arm and stopped her jerky motions. "Lena, I didn't expect... I mean—"

"Please don't say you're sorry," she said. "I don't want to hear that you're sorry." Being with him had made her feel better. For a short while, she'd even become her old self, not the bitchy brat she'd been since she'd discovered her mother's betrayal. Being with Luke made her feel wanted and worthwhile. Being with him made her forget about the father who hadn't wanted her. And she didn't want to hear that he wished it hadn't happened.

"I don't know what you're thinking, Lena." He reached out and curved his hand around her neck. "But the last thing I want to do is go back."

Lena's heart lifted and soared. In the span of a couple of hours, her whole life had changed. And she knew without a doubt that she would never be the same again.

ONCE HE'D MADE sure Lena was back at the campsite, Luke climbed the hill to Tim Anderson's Wagoneer and pulled a sleeping bag out of the back. He made his way to the tent the two of them had pitched earlier.

Tim was already inside. Opening the flap, Luke ducked in, trying not to wake him.

"Where you been?" the other boy asked, lifting up on one elbow.

"Went for a walk."

"Some walk. Who went with you?"

"Nobody."

Tim grinned. "Yeah, I believe that."

Luke rolled out the bed, then lay down on it, ignoring the other boy's baiting.

"Somebody said Lena Williams wasn't back a little while ago. She wasn't out walking with you, was she?"

"'Night, Anderson," Luke said, rolling over on his side.

Tim chuckled. "I'll take that as a yes."

It was a long time before Luke fell asleep. His mind was wide awake, thinking about what had happened between Lena and him. It had surprised the hell out of him. Everything about it.

Lena Williams was nothing like the girls he'd hung around with in the city. Most of them would have eaten her alive. But something about her appealed to him. She had guts, that was for sure, but kissing her had been the biggest surprise of all. It had just happened as if it were supposed to all along. And he'd enjoyed it. More than he wanted to admit, even now. He'd liked the way she felt against him. He'd sensed that she hadn't done a lot of kissing. He'd gotten used to girls who could show him things. He'd liked being the one to show her. And it was a rite of passage for all guys to brag when they'd been with a girl. So why hadn't he wanted to tell Tim?

Lying there on his sleeping bag, Luke avoided answering that question. He stared up at the ceiling of the tent and let himself admit that maybe Keeling Creek wouldn't be so bad, after all. There was something about the place that had kind of started to grow on him. It was even getting to his dad. He'd actually gone out and bought a calf a few days ago. A calf, of all things! When Luke had come home and found it tied under one of the oak trees in the front yard, he'd thought for sure his father must be losing it. When Luke had questioned him about it, he'd just said a farm needed animals.

Luke still couldn't get over it. Even though he hadn't let on as much to his dad, he thought it was pretty cool. This place was definitely having a weird effect on his father. And maybe on him a little bit, too.

## *CHAPTER TEN*

AFTER LEAVING THE clinic on Saturday morning,
Colby stopped by her parents' house for lunch since
Lena wouldn't be home from the camp-out until later
that afternoon.

She knocked at the back door, sending a glance
around the familiar yard. Samuel and Emma Williams had the neatest house around. They weren't
wealthy by some standards, but they took great pride
in the things they had. They loved working in the
yard together, planting bulbs in the spring and fall,
pruning bushes and keeping the lawn as closely
mowed as the golf course at the Low Valley Country
Club. People drove from as far as seventy-five miles
away just to see her mother's flower garden. An
enormous old magnolia tree stood in the front yard.
In the spring and summer, red impatiens encircled it,
thick as clover in a hay field. Fall brought out different flowers. Now, the driveway was lined with
burgundy mums, four plants wide on each side.

Standing there on the brick walkway, Colby realized not for the first time that if things had worked
out differently for her, theirs was the kind of marriage she would want. A partnership. Someone with
whom she could share all and do all. After Doug,
she'd been so busy trying to prove that she could
accomplish on her own all the things in life that re-

ally mattered that maybe she'd never really given anyone a chance. The hurt he'd caused her had shaped her adult life, and she wondered now if she'd been wrong to let him have that much power over her.

Her mother appeared at the door, a pleased expression on her face. "Colby. You're just in time for lunch."

"I'd hoped I would be." She stepped inside and gave her mother a hug. "Sorry I didn't call first."

"As if you need to. Your father's golfing this morning, so he won't be back for a while yet. Let me grab another bowl, and we'll sit down."

Colby washed her hands and tested the soup on the stove. "Um, that's good."

"Vegetable soup. Every one from my summer garden." She poured them each a glass of iced tea, and they sat down. The soup was good, perfect for an early fall afternoon.

"How's Lena?"

"The same."

"Maybe I should talk to her, honey."

"Thanks, Mom, but this is something I need to handle on my own."

"I understand, and you're probably right. But you know it's a mother's nature to want to fix whatever's wrong in her daughter's life."

"I know, Mom. And I appreciate it," Colby said, stirring some sugar into her tea.

"While we're on that subject, I ran into Phoebe at the grocery store this week. She told me she'd fixed you up with Mr. McKinley."

"It wasn't a date. You know Phoebe. She thinks I'm desperate for a husband."

"Well, he is awfully handsome."

"Handsome and engaged," Colby said pointedly.

Emma's expression fell. "She forgot to mention that part."

"Phoebe's an optimist. She considers that a minor hitch in her plan."

Emma chuckled and shook her head. "Your father said he saw your truck at Oak Hill last night, though. We thought you might have had a date."

Colby reached for some crackers and crumbled them into her soup. "Actually, I was just helping him de-skunk his dog."

"Oh."

"Not the answer you'd hoped for, I gather."

"Now, honey—"

"Mom, even if I were interested, which I'm not," she emphasized, trying not to think about last night, "the man is not up for consideration. You and Phoebe both might as well accept that."

"All right, honey. Whatever you say," she said, a curious look in her eye which Colby determinedly ignored.

IT WAS ALMOST dinnertime when Mrs. Mitchell's car pulled up in front of the house and Lena got out, wearing faded jeans and a multicolored sweatshirt. From her position at the living room window, Colby noticed that she was smiling and looked happier than she had seen her in months. The sight of it both lifted her heart and sent it plummeting.

How long had it been since Lena had smiled at her that way?

A minute later, Lena bounded through the front door, her hair tousled, her cheeks bright with color.

Colby tried to keep her voice light when she said, "Hi. How was the camp-out?"

Lena looked up, her expression closing immediately. "It was okay."

"Did they have a good turnout?"

"Yeah." Lena headed for the stairs without looking back.

"Lena?"

She stopped midway up and said, "What?"

Sighing, Colby decided then and there to take the bull by the horns. This couldn't go on any longer. She'd done everything but stand on her head to try to mend a rift she didn't even understand. "Come down here. I think we need to talk."

"I've got stuff to do."

"This can't wait."

Lena turned and clomped back down the stairs, the heaviness of her footsteps echoing her reluctance.

Colby went into the den and stood by the window. Confrontations had never been a part of her relationship with her daughter, and she wished fervently that they weren't now. "I want to know what's wrong, Lena. And don't say 'Nothing.' I've tried to be patient, hoping that whatever it was would blow over. But obviously, it isn't going to. So tell me what's going on."

Lena folded her arms across her chest and glared at her. "There's nothing to talk about."

"I don't believe that."

"Believe what you want."

Anger and hurt were neck and neck among the emotions galloping through Colby's insides. She subdued them both and said, "We used to be able to talk about everything, Lena. What's changed?"

"Nothing."

"Yes, it has. Why is it different now?"

For a long time, Lena didn't say anything. She kept her gaze locked somewhere over Colby's left shoulder. When she spoke, her voice was harsh with anger. "Why did you lie to me?"

"About what?" she asked, caught off guard by the question.

Lena turned and stomped up the stairs without answering. Stunned, Colby stayed where she was. What on earth was she talking about? Just when she started to go after her, Lena tromped back downstairs with a piece of paper in her hand. She held it out to her with a look of condemnation in her eyes.

Colby took it, glanced at it and then felt the color drain from her face when she realized what it was. "Where did you find this?" she asked in little more than a whisper.

"In your old room at Grandma's."

Dread marched down Colby's spine, followed by a crystal clear understanding of what had brought about the changes in her daughter. "Lena—"

"Why couldn't you just tell me the truth, Mom? That he didn't want anything to do with either one of us."

"Oh, Lena, it's not what—"

Tears running down her face, Lena ran back up the stairs. Her door slammed. Colby flinched. She groped for the chair behind her and sat down, feeling shell-shocked. How had this happened? All these years, she'd kept the truth from Lena, not wanting to hurt her. And now, because of one stupid letter she should have thrown away long ago...

Oh God, why hadn't she? But she knew why.

She'd kept it as a reminder to herself that she'd done the right thing. That Doug had made his choice, that he was the one who would come out the loser.

She now understood Lena's rebellion, her anger. She'd been keeping this inside, letting it build until the wall between them was so high that they might never get past it.

How could she explain this to Lena? She couldn't tell her that Doug had wanted her to terminate the pregnancy. That he'd had no understanding of Colby's refusal to do so. She couldn't. She wouldn't. Right now, she feared what that might do to her daughter more than any resentment Lena might feel for her.

She sat there until all the sunlight had disappeared from the room, torn between the need to go to her daughter and the fear that she wouldn't be able to find the right words to say. Finally, when she could avoid it no longer, she got up and climbed the stairs to Lena's room, feeling as if her feet were weighted with lead.

She knocked at the door. "Lena?" No answer. She turned the knob, surprised to find it unlocked.

Lena was sitting on the side of the bed, staring out the window that looked onto their backyard. Colby went over and sat down beside her, close but not touching. "Baby, we need to talk," she said, unconsciously reverting to the endearment Lena had recently demanded she stop using.

"What's there to talk about?"

"For starters, the fact that I love you more than life itself and the last thing I ever wanted to do was hurt you."

"Why did you tell me my father was dead, then? He's not, is he?"

Colby looked down at her hands and shook her head. "No, he isn't. At least not that I know of."

Fresh tears gathered in Lena's eyes. She swiped at them. "All these years I've wondered what he would have been like, if he would have been the kind of father I'd have wanted to take to parents' day...if I looked like him."

The lump in Colby's throat thickened. How she wished that he had been. How she would have liked for him to deserve this child's grief over not knowing him. But he *didn't* deserve it. Not once had he ever called to see whether they'd had a boy or a girl. Not once in all these years had he ever tried to contact them. Lena deserved better than that. So much better.

"Honey, your father and I were so young. He...he wasn't ready for that kind of responsibility. I wish things had been different, but..."

Lena jumped up from the bed, cutting her off and turning to stare at her with angry eyes. "Why didn't you just tell me that? That the two of you broke up? At least I would have had the option of seeing him."

"Lena, it's not that simple. I wish it was."

"Will you find him for me?" she asked, her eyes defiant.

"Oh, Lena." Colby didn't know what to say. When she'd heard years ago that Doug had married, the news hadn't bothered her in the least. Whatever love she'd thought she held in her heart for him had died the day he'd renounced any obligation to their unborn child. But for Lena's sake, she feared opening that can of worms. It was already done, though, and she couldn't close it back again. "Is that what you really want?"

"Yes," Lena said, her expression set.

In that moment, Colby realized that what Lena wanted most was to hurt her. To pay her back for keeping the truth from her. And she had found the most effective way of doing it. With a sigh of resignation, she said, "Then I'll do whatever I can to find him."

SLEEP WAS A futile effort that night. Colby lay awake thinking about what calling Doug would mean, dreading it more than she had ever imagined she would. She had no idea whether he was still in Philadelphia, but it was a place to start.

She was up before the sun rose, sitting at the kitchen table drinking coffee until almost eight o'clock when she picked up the phone and called Phoebe. She needed to talk to someone. She didn't want to call her parents. This would upset them too much.

Phoebe's hello was cheerful enough that Colby knew she hadn't gotten her out of bed. She told her, in as few words as possible, what had happened last night.

"Oh, Colby," Phoebe said when she had finished. "That's what's been wrong with her, then?"

"Yes," she said, miserable.

"So are you going to call the slime bucket?"

"I don't have a choice."

"She'd resent you forever if you didn't."

"How'd I turn out to be the bad guy in this? That's what I want to know."

"Give her a chance to judge him for herself. You'll come out smelling like a rose. Trust me."

She could only hope Phoebe was right. She would never forgive herself if this permanently marred her relationship with Lena.

She waited until nine o'clock and then dialed information.

"Directory assistance. What city, please?"

"Philadelphia. Douglas Jamison."

"I have a Douglas A. and two Douglas C. Jamisons."

Colby asked for the first Douglas C., since she had no way of knowing which was the right one. She dialed the number. After three rings, a woman answered.

"May I speak to Doug Jamison, please?" Colby asked.

A pause of silence followed before the woman said, "My husband is no longer alive."

"Oh. I'm sorry," Colby said. "I have the wrong number." She hung up, a knot in her stomach. The woman had sounded too old to be Doug's wife. Maybe that had been his parents' home, and his father was the one who had died.

Colby dialed information again and asked for the second Douglas C.

Before she had a chance to lose her courage, she picked up the phone and dialed the number. It rang twice, and then she heard his voice for the first time in more than sixteen years. She couldn't say anything for a moment, frozen with too many emotions to identify.

"Hello? Is anyone there?" he asked, irritation marking the words.

"It's Colby, Doug," she said finally. "Colby Williams."

Silence followed her admission. She heard the phone being shuffled around and then what sounded like a door closing.

His voice was lower when he said, "God, Colby. Where are you?"

"I'm at home. In Keeling Creek."

"Oh." He paused. "You're the last person I expected to hear from."

"Believe me," she said, "this isn't a social call."

"What is it, then?" he asked warily.

"It's about our daughter...she wants to see you." Blunt, but what point was there in beating around the bush?

"What do you mean?" The words held an edge, as if he were being backed into a corner.

"I had a girl, Doug. I never told her the truth about you. She found out recently, though, and she's understandably upset."

"What did you tell her?"

"What difference does it make? You weren't a part of our lives." She couldn't keep the accusation from her voice.

He was silent a moment, then said, "You can't just spring this on me and expect me to—"

"I don't expect you to do anything, Doug. Calling you is the last thing I ever wanted to do. But Lena is hurting over this. She's confused and—"

"I have a family, Colby."

On some level, she had known that he would. But hearing him say it somehow brought back a pain that she'd thought she had long ago put away. He had been nineteen when Lena had been born. He hadn't wanted marriage and a family. It hurt somehow to think that he had eventually chosen them with another woman, other children. It was illogical to feel that way, but for the first time since her confrontation with Lena, she thought she truly understood how her daughter must feel. "Are you saying you don't want to see her?"

"I don't know," he said, the words sounding as if they'd been issued through clenched teeth. Just for her own satisfaction, she pictured him fat and sweating.

"Look, Doug, I'm not asking anything of you," she said, her own voice cool. "But I will not allow you to hurt her. If you don't want to see her, just say so, and I'll think of something to tell her."

"This is too sudden, Colby. I need some time to think."

Colby laughed. She couldn't help it. It was such a ridiculous statement, and typical of the selfish person he had turned out to be. "You're right. Sixteen years is a bit sudden." As soon as the words were out, she wished she could take them back. She didn't want him to think that she'd ever spent a moment of that time yearning for him.

"I made my decision about this before she was born," he said, his voice ice-cold and impersonal to the point that she wondered if she'd ever known him. "You know what my choice was. I didn't want this child. I wanted you to have an abortion. You chose not to do that. I hardly think it's fair for you to call me up out of the blue and—"

"Fair?" she interrupted, anger scalding through her. How dare he sit there, blithely talking about an abortion as if Lena didn't exist? As if he had any idea what he had missed in not knowing her as his child? How could she have ever imagined herself in love with him? "I'm sorry to see that you haven't changed one bit, Doug. Give me a call when you've had enough time to think about this. Personally, I don't think you deserve to know our daughter. I won't tell her we talked until I hear from you." She gave him her number and hung up without saying goodbye.

She tore off the piece of paper on which she'd scribbled his number and shoved it in her pocket. To her disgust, her hand was shaking, and she hated herself for letting him get to her that way.

Fourteen different emotions assaulted her at once, anger and protectiveness at the top of the list. A few minutes spent talking to him had brought back all the old insecurities with which their relationship had left her. Doug Jamison was going to be a disappointment to his daughter. In her heart, she knew that. How would Lena handle his rejection? How could she be anything but devastated?

Colby glanced at her watch. The 11:00 church service would be starting in an hour and a half. But she didn't feel like going this morning. She needed some time to pull herself together. Deciding to let Lena sleep on, Colby wrote her a note, then grabbed her keys and left the house.

IT HAD BECOME a ritual for Ian to drive into town for the Sunday-morning paper. He arrived at Cutter's Grocery around 8:30. It was located in the middle of town, and Maude Cutter and her husband, Harvey, ran the place. Since the first time he'd set foot in the store, he'd been unable to resist Mrs. Cutter's homemade cinnamon rolls, which she made fresh every morning. The tantalizing aroma predictably tempted him as he stepped inside and poured himself a cup of coffee from the pot on the counter. He nodded at Dillard and Willard Nolen, who were sitting on the bench by the door swapping sections of the paper.

"Morning, Mr. McKinley," Mrs. Cutter said from behind the counter. "Looks like we're gonna have a nice week."

"No rain in the forecast?" he asked. This, too, had become part of the ritual—Mrs. Cutter's weekly weather bulletin.

"Doesn't look like it. We may get a few clouds by Wednesday, but they don't talk like it'll turn to rain."

"Good. I've got some work to do on the barn. And then there's all that hay that needs cutting," he said, some inner devil urging him on. Dillard and Willard both peered over their papers at him, nodding in approval. Obviously, they hadn't heard about his tractor mishap or they would have known he wouldn't be going anywhere near one. He smiled to himself and picked up the paper from the counter. "I'll take some of those cinnamon rolls, too. You've ruined my will-power, Mrs. Cutter."

The older woman beamed. "It's nice to know I can still tempt a young looker like you."

Ian chuckled and paid her, enjoying their banter. He leaned against the counter and leafed through the financial section while he drank his coffee. A little while later, he left the store with a fresh cup of coffee in his hand.

The morning was crisp and cool, the sky cloudless above him. He climbed into his car, thinking of how different his Sunday mornings had been in New York. Trying to get ahead on his work, never catching up from one week to the next, but continuing the race until the days and months ran together and he had forgotten how to stop and smell the roses altogether. That was something he was relearning here. He hoped he never forgot again.

On his way out of town, he spotted the tail end of Colby's truck behind her clinic. Common sense told him to keep on driving, but since he hadn't been listening to that a lot lately where she was concerned, he swung the Mercedes into the parking lot and sat there, debating whether or not to go in.

Since the moment she'd left his house on Friday, he'd been comparing her to Rachel in ways he shouldn't have. The two of them couldn't have been more different. Not in a million years could he have imagined doing with Rachel what he'd done with Colby. Rachel would have been horrified at the thought of helping him bathe U-2 in tomato juice. She would have thought he'd lost his mind for buying Matilda. And she didn't eat pizza.

The mere fact that he was making comparisons between the two of them should have made him turn the car around and drive away as fast as he could get the thing in gear. Instead, he got out and crossed the parking lot to the back door.

It was cracked open an inch or two. He knocked and called out, "Colby?"

No answer. He went inside and called her name again.

"I'm back here."

He followed her voice. Several dogs barked in unison, aware now that they had company on an otherwise quiet Sunday morning. He found her at the back of the building, sitting on a crate in the middle of what looked like a supply room. A bunch of smaller boxes surrounded her. A clipboard lay across her lap.

"Putting in some overtime?" he asked, leaning against the doorjamb.

She kept her face averted, running a thumb beneath each eye and not quite meeting his gaze. "I...not really. Just doing some inventory."

Her voice sounded funny, raspy and uneven. "Thought you'd be in church."

"I asked Him for a rain check this morning," she said with a bad attempt at a smile.

There was something wrong. He could see it in the tenseness of her expression. "Are you okay?"

She nodded, still not meeting his gaze, but focusing on the clipboard in her left hand.

No, she wasn't. He was surprised to realize that he knew her well enough to see it. He went over and sat down on the crate beside her, careful not to touch her. "You want to talk about it?"

Her shoulders lifted in a shrug. "There's nothing to talk about—"

"Why don't I believe you?"

Tears welled in her eyes. She tossed the clipboard on the floor and wiped the back of her hand across her cheeks. "Oh, damn."

"What is it, Colby?" He put a hand on her shoulder and tried to ignore the shock of awareness that touching her sent through him.

She didn't answer for several moments, visibly struggling for composure. "It's a long story. You don't really want to hear it."

"Hey, I don't have anywhere else to be."

She sat there, not saying anything for a while. He just waited, knowing she would get around to it when she was ready. She let out a heavy sigh and then said, "I found out why Lena's been hating me the past couple of months."

"And?"

She dabbed at her eyes with her shirtsleeve and sighed, her shoulders slumping. "I had her when I was in college. I wasn't married."

She looked up at him as though she expected him to be shocked or disgusted. He was neither. He knew she must have been young when Lena was born. But Ian had assumed she'd married and divorced.

"That was a long time ago," she said before he could respond. "Lena never knew her father. I told her he was dead."

Surprised, Ian wasn't sure what to say. "Why?"

She got up from the crate and moved to the window that looked out on the back parking lot, arms folded across her chest as if she were physically holding herself together. "We were young, and when I first found out, I had no idea what to do. Doug wanted me to have an abortion. I didn't want to, but I kept thinking about how disappointed my parents were going to be in me. He pressured me, and I was about to go through with it before I realized that I couldn't."

Colby Williams was the strongest woman Ian had ever known, and the unfamiliar fragility he sensed in her now bothered him in ways he couldn't explain. He was overcome with the urge to pull her into his arms and give her the comfort he could see she needed. He subdued the impulse with hard-won restraint. "And that's why you two didn't stay together?"

"That pretty much ended things."

Ian didn't know what to say. Part of him was amazed that any guy could be so heartless. "He didn't want to be a part of her life?"

Colby shook her head. "No. And I could never bring myself to tell her that."

"So how did she find out about him?"

"She found a letter from him to me in my old room at my parents' house. That's why she's been so different lately. Not that I blame her. I can't believe I was stupid enough to keep that letter. I've called him, asking him to speak to her, but I haven't told her in case he doesn't want anything to do with her."

"Hey," he said, tilting her chin up so she was forced to look at him. "Don't blame yourself. She's lucky to have you for a mother."

He could feel her distress as if it were his own. They stood there, staring at each other, caught up in something Ian didn't want to name but couldn't deny. Consoling her wasn't his right. It wasn't his place. But she needed comfort. And he was here. He told himself that was all there was to it as he pulled her against him. He actually believed it until the reality of her breasts against his chest shot that theory all to hell.

It felt as if she melted against him; she wrapped her arms around his waist, her hands splayed across his back.

Ian closed his eyes. His hands hung suspended behind her until the need to touch her overrode all the reasons why he should not. He let one hand rest in the center of her back while the other stroked the length of her hair. Soft and straight, it felt like silk against his palm.

Something shifted inside him, cutting him adrift from everything he had felt certain about just moments ago.

The first thought that went through his mind was that they fit somehow. Like two interlocking pieces of a puzzle. He thought of Colby Williams as a woman who could take care of herself. A woman who didn't need a man to complete who she was. But with her in his arms, he himself felt a sense of completeness that was distinctly unnerving, but equally welcome.

For long, uncountable moments, they stood there, simply holding each other. When she pulled back and looked up at him, her eyes were questioning and needy in a way that he could not ignore. He felt the shift inside him again, and of its own volition, his hand moved to smooth a strand of hair from her face. He was sure the uncertainty in her expression was reflected in his own. But kissing her suddenly seemed like something he had to do. He leaned down and brushed his mouth against hers. She made a soft sound somewhere between protest and acquiescence.

He deepened the kiss, cupping his hand around the back of her neck, holding her closer against him. He was aware of the curves and lines of her against him, surprised by how right that felt, too. It was the first time he had held her this way, and yet there was nothing strange or unfamiliar about it.

The kiss grew more hurried, more greedy, Colby as insistent as he. What had begun as consolation had become something else entirely. And yet, he couldn't stop. Didn't want to. Reason and logic had deserted him, and he wanted more of everything. Her mouth. Her skin. The soft sounds of pleasure coming from her throat.

The phone rang, the answering machine out front picking up the call. The noise was sufficient to bring some semblance of sanity to what was happening between them.

Colby pulled away and pressed the back of her hand to her mouth.

"Colby, are you there? We didn't see you at church, and I got a little concerned. No one answered at your house, so I thought I'd check here. If you get this message, give me a call."

"My mom." Colby pressed her lips together and avoided his gaze.

Ian nodded and stepped back, shoving a hand through his hair. Colby moved to the window, looking out. Her breathing was erratic, and he wondered what he was supposed to say about what had just happened when he had no idea why or how it had.

"We shouldn't have done that," she said, her voice oddly uneven.

She was right. They shouldn't have. He was in no position to be kissing her. But if anyone was to blame for this, he was. "It wasn't your fault. I—"

She turned to face him and raised a hand to interrupt. "Please. You were just being nice. I took advantage of that."

"You didn't take advantage of anything, Colby." Confusion settled over him like fog over San Francisco. He heard the guilt in her voice. He was the one who should have been feeling guilty, but of all the other emotions churning inside him, that one was absent. In all honesty, he had wanted to kiss her for a long time now—on the day she'd brought him home from the hospital and then again on Friday night when she'd left his house. From the first day he'd met her, something had been simmering beneath the surface between them. He couldn't deny that. But he'd never expected the kind of heat their kiss had generated.

"Okay, let's be rational about this," she said, one hand in stop sign mode. "You and I both know what just happened wouldn't have happened if I hadn't been upset. You were only—"

"Colby."

"—trying to make me feel—"

"Colby."

This time she stopped, meeting his gaze with what looked like a sincere attempt to convince them both that this whole thing was nothing more than a fluke brought on by need on her part and martyrdom on his. As much as he would have liked to believe that, his gut wasn't buying it. "Let's put this on rewind. Stay right there."

He backed out of the room while she watched him, a curious expression on her face. He retraced his steps to the door that opened into the parking lot and called out, "Colby?"

"In the back," she answered, sounding puzzled.

He wound his way down the hall, across the room to the window, where she stood looking at him as if she thought he'd lost his mind. "So this Doug," he said. "He's a real jerk, right? Well, I think you're doing the right thing in waiting to tell Lena that you spoke with him. That kind of thing could do a lot of damage to a fifteen-year-old's self-image. And if you ever need anyone to talk to about this, just pick up the phone and call, okay? After all, that's what friends are for.''

Colby's face broke into a smile, her eyes still moist from the earlier tears.

"All right?" he prompted.

"All right," she said.

"I'm going to go now." He backed away from her and left before he could change his mind.

# CHAPTER ELEVEN

THE SMILE LINGERED on Colby's lips long after Ian had gone.

An hour ago, she'd thought she might never smile again.

She sank back down on the crate and sighed. No matter how they colored it, what had happened here had been a mistake. Of the screwing-up-your-life-in-a-big-way variety.

Logically, she knew that to be true. So why hadn't she wanted it to stop? Why had she been sorry to see him go at the same time she'd been telling him he should?

Being friends with Ian McKinley wasn't working out exactly as she'd thought it would. Maybe she'd been crazy to think it was possible, anyway.

Considering everything that was going on with Lena right now, the last thing she needed was to set herself up as the other woman.

No, the friends thing definitely wasn't working. But it wasn't too late for damage control. She would just stay away from him. It was no more complicated than that. It was the right thing to do. The only thing to do.

IN THE WEEK following the incident at Colby's clinic, Ian was tempted to call and find out whether she'd heard from Lena's father yet. The way he saw it, the jerk didn't deserve a chance to be part of Lena's life. But he didn't call. His reasons for wanting to weren't as pure as they should have been. And he knew it.

He worked in his office each morning, then spent his afternoons working on the barn and the outside of the house. The leaves had begun to brighten toward full color now, the oak trees lining the driveway and the front of the house streaked in yellow. Somehow, in the city, the beauty of autumn had always escaped him. Here, he could only revel in it. He brought Matilda out in the afternoons and tied her beneath a big shade tree where she could watch him while U-2 raced circles around her, wanting to play.

Even though he didn't see Colby, she was never far from his thoughts. He'd gone over that Sunday morning so many times, it played like an old movie running through his head. As much as he tried to rationalize it to himself, a voice in his gut told him that a happily engaged man didn't do what he'd done with Colby Williams. Be that as it might, he found reassurance in the realization that it was one of those things that didn't have to…wouldn't…happen again.

When Rachel called on Wednesday and said she would like to come down for the weekend, he said all the right things. Of course he wanted her to come. He would be glad to see her. But when she called back on Thursday and said something had come up at work and she would be tied up all day Saturday, he was more than a little unsettled to find that he wasn't disappointed.

Then he ran across a letter from Colby on the editorial page of Friday morning's paper. The sight of it made his chest tighten and blew to smithereens any notion that he'd put what had happened between them from his mind. Without taking his gaze from the paper, he set down his cup of coffee and began to read.

Dear Editor,
On my way to work today, I found a black-and-white beagle puppy lying in the middle of the road at the top of Nolen Hill. Its small body was twisted and broken, rain pelting off its fur. It was too late for me to do anything to help it.

A few yards away, its brother and two sisters sat huddled together on the shoulder of the road, looking as if they were sure the owner who had left them there would soon return to take them home.

This isn't the first time I've seen dogs and cats who, no longer wanted by their owners, have been dropped off and left to sit by the road in that same way, just waiting.

I have to wonder how someone could have left those puppies there, knowing that they would either starve to death or be hit by a car. Their fate was certainly to be one or the other.

As anyone who has ever been to my clinic knows, I encourage the spaying and neutering of pets so that unwanted puppies and kittens won't be brought into the world. If such a thing should happen, though, please don't abandon them to the kind of fate I've just described. Bring them to our local SPCA, where they will have a chance at being adopted.

It is my dream to someday open a noneuthanasia shelter in this county where unwanted pets can stay until they are adopted. Until then, I hope I never see another animal abandoned this way.

                                    Colby Williams, DVM

The editor had included a note below the letter that read: "For anyone interested in adopting a pet, the SPCA will be holding Adopt-A-Pet Day on the lawn outside the courthouse on Saturday from 1:00 to 4:00 p.m."

Ian put down the paper and turned his chair to stare out the window. His throat felt tight, and it was hard to swallow.

The letter made him think about the choice Colby had made sixteen years ago. She had taken responsibility for her actions. Had a child and raised her by herself. Not an easy task for someone trying to get through college and then vet school. She was the same woman today that she had been then. A woman with values that she not only spoke, but practiced. Her own life wasn't exactly a bed of roses at the moment, and yet she'd taken the time to write this letter.

He read it again, and if he'd had any doubts before, he could no longer deny that putting Colby Williams out of his mind was not going to be easy.

WITHOUT LOOKING UP, Colby knew exactly when Ian walked through the gate to the Adopt-A-Pet Day on Saturday afternoon. She glanced up and found him smiling at something Stacey Renick was saying to him.

It had been almost a week since she'd seen him, and yet her awareness of him was as pronounced now as it had been before. She felt as if she had a divining fork inside her and he was the only water in a bone-dry desert.

She'd been tempted to call him a number of times, to apologize for unloading on him last Sunday, but each time she'd picked up the phone, cowardice had won out. She hadn't trusted her own declarations of indifference.

She still didn't.

For the next hour, she deliberately put herself as far away from him as she could. At one point, she looked up and found him staring at her. She swallowed, caught up in remembering the heat of their kiss, and almost, almost, lost her resolve to keep her distance.

Phoebe walked up just then. "Well, aren't you going to go over and say hi?"

"No, Phoebe, I'm not," she said, and inserted herself in a debate between a young husband and wife trying to choose a kitten. Colby convinced them to take two, since the couple had a nice barn in which the cats could earn their keep by keeping the mice away.

It was almost four o'clock when she made her way back to the gate, where Stacey said, "Boy, this was a great day. I think your letter to the paper pricked a few consciences."

Colby smiled. "Good. Who took our last little beagle?"

"Mr. McKinley. You should have seen them leaving. That little fella was as happy as a bee in clover."

"That's great," Colby said, caught off guard by the news.

Stacey laughed. "Yeah, I'd be happy if he took me home with him, too."

Colby tried for a laugh herself and failed noticeably. Here she was, trying not to think about the man, but he wasn't helping matters any. Sooner or later, he would do something to tarnish his image. Sooner or later, all men did.

HAVING A PUPPY was like having a newborn baby in the house.

On the way home, Ian had stopped by the grocery store and bought several different varieties of puppy food, wanting to make sure he found one the puppy would like.

Ian had felt guilty about not taking every single animal there home with him. He supposed he'd always known that the SPCA and other such organizations couldn't hold on to animals forever. They wouldn't have the funding to do so. But whoever had said a picture was worth a thousand words had been right. Seeing those pets, each of whom had once had a home to live in, staring up at every person who walked by with hopeful looks on their faces, had made him feel sick inside.

That explained why he'd ended up driving home with a grateful little beagle in the front seat. A beagle, of all things. Beagles weren't New York City dogs. They liked to run. And chase rabbits. There weren't any rabbits on Park Avenue.

First a calf and now a beagle. What was happening to him?

He thought about the office he'd left behind in New York and the no-nonsense person he'd been there. Would any of those people even recognize him? Would his own fiancée recognize him?

He didn't think so.

He was beginning not to recognize himself.

Back at the house, Mabel fussed over the puppy and fixed him a bowl of warm milk, clucking and persisting until he'd finished every drop.

"Pretty soon we'll have more animals roaming around here than Colby has at her clinic, won't we, Mr. McKinley?" she asked with a knowing smile.

Ian pretended to miss the innuendo behind Mabel's seemingly innocent remark and went to the sink to rinse out the puppy's bowl.

Mabel left just after six, leaving U-2 and him alone with the latest addition to the family. The puppy refused to stay in his bed. He trotted around the house and acquainted himself with his new surroundings while U-2 followed, curious and a little miffed by his presence. Ian suspected the two would soon be devoted buddies.

That night, Ian left the puppy in the kitchen with the lab. Luke was out with friends, and he didn't expect him back until late. Ian had hoped he would get home in time to meet the new puppy, but it would have to wait until morning.

He fixed the dog a basket with a towel inside it and a ticking alarm clock beneath it. He'd once heard the noise was a comfort to puppies recently taken from their mothers. He hoped it would work.

He'd been upstairs no more than five minutes when the howling started. Only it sounded more like crying. Ian gave the puppy a few minutes, thinking he'd adjust. He didn't.

Guilt led Ian to the kitchen, where he scooped the

puppy up, basket and all and took him to his room.
U-2 stayed in the kitchen as if she didn't want her
sleep disturbed again. Ian tucked the puppy back in
and kept his hand on the little guy's head until he
fell asleep. As soon as he removed his hand from the
basket, the puppy started howling again.

Ian finally dozed off at some point after eleven,
but was brought abruptly awake to a pitiful, protesting wail sometime later. "Okay, okay." He bent
down to pick up the scrawny little puppy and tuck
him beneath the covers. "You win."

"What's going on?"

Luke stood in the doorway, dressed in jeans and a
leather jacket. He glanced at Ian and then at the
puppy.

"We've got a new member of the family," Ian
said. "Come meet him."

Luke hung back for a few moments, struggling not
to appear too interested. But curiosity apparently got
the better of him. He stepped inside the room and
said, "Where did he come from?"

"The SPCA."

"Why?"

Ian heard the surprise in his son's voice and realized that it was justified. It was something he
wouldn't have taken the time to do a few months
ago. "He needed a home."

"Is he one of the puppies Dr. Williams wrote to
the paper about?"

Ian nodded. "You read the letter?"

"Yeah." Luke rubbed the sleepy puppy's ears.
The puppy got up and wagged his tail, then playfully
swatted Luke's hand with his paw.

"We need to come up with a name for him," Ian said.

"Like what?"

"I don't know. What's he look like?"

"A shrimp."

Ian smiled. "You think he'd answer to that?"

Luke shrugged and rubbed the puppy's ears again, surprising Ian with his half smile.

"Too bad we can't think of something that means 'doesn't sleep at night.'"

Luke laughed, startling Ian into speechlessness. He stared at his son for a moment, completely taken aback. How long had it been since he'd made his son laugh? Too long. Way too long.

Rubbing the puppy's back, Luke said, "What do you think about Rebel?"

The puppy licked his hand and wagged his tail like a windshield wiper on high speed.

"He does have a bit of a James Dean look to him, doesn't he?"

"Yeah, he does." Luke picked the puppy up and cradled him against his chest.

Pleasure rose inside Ian and spread outward, love for his son a pain in his heart. "He doesn't like sleeping by himself. You want to take him with you?"

Luke looked up at him, obviously pleased. "Sure."

"U-2 didn't know what to think of him at first."

"She'll like him. She'll have somebody to play with other than Matilda."

Ian smiled. "Matilda's not much on chasing rabbits."

Luke chuckled again. The sound filled Ian with gratitude, and he knew that anything he'd sacrificed in coming here had been worth it. This was the boy he'd missed with all his heart. "You can take the basket with you," he said, hearing the waver in his own voice.

Luke scooped the basket up with one hand and headed out of the room. "'Night, Dad," he said.

"Hey, Luke?"

"Yeah?" he said, turning around.

With his heart thumping against his chest, Ian searched for words and prayed that his timing was right. "Remember what you said that night at the police station? About me blaming you for your mother's death?"

Luke held the puppy a little closer against him and nodded.

"I want you to know that was never true. You were what kept me going then. I don't know what I would have done without you. I'm the one who's made some mistakes. It's kind of hard to explain why people do the things they do, but I guess I used my work as a way to get through the grief. After a while, working all the time became a way of life. I wanted to give you all the things my father never gave me when I was growing up. What I failed to realize was that I wasn't there for you in the ways that count, either. I hope you can forgive me for that, because I really want to make it up to you."

Luke looked down at the puppy. When he glanced back up, his eyes held the sheen of tears. "I haven't exactly been the world's greatest son."

"With both of us trying, we're bound to get things right sooner or later," Ian said.

Luke nodded, not quite meeting his gaze. "See you in the morning."

"'Night, son.''

Luke turned in the doorway. "Maybe we could make a house for Rebel outside next to U-2's tomorrow.''

Ian's heart swelled with love for the boy. "That'd be great, Luke. Really great.''

And for the first time since they'd moved to Keeling Creek, Ian went to sleep feeling as if he'd made some small headway in the healing process between him and his son.

LIFE WAS GOOD.

Curling iron in hand, Lena put the finishing touches on her hair, deciding that maybe her own color wasn't so bad. It was somewhere between blond and brown, and she'd stopped putting the purple streaks in it when Luke had said he thought her own color was much prettier.

Because of Luke, Lena actually looked forward to school these days. She lived for the breaks in between classes when the two of them would meet at her locker.

Since the camp-out, they had spent more and more time together. Sometimes, she still wanted to pinch herself to make sure it was true.

Lena had never known anyone like Luke. He was exciting and fun. He made her feel things she didn't understand but wanted to more than anything. And when she was with him, she didn't think about the fact that her mom hadn't brought up the subject of her father since the night she'd confronted her with the letter.

She and Luke had been hanging out together after school every day. Lena had even told her mom she was going to the movies a couple of times and met Luke, instead. Even though her mom's rule was that she couldn't date until she was sixteen, Lena justified whatever guilt she felt by reminding herself of how her mother had deceived *her* all these years. This was nothing in comparison.

Luke was easy to talk to in a way she very much needed since she and her mom were on the outs. She'd found herself telling him about it one day after school when they'd been sitting outside on the school steps. She'd somehow known he would understand. She told him about how she'd gone through her whole life thinking her father was dead. When she'd reached the part about finding the letter in her mother's closet, she'd broken off, her voice thready.

"Did you ask her about it?" Luke had asked.

Lena nodded. "Yeah, she was pretty freaked out. She's supposedly trying to track him down."

"So, do you want to see him or something?"

Lena didn't say anything for a few seconds. "I don't know," she said finally. "Yes, I want to. But I'm scared."

"Why?"

"What if he doesn't want to see me?"

"Why wouldn't he? He'd be crazy not to."

They'd sat there on the grass while a fall breeze hinted at cooler weather. With Luke, Lena felt as if she could conquer all the demons inside her, her anger at her mother, her need to know about her father. He did that to her, made her feel like more than she was. That was what she liked most about him. That, and the fact that he was the best-looking guy she'd ever seen. She felt proud to walk down the hall beside him with all the other girls, even the cheerleaders, looking at her with envy.

Lena unplugged the curling iron and stood looking at herself in the mirror. She'd never thought of herself as pretty like her mom, but maybe she wasn't so bad. She put away her things and headed downstairs, hoping with all her heart that today would be the day Luke asked her to the homecoming dance.

TODAY WAS THE DAY.

Luke was going to ask her. He'd been thinking about it for days but hadn't worked up the courage yet. When he and his dad had first moved here, he couldn't have imagined ever wanting to go to the homecoming dance. All he'd wanted was to move back to the city as fast as they could.

But things were different now. He and his dad were actually talking. About everything. His schoolwork. The books he was reading for English class. Luke had started helping him work on the house a few afternoons a week. He'd surprised himself by actually thinking it was kind of fun. They'd even gone out the afternoon before and bought an old truck for the farm together. His dad needed something to haul stuff around on, and he'd said Luke could drive it when he wanted. They'd named it Pokey because it had about as much power as a twenty-year-old lawn mower.

Things *were* different. At home and at school. Luke liked Lena. She was the coolest girl he'd ever known. And he identified with her. Maybe it was because she'd had problems with her mom the same as he'd had with his dad. Whatever it was, he just liked being with her. He felt as if he could tell her anything, that he could be himself with her.

He opened his locker and threw his books inside. He was supposed to have met Lena in the cafeteria five minutes ago. He slammed the door and swung around, almost bumping into the two guys standing behind him.

"Hey," the tall one said. Luke thought his name was Larry. He had long, stringy hair, and from what Luke knew of him, he spent most of his time in detention hall. The shorter one was Jimmy, or something like that. Like his buddy, he wasn't one of Jefferson County High's finest students.

"Hey," he said, and moved to step around them.

Larry caught his arm and stopped him, glancing over his shoulder before saying, "We heard you were connected."

Luke frowned. "Who told you that?"

The short guy shrugged. "Heard it through the grapevine. What difference does it make?"

"Are you or aren't you?" Larry prodded.

Luke stepped back, feeling sick inside. Nobody here knew about his past except the principal. Mr. Walters had promised Luke's dad that the knowledge wouldn't leave his office. He'd agreed to give Luke a second chance here. That meant there was only one person who could have told them. Lena.

"I don't know where you got your info, but you're barking up the wrong tree," he said, and then took off down the hall and out of the school.

## CHAPTER TWELVE

HOMECOMING AT Jefferson High was always the last weekend in October. Colby had been asked to act as a chaperon at the dance on Saturday night. She felt every bit the fifth wheel as she walked alone into the high school gymnasium at just after seven.

She would probably be the only adult there without a date. Being single had never bothered her the way it seemed to lately. Especially during the past two weeks, when she'd done her best to avoid crossing paths with Ian and yet heard about him at every turn. A stop at Cutter's Grocery led Maude Cutter to extol the virtues of her cinnamon rolls based on Mr. McKinley's rave reviews. And a call to Harry Pasley's farm to help out with another problem delivery had meant listening to how he couldn't get over somebody like that McKinley fella buying that calf as a pet. Needless to say, it had been impossible to erase him from her own thoughts when everyone else insisted on talking about him.

She'd planned to drive Lena and Millie to the dance tonight, but that afternoon, Lena had announced she was going over to Millie's to get ready and that Mrs. Mitchell would be taking them.

If possible, Lena had become even more withdrawn and upset in the past couple of weeks. Colby still hadn't heard from Doug. She could have choked him for that. She'd told herself she would hold out for a while longer, mainly because she wanted him to contact Lena on his own terms, but also because she didn't know how she was going to explain it to her daughter if he didn't want to see her.

When Colby had suggested picking her up after school one afternoon to look for a dress, Lena had refused. And when Colby had come home a few nights later to find a new one on Lena's bed, Lena had said she'd gone with Grandma Williams to pick it out.

Her daughter's deliberate attempts to hurt her were clear. She told herself not to dwell on them. Lena was hurting, and someone had to be the target of that hurt.

One afternoon when she had needed to get away for a while, she had driven to Charlottesville by herself, hitting a total of eight stores before she found something suitable for the dance. The dress didn't sparkle and it wasn't weighed down with frills. Its simplicity was what had caught her eye. It was black with cap sleeves and a V-neck that hinted at cleavage but didn't actually reveal any. The skirt of the dress fit close against her hips, and even though it was totally different from her normal wardrobe, when she'd glanced in the mirror, she'd realized it was very flattering.

She'd actually caught herself wondering if Ian would like it. But she hadn't bought it with him in mind. It was unlikely that he would even be here.

She hung her coat on one of the racks in the cloakroom, making her way into the gym. Standing by one of the bleachers, talking with Randall Walters, the high school principal, was Ian. All the willpower in the world couldn't have made her pull her gaze away from him. Since he was unaware of her watching him, she took advantage of the moment. While most of the men here were far more at home in jeans and workshirts than a suit, Ian looked as if his had been made for him. It was dark blue with a tastefully muted tie knotted at his throat. His face was tan from the work he'd been doing outdoors. He definitely stood out among the other men in the gym, but then, he would have stood out in a room full of Hollywood's leading actors.

Memories of the last time she'd seen him alone assaulted her. Her mouth tingled with the recollection of his kiss. Warmth spread through her and set butterflies astir in her midsection.

He glanced up and caught her staring. She looked away too hastily to be anything but guilty. She headed toward a table set up with punch bowls and poured herself a glass.

The gym had been decorated earlier in the day. Lena had come over for a couple of hours to help. Balloons hung in clusters from the ceiling. Banners announcing the names of this year's homecoming queen and king were draped across the front and back of the gymnasium. The one thing conspicuously absent, however, was the band.

Colby wandered over to a group of parents, most of whom she knew. They all greeted her with smiles. She'd been chatting with them for a couple of minutes when the principal approached them. Ian was right behind him.

"Evening, folks," Mr. Walters said. "Have most of you met Ian McKinley? His son, Luke, is a senior here this year."

Ian shook hands with everyone. When his gaze finally met hers, she knew that he, too, remembered that morning at the clinic.

"Our band for tonight went to the wrong state. Right now, they're in Jefferson County, North Carolina," the principal said, shaking his head. "So, we're without music. Ian was nice enough to make a few calls to the local radio stations. Both DJs are booked for wedding receptions. I really don't know what to do."

"Does the school have a stereo system, Mr. Walters?" Ian asked.

"Yes. A pretty good one," the principal said.

"I'd be willing to play DJ if we can set it up in here."

Looking pleased with the suggestion, Mr. Walters said, "That would be great. You'd be a lifesaver. I'd hate to think what would happen if all the kids showed up and we didn't have any music. Colby, would you mind helping out?"

A quick refusal sprang to her lips. "I don't know very much about the kind of music the kids like."

"Yes, you do." Mr. Walters smiled. "I'll bet Lena's room is full of CDs."

He was right. It was. And she knew most of them by heart. It would be silly to refuse Mr. Walters's request simply because she had promised herself she would stay away from Ian. "Well, maybe I do know a little."

"Terrific."

Ian glanced at his watch and then looked at her. "We could run by our houses and grab some CDs from their rooms. What do you think?"

Colby had to admit it seemed like a good idea.

And since their options were limited, there was little else to do. "Sure. I'd be glad to help."

The other parents chimed in, too, several offering to run home and confiscate their teenager's music collection.

Agreeing that it might be quicker to go separately, Ian and Colby took their own cars. Colby was back before he was. Mr. Walters had set up the stereo while they were gone. Once Ian arrived, the principal gratefully left them to it and went off to put out the most recent fire.

They worked in silence for the first few minutes, stacking CDs in alphabetical order and asking parents to write their children's names on the cases as they put them on the table. Within twenty minutes, they had the situation under control.

Ian turned to look at her. "Think we can pull this off?"

The question startled her. They hadn't said anything for the last ten minutes, both of them feigning intense concentration on the task at hand. She'd been on pins and needles the entire time. "If we don't, we may have a rebellion on our hands," she said, glancing toward the door where couples had begun to file in. It was almost 9:00. The dance officially started at 8:00, but no one came that early. "Good thing it isn't cool to get here on time, huh?"

Ian smiled. "Yeah. We might have been reduced to singing."

With the atmosphere between them considerably lighter, Colby laughed. "*That* would have been a disaster."

"And you haven't even heard me sing," he said in mock dismay.

"I was speaking of my own lack of talent."

His gaze lingered on her. "You look incredible tonight, Colby."

"Thank you," she said, realizing how much she had wanted him to notice. She would have been lying to herself to deny it. "You look nice yourself."

"Well, it's one of the few times you've seen me without mud or tomato juice on my shirt."

She smiled while awkwardness descended upon them in a grip every bit as crippling as any she had ever experienced as a teenager.

For the next forty-five minutes or so, they played music and made small talk. A couple of their first selections got a few boos, but several songs into the mix, they apparently hit the right combination. The dance floor was packed, and no one seemed to be missing the band at all.

Several times, Colby searched the crowd for Lena, finally spotting her on the other side of the gym. She waved, certain that Lena was looking right at her. Lena turned away without waving back. Colby's heart fell. She turned her attention to restacking the CD cases in front of her, determined not to let it ruin the night.

"They can put a knife through your heart, can't they?" Ian asked in a quiet voice.

Colby looked up, started to deny it, then decided there was no point. He was right. And she knew he understood. "I never thought being a parent would be this hard. Even when she was a newborn and I was trying to go to college, it wasn't this difficult."

"Caring is what makes it hard. I imagine it would be a lot easier if we didn't love them so damn much."

"You're right," she said, sighing. "How are things with you and Luke?"

"Better than they've been in a long time. We're actually talking, and it feels really good."

"I'm happy for you. That's terrific."

"Thanks." He paused, then said, "Any word from Lena's father?"

She shook her head. "No. And if someone throws a match anywhere near our house, it's going to blow."

Ian reached out and squeezed her shoulder. It was a gesture of comfort. Or at least that's what Colby told herself. That did not explain, however, her own response to it: the desire it conjured up, the yearning to be alone with him, away from curious gazes, to pick up where they'd left off that Sunday morning in the storage room of her clinic.

He took her arm and tugged her toward the dance floor. "Come on. What do you say we test our selection?"

Colby didn't have time to protest. Before she knew it, they were in the middle of the throng of dancers. The song was one of the Nirvana numbers Lena loved and Colby had no idea how to dance to. She gave it her best shot, though, and after a minute or so, forgot about her inhibitions and relaxed.

Ian was a surprisingly good dancer. She'd always thought men of his height and breadth had a disadvantage when it came to looking good on a dance floor. He proved her wrong. They finished out two fast songs. Randy Travis was next with a toe-tapper about the woman of his dreams. "I don't think I know how to dance to this one," Ian said.

"You were the one who wanted to come out here.

You're not getting off that easily. Come on. I'll show you the two-step." Colby took his hand and walked him through the motions. When he looked impressed that she knew it, she said, "That was the one thing I got out of my date with Tip LaPrade before he showed me the prenup agreement."

Ian laughed, and the sound of it was glorious to her ears. Rich and full and undeniably seductive.

He caught on quickly, and she said, "Let me guess. You own stock in a dance studio."

Ian smiled. "Right. I've also got a couple of bridges in Nevada if you're interested."

Colby laughed. They finished out the Randy Travis. Billy Ray Cyrus was next, and someone started a line dance. Everyone knew the steps except Ian. "You'll catch on in no time," she told him when he began to look doubtful.

He was a good sport, following her lead but missing every other step at first. His forehead was wrinkled with the effort of concentrating, while the line of dancers moved gracefully in one direction and then the other. He started laughing at one point and said, "Clueless in Keeling Creek. That's me."

Colby laughed, too, until tears threatened to ruin her mascara. She wiped at her eyes, smiling and refusing to let him give up. "No, you're not. You've almost got it."

"Doesn't that only count in horseshoes—"

"—and hand grenades," she finished.

They both laughed again, and by the end of the song, he nearly had the hang of it.

When that song ended, something slow and bonemelting followed. Alarm bells went off inside Colby. Time to get back to work. Distance between them was one thing. Dancing as closely as this song called for was something else altogether. Colby turned to head back to the table, but Ian stopped her with a hand on her arm. From the look in his eyes, he, too, knew it wasn't wise, but that didn't stop him from saying, "One more?"

If she'd had an ounce of honor inside her, she would have turned him down. But there in the middle of the crowded dance floor, his gaze held hers, said things that didn't need words for expression. The message couldn't have been more eloquent. Her own response echoed inside her, compelled her to take his hand, to move into the circle of his arms, the last place on earth she should have been.

He held her close, closer than he should have, closer than she should have allowed him to.

The music echoed her pulse rate. Sensation heightened her awareness. She was conscious of each and every place their bodies touched in mirror alignment, her left shoulder to his right, her hipbone to his thigh, their knees grazing with each half turn. She was aware of the silk of her dress smoothing across her skin with each movement, the brush of his cotton shirt on her arm.

To Colby, dancing had always seemed an act of intimacy, but this was another thing altogether. Here in his arms, they might have been the only two people in the room.

Neither of them said a word throughout the entire song. They didn't have to. Their bodies did the talking, and Colby knew there was no point in denying what they were saying. Yet she was dancing with a man who was engaged to another woman. A man who made her question her own choice to be alone all these years. And she couldn't make herself step out of his arms and walk away.

They swayed to the music, their bodies in tune with the rhythm, in tune with each other. The song seemed to go on forever, but when it ended, Colby wished it hadn't. They lingered for a moment under a spell of confusion, but the silence following the song jolted them both back to awareness. The CD player had stopped. Everyone on the dance floor was staring at them.

Blushing, she turned and headed back to the table. Ian followed her, pacifying the crowd with a promise that the music would be on in a second.

Luckily for them, the problem was nothing more than an electrical cord someone had knocked loose. Ian got the music started again while Colby went off to get herself some punch. She wasn't thirsty, but she needed the time to collect her thoughts.

She stayed away as long as she could manage without totally deserting him, talking to anyone she recognized. When she could avoid it no longer, she returned to the table, where Ian stood watching her with knowing eyes.

"You didn't have to do that, you know," he said.

"Ian, I don't think it's a good idea for us to—" She broke off, thinking maybe she'd assumed too much.

"You're right." He held up a hand. "It wasn't." And with that, he turned around and walked away.

LENA COULDN'T BELIEVE IT.

Her mother acting as DJ! With Luke's father!

And the two of them dancing together a little while

ago. It was awful. They'd been looking at each other as if they couldn't pull their eyes away.

Her mother was deliberately doing this to embarrass her. As if she didn't have enough to deal with, anyway.

Lena stood in the shadow of a set of bleachers, her gaze on the dance floor where Luke was swaying to a slow song with Melanie Cundiff.

She felt as if her heart were breaking into little bitty pieces, one grain at a time.

What did he see in her, anyway? Melanie had one of the worst reputations at Jefferson High.

Lena glanced down at her dress and wished she could disappear. What a fool she'd been to let Millie convince her that she should show up without a date in the hope that he would be alone, as well. She deserved to feel this way. It served her right.

Why was it that girls like Melanie always got the guys? Melanie already had more boyfriends than Lena dreamed of having in a lifetime.

But then, she knew the answer to her own question.

Sex. It was always about sex. Melanie put out. And everybody knew it.

Since she'd met Luke, Lena had thought about making out a lot. But whenever her thoughts had reached the sex part, they'd shied away. She couldn't imagine that it could actually be fun. She'd grown up seeing animals do it, and to be honest, she'd always felt kind of sorry for the female. How could it be much different with humans?

Luke and Melanie danced into her line of vision again. Melanie's arms were tight around his neck, her breasts to his chest, her thighs against his. Obviously, Lena was wrong. There had to be a lot more to it than she'd imagined.

So maybe it was time she tried it herself. She was almost sixteen. Several of her friends had already done it. The others were talking about doing it. What was the point in waiting, anyway?

If sex was what it took to get Luke McKinley, then she would do it.

But she would never make the mistakes her mother had made. Never.

## CHAPTER THIRTEEN

It was almost 1:00 by the time the last few kids left the dance.

Colby should have been tired, but she wasn't. She was strung as tight as a banjo string. She and Ian had barely said two words to each other since he'd left the table earlier, returning a little while later with a set look on his face. She had danced with the principal and a couple of other acquaintances, all of whom were married. Each of them had teased her about the silent music she and Ian had been dancing to. Colby had made light of their joking, while inside she cringed at the thought of how it must have looked.

Ian hadn't asked her to dance again. In a way, she was relieved. She didn't think her nerves could handle being that close to him. She wasn't a good enough actress to pretend indifference.

Lena had come by the table earlier and said she was spending the night with Millie. The gym was so crowded that Colby had barely caught a glimpse of her the entire night.

Some of the other parents helped them clean up and put away the stereo equipment. Once they'd finished, she collected her purse and coat and deliberately avoided looking at Ian. "I'm calling it a night. 'Bye, everybody."

She'd just reached the parking lot when a voice behind her said, "Colby. Wait up."

She turned around to find Ian walking in her direction, his hands shoved inside the pockets of a long black wool coat that made him look even more appealing than he had earlier. He held her gaze for a moment before saying, "I'm sorry for being such a jerk in there."

"You weren't."

"I was."

"Okay, so you were."

That got a crooked smile out of him.

She looked away. "I have to go. Good night, Ian."

"Would you like to take a drive?"

Tentative though the question was, it surprised her. She met his gaze and shivered in the chill October air. "I really should get home," she said, stepping back.

"Just to talk? For a little while?"

Common sense told her that going anywhere with him at this hour was asking for trouble. "It's not a good idea."

"Probably not."

Put that way, with that particular look on his too handsome face, Colby ignored logic and walked with him through the parking lot. She climbed inside the vehicle when he opened the door, then sat waiting for him to come around to the other side.

They left the high school parking lot and headed out of town. They drove for a long time without saying anything. The tension between them all but hummed.

Blue Mountain Lake was located some ten miles outside of town. She recognized the turnoff to the dam as soon as Ian swung onto the narrow paved road that led to the lookout. It had been years since she'd been out here. During the day, the views were spectacular. She'd never seen it in moonlight. Until a couple of years ago, it had been closed off at night.

They pulled into the left-hand corner of the lot. Ian cut the engine, and everything went black. He looped his arms over the steering wheel and stared out into the night. "I have no excuse for acting the way I did tonight. I had a good time. Maybe too good. And that was the problem."

"You don't have to apologize."

"Yeah, I do." He hesitated and then said, "The only excuse I have is that I wanted to kiss you so badly I couldn't stand it."

She considered that, a little shocked by his honesty.

"I still do," he added, turning to look at her.

Colby's pulse began a slow, rhythmic thud. It was cold inside the vehicle, and yet she was suddenly warm, too warm. She loosened her coat and twisted the ring on her right hand. "Ian...you shouldn't be saying that."

"No, I shouldn't."

She could feel the force of his gaze on her in the darkness, the heat of it, the directness that told her she hadn't imagined the chemistry building between them throughout the night.

When he moved toward her, she leaned across the seat to meet him, barely conscious of doing so. It was as if some irresistible force were pulling them together.

His hand slid behind her neck, his thumb caressing the side of her throat.

"I've done my damnedest not to think about you. About this," he said, his voice low and ragged. "And it's been driving me crazy."

They sat there, mere inches between them, suspended between "Should we?" or "Shouldn't we?"

When he pulled her against his chest, she could no longer deny that they had been headed toward this all night. Pretensions of anything else fell away, leaving nothing between them but raw, honest feelings. All the lectures she'd given herself these past weeks about getting involved with a man who wasn't free collapsed beneath the reality of being in his arms. They kissed like two people who had been thinking about it for far too long, their mouths open and seeking, their arms locked tight around each other.

Colby had been kissed before. She was a grown woman. She had a teenage daughter. But in Ian's arms, she *felt* like a teenager. His touch made her forget all else. Pure, undiluted physical attraction caught her in its grip, and she felt full and ripe, like a peach ready to fall from the tree.

Ian had taken his coat off before they'd left the school, but he was still wearing his suit jacket. Her own coat suddenly felt too cumbersome, too confining. As if reading her thoughts, he reached for the belt at her waist and untied it, slipping his hands inside to curve around her waist.

All the while, they kissed and the clock on the dashboard ticked, ticked.

Colby's hands found their way inside Ian's jacket, around to his back, where she smoothed her palms across corded muscle, then up to his shoulder blades. Her breasts were crushed against his chest, the silk of her dress thin enough to accentuate the sensation.

His hands cupped her face, tilting her head back while he nuzzled the line of her jaw. "You smell so good," he said, his voice whiskey-hoarse.

The words were intoxicating. Colby sighed, and something inside her went warm and liquid. His lips followed the curve of her neck, paused at the hollow of her throat while his thumb stroked her pounding pulse point.

The backs of his fingers followed the neckline of her dress, grazing the upper softness of her breasts. A sound of longing slipped past her lips, unbidden. Ian made a similar sound and undid the first few buttons of her dress. He pushed the shoulders down, revealing the terracotta silk bra she'd splurged on when she'd purchased her dress. His gaze fell on her breasts, and when he met her eyes again, she felt as if she'd been singed. No one had ever looked at her with such appreciation, such heat, such wanting. It was heady and gratifying and unbelievably empowering.

He reached out and touched her left breast with his knuckles before turning his hand over and testing the full weight of it. The heel of his palm tormented the lace-covered tip. He leaned down and kissed her while his hand continued its magic, and the world tilted on its axis. She should stop him. Really. But it had been so long since a man had touched her this way. Since she had wanted a man to touch her this way. "Ian—"

"I know," he said. "I know."

She loosened his tie and marveled that her fingers could still function when her insides were shaking. She couldn't remember the last time she'd done such a thing. With the tie out of the way, she undid the buttons of his shirt. Surely she would die if she didn't touch him. Now. Now. Her hands found him. Ah. Hair-roughened skin over contoured muscle. He felt as wonderful as he looked. Her hands tugged the sides of his shirt free from his pants.

"Colby—" Her name on his lips was a low moan, his breathing as uneven as her own. She couldn't think for wanting him. All the reasons why they shouldn't be doing this had slipped out of her grasp. Nothing was more important than following the road before them, finding out where it led. Their movements became more frantic, as if neither of them could get close enough, touch enough. Like a blaze too far gone to be contained, they were both out of control, desperate for more....

The sound of crunching gravel hit her like a blast of cold air, jolting her back to reality. Headlights flooded the back of the car. "Oh, no," she said. "Who could that be?"

"I don't know." He adjusted her dress and pulled her coat around her shoulders.

He took care of his own clothing while Colby hastily refastened her buttons, hoping she'd gotten them straight. A flashlight shone in through the driver's-side window. She looked up, completely blinded by the glare.

"Jefferson County Sheriff's Department. Step out of the car, please," the voice behind the light said.

Ian opened the vehicle door and slid out. "Is something wrong, officer?"

Fear should have been her overriding emotion. But mortification left it in its dust. She recognized the deputy's voice. Joe Middleton. They'd gone to high school together.

He bent over and directed the light inside, once again blinding her. "Is that you, Colby?"

"Hi, Joe. I apologize if we were trespassing. We were, ah, just looking for a quiet place to talk."

Joe chuckled, diverting the beam toward the other end of the darkened lot. "Yeah, you and the rest of the homecoming dance."

In the arc of light, she caught a glimpse of a few other cars, teenage boys standing outside the doors while two deputies questioned them. She closed her eyes and pictured the headlines in Monday's paper. "Local Vet Arrested for Parking at Blue Mountain Dam." A second later, she added, "With Engaged Man."

Ian had stepped away from the car with Joe. They talked for a couple of minutes, but she couldn't make out what they were saying. When Ian got back in, Joe leaned down and said, "'Night, Colby. See you around."

Joe got into his car, following the other vehicles out of the lot.

"I told him we would head out in a few minutes," Ian said.

Colby pushed her hair back from her face. "I've already written the article in Monday's paper. I'd just gotten to the part where I was trying to explain this to Lena."

Ian dropped his head back on the seat, a low chuckle rumbling from his chest. She laughed, too.

He sobered first, and even in the dimness she could see the light in his eyes. He shoved a hand through his hair. "I'm sorry about this. But I'm glad you're the kind of woman who can laugh about it." He sobered, holding her gaze for several long moments.

"You know, I've laughed more with you in the past couple of months than I have in years."

"I think we both got caught up in things tonight," she said, striving for reason. "The dancing. Being all dressed up—"

"I wish it were that simple," he interrupted, his voice serious now. Not knowing what to say, she sat there, fighting a feeling that was about as easy to ignore as a tidal wave coming in from the Pacific.

Still looking at her, his eyes dark and intent, he said, "I don't know what's happening, Colby. I feel like my life's done a one-eighty, and I don't know what to make of it, anymore."

The admission took her by surprise. "What do you mean?"

With the engine still running, he slid sideways to face her, his left elbow propped on the steering wheel, his right knee on the emergency break. "I came here with my life all mapped out for the next year. Since I met you, not one thing has gone the way I planned it. When I'm around you, I find myself doing things I never intended to do. Like asking you to come out here tonight."

"I shouldn't have agreed. You're not entirely to blame."

"I can't think when I'm around you. And when I'm not around you, you're all I think about."

"I...I don't know what to say to that, Ian. I conveniently let myself forget that there's another woman in your life. And that was wrong. I can't be part of messing up someone else's future. I'm a practical woman. And practical women don't have affairs with unavailable men."

"Colby, I wasn't asking you to—"

"Then what were you asking me? We've agreed to be friends, but friends don't do what we just did. And they don't want to do what we wanted to do but didn't get around to doing." If she hadn't been so frustrated, she would have laughed at herself. But she *was* frustrated and a little angry now because he wasn't hers to want. And she *did* want him. That was what made all of this so awful.

If she let this play out any further, she was going to lose her heart in a big way. And she couldn't afford to do that. She'd tasted rejection once. If she'd learned anything from it, it was that hopeless situations were hopeless. "I'd like to go back now," she said.

He didn't say anything, merely watched her a few moments longer. "Okay," he said finally, shifting in his seat and turning the key in the ignition. Disappointment assailed her as he pulled back out onto the main road. The feeling was inexplicable, unjustifiable. He was doing as she'd asked. Why did she feel so miserable?

The drive back to the high school parking lot seemed to take forever. Colby ached for him to touch her, to take her hand in his, wrong as she knew it to be. She focused on the road ahead, telling herself she'd done the right thing. When he pulled up beside her car, she slid out of the passenger side and held the door open. "I think it's better if we don't see each other anymore. For all concerned."

"Colby—"

But she wouldn't let herself stop and listen to him. She turned to her truck, fumbling to get the key in the lock. He called out again, but without looking back, she tore out of the parking lot while she still had the will to leave.

## *CHAPTER FOURTEEN*

IT WAS NEARLY 3:00 a.m. when Colby pulled into her driveway. Phoebe was sitting on the front porch waiting for her, huddled up in Frank's old varsity football jacket.

Colby got out of the truck and jogged across the yard. "Phoebe, are you all right? What's wrong?"

Phoebe sniffed and wiped the back of her arm across her cheek. "How about what's not? It'll take less time."

Colby sat down on the step and put an arm around her friend's shoulder, almost welcoming the distraction from her own troubled thoughts. "Come on, tell me about it."

"There's not much to say. One day I thought we had a great marriage, and now...now everything's a mess," she said with a broken sob.

Colby hugged her closer. "Where are the kids?"

"At their grandma's."

"Come on, then," she said, getting up and pulling Phoebe to her feet. "I'll make coffee. You'll talk."

Phoebe followed Colby into the kitchen and sat down in the chair she pulled out for her. In a couple of minutes, Colby had the coffee made, filling a cup for each of them. She took a fortifying sip. "What happened?"

Phoebe's face crumpled. "He said he had some

kind of business dinner tonight. And he wasn't home when I left at midnight.''

"He could have had a flat tire. Anything could have happened.''

"He always takes me with him if he has business on the weekend.''

"Have you talked to him about any of this, Phoebe?''

"I'm afraid to. What if he's having an affair? I don't think I want to know. And, on the other hand, I think I'll die if I don't find out something soon.''

"What good does it do to assume the worst, Phoebs?''

"What else could it be?'' She sighed, looking miserable. "Our fifteenth wedding anniversary is coming up next week. I never thought I'd be celebrating it like this.''

Colby hadn't wanted to believe Frank could ever do such a thing. But maybe she was just being naive. Why was it so hard to believe? Why had she thought him any different from most men? Any different from Ian McKinley, who had kissed her tonight, who had wanted more than that? Ian McKinley, who belonged to someone else.

She'd driven home, ridiculing herself for letting things get so out of hand. How far would they have gone if they hadn't been interrupted? She would like to think she'd have come to her senses, but who was she kidding?

She forced her attention back to Phoebe. "Did you leave him a note?'' she asked.

Phoebe nodded, sniffing.

"Then why don't you stay here tonight? Lena's staying at Millie's. You can sleep in her bed.''

"Are you sure I won't be putting you out?"

Colby squeezed her shoulder and said, "Never."

PHOEBE STAYED UNTIL almost 10:00 the next morning. The two of them were up early, though, talking and drinking coffee. Colby listened while Phoebe talked. Hearing the strain in her friend's voice, she realized Phoebe had been holding her worries in for a long time, hiding behind her usual front of good spirits. She felt guilty for not having taken Phoebe's concerns more seriously. She'd felt sure there was some explanation for Frank's behavior, but now, she honestly didn't know.

Once Phoebe had left, she straightened up the house, admitting to herself that she didn't know about a lot of things anymore. Her relationship with her daughter. Her growing preoccupation with an unavailable man.

What had happened to her steady, if somewhat predictable, life? How many times had Phoebe accused her of being set in her ways? Of refusing to open herself up to the possibility of falling in love? If that meant she didn't have to walk around with a knot in her stomach and a yearning for something she couldn't have, then she'd choose that option any day of the week.

She took a shower, got dressed and drove to the clinic to check on a springer spaniel named Hermie that had been hit by a car on Friday. The dog had been badly hurt. He had some internal injuries and a broken leg. Andrea Morris, the dog's owner, absolutely doted on the dog and had been nearly hysterical when she'd brought him in. Colby opened Hermie's cage now and stepped inside. He raised his head and looked glad to see her, his eyes noticeably more alert than they had been yesterday. She bent down and rubbed his ears. "Hey, fella. Glad to see you're feeling better this morning."

The dog whimpered again. She stroked the fur beneath his chin, and he tipped his head back a little farther, obviously enjoying the attention. She looked at the cast on his leg, checked his temperature and was glad to see it was normal. He had also eaten some of the food in his bowl, another good sign. She went to her office and called Mrs. Morris to tell her that Hermie was doing much better. The woman's relief was tangible.

"If you'd like to come see him, someone will be here. Just knock at the back door."

"Thank you, Dr. Williams. I'll do that."

Colby hung up, taking satisfaction in knowing she'd relieved the woman's worries. She drove back home and spent the rest of the morning preparing lunch for Lena, who was supposed to be home by 12:00. But her mind was only half on what she was doing. She kept reliving last night, hating herself for it but unable to stop thinking about Ian. She wasn't naive when it came to chemistry between a man and a woman. And there was definitely chemistry. That and then some.

The memory of last night was both sweet and poignant. Poignant, because she knew it couldn't happen again. She was a God-fearing, churchgoing, small-town veterinarian and mother. Women like her didn't have affairs with engaged men from Manhattan who looked as at home in tailor-made suits as she did in manure-spattered rubber boots. An affair was all it could be. And in the light of day, she had to admit that an affair was out of the question.

The front door opened, then closed. "Lena. Is that you?" she called out.

No answer. Lena appeared in the kitchen doorway, her expression stony.

"Hi, honey," Colby said cautiously. "Did you have a good time last night?"

Lena folded her arms across her chest and stared at her. "I was about to ask you the same question."

She faltered under the criticism in Lena's voice. "What do you mean?"

"Mom, how could you? The whole town's talking about you and Mr. McKinley. Everybody knows he's engaged, and the rumor is that you're moving in on him."

The attack left Colby stunned. "What?"

"Well, aren't you?"

"Where did you get that idea?"

"Maybe from the way you were hanging all over him at the dance last night. I guess that's why you haven't gotten in touch with my dad yet. You're too busy trying to steal Mr. McKinley from his fiancée to bother."

The injustice of the accusation cut like a knife. Colby had been walking on pins and needles for the past few weeks, waiting for Doug to call, hoping he would want to meet his daughter. "Regardless of whatever resentment you're feeling toward me, Lena, I'm your mother, and I won't tolerate that kind of disrespect."

Lena's mutinous expression wavered a bit. Colby couldn't remember ever speaking to her daughter in that tone of voice. But she'd just about reached her saturation point. She turned around and went outside, sitting down in the rope swing attached to the maple in their backyard.

She pushed off with her feet, taking the swing higher and higher. Higher than she'd ever allowed Lena to go. Higher than she should have.

The rebellion felt good. It eased the anger inside her, anger that was quickly followed by an avalanche of guilt. How had things with Lena gotten so out of control? She ached for the kind of relationship they'd once had. For the way in which she would have talked to her daughter about last night. For the light-hearted moments in which she had joked with her about bad dates and bad days.

Not once had she ever imagined things would be like this between them.

Lena's accusatory words played through her mind again. *Maybe from the way you were hanging all over him at the dance last night.*

Had she been hanging all over him? Was the rest of the town thinking that, as well? If her face revealed the feelings swirling around inside her, then they couldn't be thinking anything else.

She had fallen for a man who belonged to another woman.

It was true. She had. She, who had been perfectly content with her life. She, who had not gone out looking for this. Who had considered herself immune to the kinds of feelings she'd known last night in Ian McKinley's arms.

She'd let things get out of hand. Way out of hand. She'd embarrassed her own daughter and made a fool of herself in front of half the town if what Lena had said was true.

She stopped the swing with her feet and sat staring at the grass beneath her shoes. She'd been right to tell Ian they couldn't see each other anymore. As much as she might have wished for things to be different, it was simply a case of what might have been the right man at the wrong time.

ON MONDAY, LENA skipped school and hitched a ride to the health department in the next county.

Getting the appointment with a doctor had been a breeze. She'd called that morning from a pay phone and had been told that the doctor could see her at 2:00.

She arrived at the clinic two hours early and sat in a diner across the street, drinking lemonade and trying to still the butterflies in her stomach.

There were a couple of moments when she nearly chickened out and headed home. But this was the right thing to do. If she wanted Luke McKinley to like her, it was the *only* thing to do.

COLBY HAD JUST gotten in from work on Thursday when the phone rang. She dropped her grocery bags at the door and dashed for it.

"Hi, Dr. Williams. This is Millie. Is Lena in?"

"Hi, Millie. Just a minute. I'll check." She covered the phone and called up the stairs for Lena. No answer. "She must have gone out for a run or something."

"Oh, shoot. You don't see her algebra book anywhere nearby, do you? I need to borrow it if she brought it home with her."

She craned her neck for a glimpse of Lena's book bag and spotted it on the living room couch. "Just a sec." She put down the phone and reached for the backpack. There were two books inside. English Lit and Algebra. She put the bag back on the couch. It caught the side of a cushion and slid to the floor, spilling the contents beneath the coffee table.

She sighed and picked up the phone. "It's here, Millie."

"Great. I'll call her back in a little while and come over and get it."

Colby hung up, then went back to pick up the contents of Lena's bag. She dropped to her knees and gathered up what she could readily spot: pencils, paper clips, a notepad. She put everything back inside and zipped the bag. Just as she was getting up from the floor, she saw the edge of something sticking out from the other end of the couch. A thin plastic container with Lena's name and address on front. She turned it over in her hands, then snapped the lid open. Her stomach dropped. Birth control pills. What in the world was Lena doing with birth control pills?

Feeling as if she'd just had the wind knocked from her, she sank back onto the floor. The container was full. A thousand thoughts ran through her head. Had she started taking them yet? *Why* was she taking them?

The questions had no more than formed in her mind when Lena sprang through the front door. At the sight of Colby sitting on the floor with the packet in her hands, her face froze.

A hundred different emotions assailed Colby. Anger. Fear. Hurt. Denial.

Lena strolled into the living room and draped herself across the closest chair, defiance etched on her face.

"Millie called," Colby said in a stunned voice. "She wanted to know if you brought home your algebra book. I checked your bag for it, and these fell out."

Lena didn't say anything. She just sat with her arms folded across her chest, staring out the window.

Colby held up the packet. "What are these for?"

Lena met her gaze, her eyes narrowed. "What do you think, Mom? They're to keep me from ending up like you did! Pregnant and dumped."

Until that point, Colby had no idea that hurt could run so deep. It stabbed through the core of her and then spread outward in a white-hot spasm of pain. "Lena, you're not even dating yet."

"I will be soon. And if it weren't for your ridiculous rules, I already would be."

"Who are you taking these for, Lena?"

Lena turned around and looked her straight in the eye. "Luke McKinley. And don't worry, Mom. I know all about sex. I don't intend to make your mistakes."

Colby stared at her daughter, feeling as if she were talking to a stranger. She didn't know this child. Only she wasn't a child. She was a young woman who had decided that it was time for her to have sex. She'd seen a doctor on her own, without consulting her.

None of this would have happened if Ian McKinley and his son had never come to Keeling Creek. Colby dropped the pills on the couch and left the room.

IT WAS THE last place on earth she wanted to be.

With her hands shoved inside her coat pockets,

Colby stood outside of Ian's newly painted front door. Her breath made little puffs of smoke in the cold night air. Righteous indignation simmered inside her. The more she thought about it, the more convinced she became that she was right. Ian McKinley, with his city-wise ways, was wreaking havoc with her life. And now his son was doing the same to Lena's.

She'd started to call instead of coming over, but hadn't wanted to take a chance on Lena overhearing the conversation. She would only stay long enough to say what she had to say, and then she'd be on her way. Drawing in a deep breath, she knocked on the door and reminded herself that she was a grown woman who could handle this situation with decorum even if she had acted like a sex-starved nymphet in the front seat of the man's car. Even if the Jefferson County Sheriff's Department was probably still chuckling about Colby Williams being caught parking with an unavailable man. She would just have to get past that. She—

The door opened, and suddenly she was looking up at him. Despite the forty-degree temperature, she broke out in a sweat. "I need to talk to you, Ian. Do you have a few minutes?"

"Sure. Come in," he said, looking surprised to see her. He pointed toward the half-painted living room just down the hallway and followed her inside, closing the French doors behind them. "Sorry about the mess. I'm still under construction here."

Her anger did wonders for subduing the awkwardness she would have otherwise felt at seeing him again. "I won't stay long."

"Colby, you can look at me. I won't bite. Really."

She met his gaze and realized why she'd been avoiding doing so. It was his eyes. They got her every time. Focusing on her anger, she said, "I'm here about Lena and Luke. I accidentally discovered a packet of birth control pills in Lena's backpack today. Apparently, they're seeing one another."

"They are?" He was obviously surprised.

"I think she just started taking them. I don't know that they've... I think she was planning ahead."

"Oh," he said. "Oh. I'm sorry, Colby. I don't know what to say."

"Until your son came to town, Lena wasn't even interested in boys," she said, an edge to her voice.

Ian looked at her for a moment. "Are you saying Luke somehow coerced her into—"

"I think it's obvious that he's more worldly than she is."

"So you think he's corrupted her?" Ian asked, looking incredulous.

Ignoring the voice inside her that questioned whether she was being fair, she said, "Sex was never an issue until she met him. Lena isn't supposed to date until she's sixteen, which is a couple of months from now. I'm going to stand by that. I'd appreciate it if you talked to Luke and asked him not to see Lena outside of school until then."

"You know that if it's what they really want to do, we're not going to stop them. It's the Romeo and Juliet thing."

"Please back me up on this," she said, her voice remarkably cool for all the turmoil inside her. And then she fled from the living room as if the devil himself were after her.

# CHAPTER FIFTEEN

FEELING LIKE the devil incarnate, Ian went after her, started to call her back, then stopped when another set of headlights arced across the driveway.

He let out a deep sigh and dropped down on the front porch steps, watching Colby's taillights disappear around the bend as the cool fall air quickly seeped through his shirtsleeves. He stared up at the clear, star-sprinkled sky he had grown to appreciate so much since moving here. Colby's angry accusations had thrown him. He hadn't seen her since the night of the dance, and as many times as he had imagined what he would say to her when he did, he had never envisioned this scenario.

Luke might be more worldly than Lena, but Ian was certain the boy wouldn't try to talk her into doing anything she didn't want to do. He'd had the distinct feeling that Colby was thinking as much about the two of them as about their son and daughter.

The car stopped in the driveway, and Luke got out of the passenger side. No time like the present to talk to him about the situation. He hadn't been surprised to hear that Luke might be having sex. He was like any other parent who hoped his child saw the wisdom in waiting until reason held some measure of control over hormones. Luke was seventeen, though, and reason had a few years to go. But the girl in question was Colby's fifteen-year-old daughter.

The car turned around and headed back down the drive. Luke strolled across the yard and stopped at the bottom of the stairs.

"How was the movie?" Ian asked.

"The special effects were good. What are you doing out here?"

"Thinking."

"Aren't you cold?"

"Not too bad. Can you sit down for a minute?"

Luke dropped his book bag onto the brick walkway and sat down on the step beside him. "Was that Dr. Williams leaving just now?"

"Yeah, it was. She found some birth control pills in Lena's backpack." So much for a lead-in.

Luke's eyes widened. A few seconds passed before he said, "So?"

"Lena said she started taking them for you."

When Luke didn't say anything, Ian felt compelled to fill the silence. "We've talked about this before, son. Pregnancy isn't the worst thing that can happen to sexually active kids today."

Luke sighed. "Dad, you gave me the lecture on safe sex a long time ago."

"I know. And I'm not giving you one now. I just—"

"I don't know why she told her mom that," Luke interrupted, throwing up his hands. "We're not seeing each other anymore."

"But you were?"

Luke shrugged and nodded.

"What happened?"

Another silence followed the question, but this

time Ian sensed Luke would answer him when he was ready. "I trusted her. I told her about what happened in New York, about me getting into trouble. She said she wouldn't tell anybody, and then, all of a sudden, I've got two goons in my face wanting to know if I'm connected."

"And you think she told them?"

"It had to be her. Nobody else knew."

Ian put a hand on his son's shoulder and squeezed. He heard the pain in the boy's voice and wanted more than anything to take it away. Even though Luke hadn't wanted to come here initially, Ian somehow knew that he would like to put the past behind him, that something about this place had touched a chord inside him, too. "Did you ask her about it?"

Luke shook his head. "What's the point? She lied. Apparently, she's pretty good at that."

"Lena's having a tough time."

"You mean because of her dad?"

Ian nodded. "Her mom doesn't want her to date until she's sixteen. Maybe what she needs more than anything right now is a good friend."

Luke considered that for a moment, then reached for his book bag and got up. "I'll think about it." At the top of the steps, he turned. "Is that all you and Dr. Williams are? Good friends?"

The question caught Ian by surprise. "I'm not sure how to answer that, Luke."

"You know, I ought to be the one giving you the lecture."

Ian raised an eyebrow. "How do you figure?"

"I saw you with her at the homecoming dance. I've never seen you look at Rachel the way you were looking at her."

"Luke—"

"It's because of Mom, isn't it?"

"What do you mean?"

"I might be a kid, but I'm smart enough to know you've never let yourself love anybody since Mom. Loving somebody means you'll have to hurt if you lose them. You don't love Rachel like that, do you?"

Stunned, Ian said, "Luke, I don't know what to say. I—"

"What if we stayed here, Dad? What if we didn't go back to the city?"

Ian leaned against a post, the question surprising him. "You mean permanently?"

Luke shrugged, his posture and tone nonchalant. But something told Ian the boy had been thinking about this a lot.

"You know I've intended to go back all along."

Luke shoved his hands into his jacket pockets. "I know. But I just like the way things are here better. With us and everything."

It was a hell of a statement. Ian had no idea how to respond to it. Before he could say anything, Luke said, "You're different since you met her, Dad. That ought to tell you something." He turned and went inside the house.

More than a little amazed, Ian sat there on the steps, staring after him. Since the moment he'd dropped Colby off at the high school on Saturday night, he'd been miserable. For the past few days, he'd done little more than mope around the house. When Mabel had finally asked him what on earth was bothering him, he'd waved away her concern, not wanting to talk about it. Apparently, Luke had been doing some observing of his own.

The truth was that he couldn't stop thinking about the dance and what had almost happened between Colby and him. Or the reasons behind it. He had always prided himself on being honorable. There was nothing honorable about infidelity. If he hadn't been unfaithful to Rachel in the complete physical sense, he couldn't deny that in his heart, the breech felt complete. Somewhere along the way, he had begun to feel that the real relationship in his life was the one he had with Colby.

He'd never intended for it to happen. They'd started out as friends. He wasn't sure when that had changed. But it had.

Colby had helped him rediscover a piece of himself that had been missing for a long time. The part of him that had finally remembered that life had more to offer than work. The part of him that had finally begun to build a bridge back to his son.

He felt good when he was with her. Alive. Like a man who was living his life rather than just racing his way through it.

Sitting there under the stars of a clear autumn night, he let himself admit that his son was right. For the first time in seventeen years, his heart was ruling his head. His confusion over Colby wasn't about Rachel. As much as it should have been, it wasn't. It was about the fact that Colby scared the hell out of him. With her, he felt things he'd been determined never to feel again. Ashamed as he was to admit it, Rachel had made things easy for him. With her, there had never been any threat of putting his soul on the line.

But Colby, with her caring heart, left him defenseless. She made him want to do exactly what his son had just suggested a few minutes ago. Through her, he had rediscovered some vital and critical links to who he was and what he wanted his future to be. She made him yearn for things he had never known he wanted. Little things that had nothing to do with money or status. Quiet moments and days filled with laughter and silliness. She had shown him that some of life's best pleasures were found in the simple things. In watching a baby calf be brought into the world. In bathing a dog in tomato juice. In learning the two-step on a crowded dance floor.

He realized then that it would be wrong to marry Rachel. On some level, maybe he had known that for a long time.

He didn't know what the future held for Colby and him—or if it held anything at all. She wasn't even speaking to him now. But he wasn't the same person he'd been when he arrived in Keeling Creek. He'd come here to change his son and had ended up changing himself. And with a conviction he couldn't explain, he knew there was no going back.

THE NEXT MORNING Colby waited at the breakfast table for Lena to come down. Her stomach jangled with nerves, and she debated about the best way to handle this situation. She wasn't anywhere close to reaching a conclusion when Lena came in, went straight to the refrigerator and poured herself a glass of juice.

With her back to her, Lena said, "I wasn't completely straight with you last night, Mom."

Colby leaned forward in her chair. "About what?"

Lena turned around, clasping her glass in both

hands and not quite meeting Colby's gaze. "I got the pills because of Luke, but we're not... we haven't..."

"I see. Are you talking about it?"

Lena shrugged. "Not exactly."

"Then why did you say they were for him?"

"Because that's the only way a girl can get a guy!" Lena's eyes filled with tears, and Colby had to force herself not to go to her.

"Why do you think that, Lena?"

"Because it's true. That's all guys care about."

"Did he say that?"

"No. But he took Melanie Cundiff to the homecoming dance, and everybody knows she puts out."

"Oh, Lena. I think you and Luke need to have a talk. I'd be willing to bet things aren't what you think they are."

"Why do you say that?"

"Because he seems like a nice boy," she said, meaning it. She'd flown off the handle last night. In the light of day, she would admit that she'd been lashing out at Ian in frustration over what was going on between them as much as she had been over Luke's part in Lena's sudden interest in sex. And that was grossly unfair.

Lena didn't say anything for a few moments. "I'm sorry for what I said last night. About not turning out like you. I didn't mean that," she said at last.

Some of the sadness inside her lifted with Lena's apology. "Thank you. I needed to hear that."

From the uncomfortable look on Lena's face, Colby knew she was aware of how deeply she had hurt her.

"Since we're clearing the air, Mom, have you talked to my father?"

Colby blinked, surprised by the question. "Lena, I—"

"You got in touch with him, didn't you?"

"Lena—" Colby began again.

"Mom, just tell me the truth. Until now, I've been too scared to ask you. But I'm a big girl. I can take it."

For a moment, Colby considered not telling her daughter the truth, but she didn't want any more lies between them. "He wanted some time to think."

"He hasn't called back, has he?" The question held a mixture of pride and fear, giving Colby a glimpse of the little girl she had once been, and in many ways, still was.

"No, honey, he hasn't," she said, her heart aching for her daughter. Above all else, this particular chapter of their lives would have to be closed before the two of them could really begin to mend their relationship. And Colby wanted that more than anything. That meant Lena had to have some kind of resolution with her father, whether he wanted it or not.

Lena looked down at the floor. "He doesn't want anything to do with me, does he?"

Colby pressed her lips together, wishing she could take the pain away from her, suffer through it herself. "It's not that. It's—"

"It *is* that, Mom. Just admit it. There's something wrong with me!"

Wheeling around, she tore out the back door before Colby could stop her.

That was it. Colby decided she wasn't waiting another minute for that asinine—

She picked up the phone and punched in the number she had memorized so Lena wouldn't find it.

Three rings, and the maid picked up, telling her that the Jamisons were on vacation.

Colby slammed down the phone so hard that her arm tingled. She stood at the sink with her hands planted on the counter, wishing for all she was worth that she could get her hands around Doug's selfish, self-centered neck.

ON FRIDAY NIGHT Colby and Lena left their house and headed for Blue Mountain Lake. Colby had received a mysterious phone call from Frank on Monday inviting Lena and her to a surprise party he was giving for Phoebe. She'd wanted to ask him if this was something he was doing out of guilt but had curbed her tongue. He made her promise not to breathe a word to Phoebe, and she could only hope that whatever problems the two of them had been having were no longer cause for concern.

"Whose house is this?" Lena asked as they pulled into the driveway of the address Frank had given her.

"I don't know," Colby replied. It was the first thing Lena had said during the entire drive. She'd been quiet and withdrawn over the past few days, spending most of her time in her room when she wasn't in school. Colby had wanted to ask her if she'd talked with Luke, but she'd refrained from doing so, hoping Lena would discuss it with her when she was ready.

Colby's own spirits had been pretty low, too, but she'd tried not to let it show. She didn't have a right to feel bad, anyway. Ian had never been available in the first place, so it wasn't as if she'd really lost anything.

But it sure felt that way.

She marveled at the house as she and Lena got out of the car. It was beautiful. Sprawled across an enormous lot, it looked like a beach house, bright and cheerful, with a white fence enclosing the perimeter. It was obviously brand-new. The yard was still covered in straw, and bits and pieces of building paraphernalia still lay scattered here and there.

At the front door hung a sign that read:

Welcome Everyone!
    Please go in and make yourselves at home. The bartender will be happy to make you something to drink. There's food set up in the kitchen and living room.

    I'll be arriving with Phoebe around seven. Please take this sign down about ten minutes before. Knock her socks off with a big "Surprise!"

                                        Frank

Inside, Colby smiled and said hello to the familiar faces. Parents and teenage children all but filled the living room and kitchen. Lena wound her way toward Millie, who was standing in the kitchen next to a bowl of chips. Colby soon discovered that she and Lena weren't the only ones in the dark about the party. No one seemed to know whose house this was.

The furnishings weren't complete, although most of the basics were in place—a sofa, some chairs, the kitchen table. The living room opened onto a deck, where several couples were talking, looking out at the lake beyond.

She had just asked for a glass of white wine from the bartender when she glanced up and spotted Ian in the kitchen. Standing next to him was Rachel. Colby's heart dropped somewhere within the vicinity of the floor.

The bartender handed her the wine with a smile. She took it, tried to smile back and failed miserably. She couldn't take her gaze off the two of them. How right they looked together. So right it hurt. It shouldn't have, but it did. Colby thought of the things she'd shared with this man in the past few months and realized that he had become a part of her life. It wasn't as if she could take any of it back, pretend it had never happened. And because of her own stupidity, she had to stand here and watch him with his fiancée.

Ian and Rachel left the kitchen, moving in her direction. Rather than turn and run, as she would have liked to, Colby stayed where she was, fixing a smile on her face when Rachel said, "Oh, hello. You're the pie lady, aren't you?"

Colby stuck out her hand, keeping her smile in place. "You have a good memory. Hello, Miss Montgomery."

"Rachel, please. After all, it won't be Montgomery much longer."

The dart, intended or not, reached Colby's heart. She looked up at Ian. He looked every bit as uncomfortable as she felt. Optimist that she was, she might have even called it miserable had she not been aware of her own bias. "I don't suppose you have any idea why Frank's having a surprise party for Phoebe in a house no one's ever seen before?" she asked, desperate to fill the silence.

He shook his head, his gaze holding hers with pained intensity. "Not a clue."

"Shhh!" Mary Simmons, Phoebe's sister, was standing by the window, peering around the edge of the curtain. "I think they're here," she said.

Everyone shuffled around, trying to find a place to stand where Phoebe wouldn't see them immediately. Colby stayed where she was. Unfortunately, so did Ian and Rachel. The room was pin-drop quiet. The car engine outside cut off, then two doors slammed. Phoebe's voice could be heard saying, "Frank Walker, what on earth is this all about?"

"Be patient, honey," he said.

The doorknob turned, and Phoebe stepped inside the hallway, Frank behind her.

"Surprise!!!" The room erupted in a roar. Phoebe let out a startled scream, one hand going to her chest. She looked at the roomful of people in front of her, then back at Frank, who was grinning ear to ear, and promptly burst into tears.

Frank put a hand on her shoulder. "Now, Phoebe, that's not exactly the reaction I was hoping for."

Laughter rippled through the room. Frank held up a hand, then leaned forward and kissed Phoebe on the mouth. "Happy fifteenth anniversary, honey," he said, one hand sweeping the expanse of the room. "You're standing in your present."

Phoebe looked down at the floor, then up again, realization dawning. "This house is my present?"

Frank nodded, looking so proud Colby thought he might actually split at the seams. "You always wanted a summer house. I'm a little late for this year, but now you know where I was all those nights when you were wondering."

Phoebe stared at him for a moment before her tears started again. She turned and took off down the hall to their right, leaving Frank at a loss. Knowing what was behind the tears, Colby went after her. The bathroom door off the master bedroom was closed, and she could hear Phoebe's sobs interspersed with hiccups. She knocked. "May I come in, Phoebe?"

She turned the knob, and the door swung inward. Phoebe was sitting on the side of an enormous tub, a wad of tissue in her hand. She looked up. "How could I have been such an idiot, Colby? All this time, I thought he was having an affair and he was building me a house."

Colby sat down on the tub and put a hand on her friend's shoulder. "It was an honest mistake."

"But I should have trusted him."

"I guess that's the lesson to be learned here."

"How am I ever going to go back out there?"

"How can you not? Your husband, who happens to adore you, has just gone to an awful lot of trouble to throw you a surprise anniversary party. I think the least you can do is go back out there and give him a big kiss."

Phoebe got up and turned on the water faucet. She rinsed her hands and dabbed at the mascara smudges beneath her eyes. "What will I say to him? To everyone out there? Oh God, I can't believe I thought he was having an affair."

"Just go back and tell them you were overwhelmed by what he did. It's certainly understandable. No one has to know the other part. Not even Frank."

"I've been so awful to him."

"Then I suggest you make it up to him here in your new house after everyone else goes home."

Phoebe caught Colby's gaze in the mirror and

smiled. "That sounds like something Dr. Green would say."

"So maybe I should have been a radio psychiatrist." Colby managed to smile back at her.

"I take it that's Rachel with Ian," Phoebe said, her disappointment obvious.

"Yes. His fiancée. The one you didn't believe existed."

"Oh, her."

"Yes, her."

"I might have been blind to my own situation, Colby Williams, but I can see as plain as the nose on my face that you're crazy about that man. When are you going to admit it to yourself?"

Colby moved to the other mirror and feigned intense concentration as she finger-combed her hair. As it turned out, Frank had been unjustly accused. But Ian had turned out to be just like Doug, after all. Nothing he'd ever said or done had meant a thing. There was another woman in his life. And Colby was the intruder. It wasn't a role she had any desire to play. "Phoebe, think of how you've felt these past few months, thinking Frank had someone else. I don't want to be the other woman. If I ever find the right person, I want to be the only one for him. I want what you and Frank have or I don't want anything at all."

Phoebe started to say something, then stopped. She put her arms around Colby and hugged her. "I'd like to argue with that, but I can't. I want that for you, too. He could have been the one, though. I just know it."

"He could have been," Colby admitted. She pulled back and tried for a bright smile.

Phoebe sighed. "Back into the fire?"

"Let's go."

FOR THE NEXT couple of hours, Colby stayed inside and mingled. Finally, she made her way out to the deck and breathed in the crisp night air, grateful to be alone so she could wilt for a moment without anyone noticing.

Maybe seeing Ian with Rachel was the cold dose of reality she had needed. Facts were facts, and when they were staring you in the face, they were awfully hard to deny.

And the fact was, that as easy as it had been to pretend otherwise these past few months, Rachel Montgomery would soon become Mrs. Ian McKinley.

"Colby?"

She swung around, startled. "Ian! What are you doing out here?"

"Looking for you."

"I don't think that's wise."

"Colby, I wanted to explain—"

"There's nothing to explain."

"There is. This isn't what you—"

"If you remember, I'm the one who told you I didn't want to see you anymore," she said, the two glasses of champagne she'd hastily swallowed earlier boosting her courage. "You really didn't need to draw me a picture tonight. I was quite clear on how things are."

She moved to step around him and go back inside.

He reached for her arm and pulled her to a stop. "Colby—"

"Ian?"

Rachel stood at the patio doors, looking at them with a question in her eyes. "I think they're getting ready to cut the cake."

Colby pulled her arm free of Ian's grasp, ignoring the look of frustration on his face. "I'd better go lend a hand," she said, and left them alone.

As soon as Lena had seen Luke come through the front door, she'd found a place in the back of the room where she hoped he couldn't see her. She stayed inside until Phoebe arrived, then slipped out to the backyard when no one was looking.

How would she ever face him? She'd been avoiding him in school for days now. If she had known he'd be here, she would have pretended to be sick and stayed home.

It was cold outside. Lena shivered and pulled her coat closer around her, shoving her bare hands in her pockets. Some fifty yards from the house sat a gazebo of sorts. She hurried across the yard and let herself inside. A shaft of light shone on the benches that circled the gazebo walls. Lena went to the back of the building and sat down in the shadows.

She'd been out there for no more than a minute when she heard footsteps outside the gazebo door. Great. Who could that be? She tucked herself into the shadows and stayed quiet.

"Lena?"

Oh, no. Luke's voice. What was he doing out here?

The door opened, and he stuck his head inside. "Lena, I know you're in here. I saw you from the deck at the house."

"Go away, Luke."

He closed the door behind him, cutting off the only light. "I'm not going away. Why have you been avoiding me?"

She made a sound that was half laughter, half disbelief. "I haven't been avoiding you."

Even in the dimness she could see that he didn't believe her. "My dad said your mom found birth control pills in your backpack. And since I was accused of being the reason why you had them, I'd say I'm not out of line in asking about it."

Lena's whole body went warm with embarrassment. She was thankful for the darkness. How had she ever gotten herself into this? "I decided it was time for me to have sex. Everybody else does. And obviously, you aren't interested in girls who don't."

"Why do you say that?"

She tilted her head to the side and gave him a look.

"You mean because of Melanie?"

Again, she said nothing.

"I never would have taken her to the dance if you hadn't broken your word to me."

She looked up in astonishment. "Broken my word? About what?"

"I trusted you not to tell anyone about my past. Then all of a sudden I'm getting tracked down by the school dopeheads looking for a connection."

Lena had no idea what he was talking about. She hadn't told anyone. "But I didn't..." And then she remembered. "Oh, Luke. I'm sorry. I did tell Millie. She's my best friend. And she swore on her life that she wouldn't... I'm sorry."

He studied her for several long seconds, a torn expression on his face. He'd trusted her, and she had let him down. She felt about two inches tall. She deserved his anger and more.

"I wanted to ask you to the homecoming dance," he finally said, "but I was mad at you for not keeping your word."

"I don't blame you. I'd be mad at me, too."

"Why'd you tell your mom we were having sex?"

"I didn't exactly. She just assumed it."

"You must have said something to make her think—"

She dropped her gaze to the floor. To her horror, tears welled up in her eyes and trickled down her cheeks. She wiped them away with her hand, hating herself for not being able to hold them back. "I figured that's why you took Melanie to the dance."

He looked at her in astonishment. "Well, it wasn't. We didn't."

Immense relief flooded through her. She looked up. "You didn't?"

He shook his head. "And if you're honest with yourself, you'll admit that part of your reason for getting those pills had something to do with your mom. Didn't it?"

Lena didn't say anything for a few moments. He was right. "I guess I wanted her to know I would never let what happened to her happen to me."

Still holding on to her arm, he pulled her against his chest and hugged her. He smoothed his hand across the back of her hair and held her while tears slid down her cheeks. "Your mom's a nice woman. My dad sure is different since he met her."

"What do you mean?"

Luke shrugged, his hand rubbing the center of her back. "I don't know. He makes time for stuff. He didn't used to do that. And things are a lot better between us.''

"I'm glad, Luke. I wish things with my mom could be the way they used to be.''

"Can't they be if you want them to be?''

"I don't know.''

"My dad wasn't around as much as I would have liked when I was growing up. He worked all the time. Rather than talk to him about it, I just bottled up all my anger. When I got into trouble, I guess I figured that was one way to get him to notice me. I know now that it wasn't the right way.''

Lena pressed her face to his chest. She knew what he was trying to say to her. That it was up to her to fix things with her mom. She wanted to. She really did. She just didn't know where to begin.

DURING THE DRIVE back to Oak Hill, Ian and Luke said very little. Rachel did all the talking.

"I bet you two will be glad to get back to the city. The people here are as nice as they can be, but things are certainly different. You can't tell me you haven't been getting bored," she said, looking over her shoulder at Luke in the back seat.

When Luke didn't respond, Ian said, "Actually, we haven't. There's plenty to do around here.''

"Like what?'' she asked with a laugh. "Once you've rented all the movies at the local video store, I'd imagine you're in trouble.''

Logically, Ian knew Rachel was half joking, but her comments irritated him. She'd written Keeling Creek off as a backward hick town. But then, maybe a few months ago, he would have, too. He was the one who had changed. The realization made him more sure than ever that what he was about to do tonight was the right thing.

He'd been on edge all week, having decided not to see Colby until he had talked to Rachel. He'd tried to get in touch with her earlier in the week with no success. Her secretary had said she would be in California with a client for most of the week. He'd left numerous messages at her hotel, and the two times she had returned his call, he had been out. This afternoon, she had shown up at Oak Hill to surprise him. And she had.

At the house, Luke went straight upstairs, leaving them alone. They went into the kitchen, where Ian put on some coffee. "Would you like a cup?" he asked.

"You know I don't have caffeine after six."

"Sorry. I forgot."

She studied him for a moment. "You've been forgetting a lot of things lately. Like remembering to call me."

He met her gaze. "We have to talk, Rachel."

"So you said in your messages. When I got back from California and heard that you'd been trying to reach me for days, I thought something must be wrong. That's why I came straight here. Something *is* wrong, isn't it?"

"Rachel, I don't think there's any easy way to say this—"

"You didn't want to take me with you tonight," she interrupted. "I have the distinct feeling you wouldn't have if you hadn't promised to be there early and open the house for your friend. After I showed up at the last minute, you could hardly leave me here."

"Rachel—"

"It's that woman, isn't it?" she said. "Your little country vet."

"Her name is Colby," he said in a quiet voice. "And in every way that counts, this has nothing to do with her."

"Then what does it have to do with?"

"Me. Changes."

"If you're talking about your life here, that's not going to be forever. You'll come back to New York and things will be like they always were."

"No, they won't. *I've* changed. In ways I never imagined. I came here a workaholic, Rachel. For too many years, I haven't spent ten seconds thinking about anyone but myself and my work. And for that, I almost ruined my relationship with my son. Since I've been here, I've realized how much I've been missing out on. With Luke…and, well, just living."

"Then we'll change things when you get back," she said quickly. "You won't work as much. We'll go away more."

"But that's just it. I don't want to keep leading a life I have to escape from."

Rachel drew in a deep breath, then let it out slowly. "And I'm part of that life."

"You deserve someone who wants the same life that you want. I'm not that man anymore."

"Stop," she said, looking away and pressing the back of her hand to her lips. "You can deny it all you want, Ian McKinley, but you're in love with that woman. And unfortunately, I can't fight her, because I don't know what her weapons are. Apparently, she has something I don't."

"Rachel—"

She held up a hand. "I guess I knew this was coming when I flew down here this afternoon. I just didn't want to let myself admit it. I'll sleep in the guest room."

Ian stood in the dimly lit kitchen, listening to the sound of her footsteps on the stairs. He heard the bedroom door open, then click closed. He felt a wave of sadness for the hurt he had caused her. He waited for a surge of regret to swamp him, but when it didn't come, he knew that he had done the right thing.

# CHAPTER SIXTEEN

COLBY HAD JUST gotten out of the shower Saturday afternoon when the phone rang. Lena and Millie were at a track club meeting, so she grabbed a towel and ran for the bedroom.

It was Phoebe.

"You sound winded, Colby."

"I just got in from the clinic a little while ago. I was in the shower. So how was your anniversary?"

"Wonderful. Better than wonderful. Oh, Colby, I was such an idiot. All those things Frank was doing, the new suits, the working out, they were all for me. He thought he'd started to let himself go, and he didn't want me to lose interest in him."

"So much for Dr. Green's theories, huh?"

"Yeah. Things aren't always what they seem. Sometimes people do things for one another just because they love them, right?"

"Right," Colby said, truly happy for her friend despite her own misery.

"I have a big favor to ask of you," Phoebe said.

"What's that?"

"Frank had to run back to town for something that came up at work. He'd planned to come back out to the lake, but he's stuck there and I don't have a ride. Could you come get me?"

Colby had spent the morning working on a golden

retriever who had been near death when his owner brought him in. The dog had been almost comatose and was having great difficulty breathing. After questioning the woman and discovering that the retriever might have had access to rat poison in a nearby barn, Colby had done a quick blood test which showed the dog's blood wasn't clotting, confirming her suspicions. It was a nasty way to die, and luckily a dose of vitamin K and a blood transfusion had saved the dog's life. It had been a stressful morning, and Colby had planned to spend the afternoon relaxing. But she couldn't very well leave Phoebe stranded. "Sure. Lena's at Millie's for the night, so I don't have anything planned for the rest of the day."

"Great. Can you be here around five? That'll give me time to finish cleaning up."

"No problem. See you then."

THE DRIVE OUT to the lake was a pretty one, but it gave Colby too much time to think. Too much time to wonder what Ian and Rachel were doing. Too much time to remember how painful it had been to see them together last night.

After she'd left Ian on the deck, she'd been miserable for the rest of the party. As soon as she'd been able to do so, she'd said good-night to Frank and Phoebe, all too conscious of the knowing look in her friend's eyes. She knew she had no right to feel the way she did, but the feelings were there, nonetheless.

She almost passed the turnoff to the lake house, but spotted it just in time. She parked her truck in the driveway and got out. She knocked twice, and when there was no answer, rang the doorbell. "Phoebe?" she called out.

She knocked again. Still no answer.

A car engine sounded from the end of the driveway. Colby turned around. Maybe that was Frank. But a second later, Ian's car appeared around the bend. Her stomach dropped. What was he doing here?

He parked behind her truck and got out, looking as startled as she felt. "I didn't expect to see you here," he said, a note of uncertainty in his voice.

She did her best to mask her feelings, even though the wound was still raw. "Phoebe called and asked me to pick her up, but she's not answering the door."

"That's strange. Frank called a little while ago and asked if *I* could pick her up."

"Oh. Well, maybe we had some kind of misunderstanding, but no one seems to be here."

Ian jogged up the steps and pushed the doorbell again. Still no answer. He turned the knob and opened the door. "Phoebe?" he called out.

They stepped inside the house. The lamps were on, and music was playing, something soft and alluring. A wonderful aroma drifted toward them. Someone was cooking.

"What's going on?" Colby asked. They went into the kitchen, where a bucket of icy champagne sat on the island in the center of the room. Propped beside it was an envelope.

With a sinking feeling, Colby pulled out the card and read it in silence.

Just so you know, Frank refused to participate in this. So if it works, he gets none of the credit. If it fails, I guess I'll take all the blame. I'm hanging up my matchmaking hat after this,

Colby. Really. I promise.

The Jacuzzi's off the master bedroom. Dinner is in the oven. And the champagne is right in front of you.

No need to worry about Lena, since you said she's spending the night at Millie's. And, Ian, I'll make sure Luke knows where you are.

                                        Phoebe

Colby closed her eyes. "This time I really will have to kill her."

"What is it?" Ian asked.

She handed the note to him. He read it, then looked up and said, "Frank must have told her."

"Told her what?"

He paused before he said, "Rachel and I aren't getting married. I told him when he called to see if I could pick up Phoebe."

Surprise ricocheted through her. "You're not?"

He shook his head. "No."

"Why?" she asked, taken aback.

Ian put the card on the counter and looked at her. "When I asked her to marry me, it wasn't for any of the right reasons. After Sherry died, I guess I stopped believing in fairy-tale love. What Rachel and I had always felt like more of a merger than anything else."

"Oh." She couldn't think of anything else to say. She felt hot and cold at once. This was the last thing she'd expected to hear.

"But then I met someone who made me believe again."

"You did?" Her voice was little more than a whisper, her heart pounding against her chest.

"Yeah, I did. She's incredible, this woman. She's smart and funny and warm, and Lord, does she know how to kiss...."

"She does?" Colby managed to whisper.

He nodded, a smile touching his lips. "And as much as I tried, I couldn't stop thinking about her. She's the kind of woman a man waits his whole life for, and when he finds her, he just knows it's right, no matter how much he tries to deny it."

She wanted to believe him. More than anything, she wanted to believe him. But the old wariness was still inside her, questioning her, torturing her with what-ifs. What if this was just temporary? What if his feelings changed, the way Doug's had changed? What if—

"I can read your thoughts," he said softly. "The doubts are there in your eyes. I know how much he hurt you, sweetheart. And I know how hard it's been for you to put that behind you. But I think that's one of the things that drew us together. My hurt was different from yours, but it had the same effect. We've both refused to really let ourselves feel anything all these years. And I think, somehow, someway, I was waiting for you."

Tears welled up in her eyes. "Oh, Ian—" She was unable to go on. Happiness rocketed through her. She couldn't believe they were really here. That he was saying these things to her. But he was. The armor with which she'd shielded herself from him these past months fell away, and she was left standing before him, fully aware of how desperately she needed to hear those words. How very much she wanted him. She could no longer pretend otherwise. To herself or to him.

They moved toward each other simultaneously. She slipped into his embrace, her arms locking around his neck, her cheek to his chest. His arms secured her to him. And in that moment, she felt as if this was where she'd been headed all her life. She knew, without doubt, that all these years, she had been waiting for this one good man to come along. This man with whom she found such satisfaction in simple things, in laughing just for the sheer joy of it, in kissing. Ah, in kissing. This man with whom and from whom she wanted so much more.

She pulled back and cupped the side of his face with the palm of her hand. "I think I've been waiting all my life to hear you say that."

"And I've been waiting all my life to say it."

The admission filled her with a sweet mixture of gratitude and awe and other emotions too tangled to identify now.

"I wanted to call you this morning," he said, his voice low and uneven. "Hell, I wanted to call you last night. But I didn't think I should so soon—"

"Phoebe's never been known for her patience."

Ian smiled. "Right now, I'm glad about that."

"I'll never admit it to her, but so am I."

Darkness had descended outside, and the kitchen was shadowed with light from the lamps in the living room.

Ian nodded toward the champagne. "It would be a shame to waste that now that we're here. Would you like a glass?"

"I'd love one," Colby said, welcoming the diversion.

He found a dishcloth in one of the drawers, then pulled the bottle out of the ice and wrapped the towel around it. He loosened the foil, then the wire and pointed the cork toward the ceiling. "Heads up." The cork zinged out of the bottle, slammed off the ceiling and shot back past them. They both ducked, shoulders colliding, champagne sloshing from the bottle and onto their clothes as their surprised laughter filled the room.

"You could take a girl out with a power shot like that," she said.

Ian grinned. "It packed a little more punch than I expected." He reached for the glasses that Phoebe had thoughtfully placed next to the ice bucket. He filled them both, then handed one to Colby and raised his own in a toast. "To meddling, good-intentioned best friends."

Colby smiled. "Here, here."

The champagne was crisp and cold and glorious. Now she stood mere inches from this man who had captured her heart and would forever hold it prisoner, and this was the only place on earth she wanted to be.

Another song started on the CD player. This one, too, was slow and easy, and it flowed over Colby's skin like the finest silk. Goose bumps danced down her arms.

"Rumor has it you're a pretty incredible dancer," he said.

"Well, I'd hate to let Phoebe's efforts go to waste."

He put his glass on the counter, reached for hers and set it down, too. And then he reached for her. She moved into his arms, and there, in the middle of the kitchen floor, they found the beat of the music, swayed and flowed to it, their steps in perfect unison.

It was torture of the sweetest, most painful kind. He held her loosely, but with every turn, their knees would brush or his thigh would graze her hip. And when the tips of her breasts encountered the wall of his chest, sensation flooded through her.

He stopped moving, and from the look in his eyes, she knew he'd found the dancing as intoxicating as she had.

"I want to kiss you so badly I think I might die if you don't let me," he said.

"Good. Because I'm going to die if you don't stop talking about it and just do it."

A smile on his lips, he pulled her to him, his hands splaying across her back, his palms wide and encompassing and urgent. Her own hands found the back of his neck and wound through his thick, soft hair.

His head dipped toward her, and his lips found the curve of her jawline. Gentle, butterfly kisses at first, soft and easy. Her eyes closed and her breathing quickened as his hands skimmed the length of her arms and cradled her neck while his thumbs brushed the hollow of her throat. He cupped the back of her head and kissed the tip of her chin. She turned her mouth toward his, needing his kiss. But still he evaded her seeking mouth and found the soft spot beneath her right ear. His tongue tested and tasted the lobe, and a thousand shivers danced up her spine.

"Ian." His name slid past her lips, softly pleading.

The kiss, when it came, was worth waiting for. Their mouths met and melded, preliminaries ignored in a frantic attempt to experience each other completely. Surely kisses didn't get any better than this. She wanted more. Forever and ever. She tightened her arms around his neck, and he gathered her closer against him. This was the kiss that made up for all the years when she had thought she would never again know this kind of physical chemistry. Years of dates endured only because it didn't seem normal for someone her age not to go out once in a while. This was what kissing should be, an act of intimacy that signals rightness, that prompts an internal message that says, *This is where I belong.*

In his arms, the message was as impossible to deny as the stars in the sky.

The kisses soon became more urgent, their body language communicating more clearly than words that it wasn't enough. He drew back and looked into her eyes. "Are you sure this is what you want, Colby?"

"Yes," she said. "I'm sure."

To her surprise, he picked her up and continued kissing her while he carried her though the living room and down the hallway. Cradled against his chest, she kept her arms around his neck, one hand laced through his hair.

He stopped at the first door on the left, and they reluctantly pulled apart long enough to give their surroundings a cursory glance. Shadows draped the room, but the enormous bed in the center of the floor was hard to miss.

"Candles," Ian said.

Colby shook her head. "Phoebe thinks of everything."

He smiled and set her down at the side of the bed. He kissed her again, long and slow, one hand at the base of her spine, massaging, enticing, the other winding through the back of her hair. "Don't go anywhere," he said, his voice uneven.

Smiling, she said, "Phoebe probably has a booby trap rigged to go off if I step back out that door."

He laughed. Maybe that was what she loved most about him. The sound of his laughter. It was the kind of sound she would like to know for the rest of her life. Over the breakfast table. In crowded movie theaters. At night just before she fell asleep.

The enormity of her admission hit her then. She loved him. Loved him as she had never loved another. She loved him for his generosity. For changing his life for his son. For passing those grits around at the church breakfast when he'd never even heard of them before. He was a genuinely good man, and regardless of what happened here tonight, or how things ended up, she loved him. How simple that was. How profound.

Ian had found a match and lit the oversize candle on the nightstand. The scent of honeysuckle drifted toward her. He picked up the card that lay beside the candle and read it, then passed it to her. "Necessaries are in the drawer. Just in case. Phoebe."

He grinned and shook his head. "She really *does* think of everything, doesn't she?"

Exasperated and amused, Colby said, "Phoebe prides herself on being a modern woman."

"Well, because of a promise I made to Luke a few years ago, I would have been ahead of her on that one, anyway," he said, patting the wallet in his back pocket. "When I had that talk with Luke, I told him responsible men were always prepared. I said I'd carry one with me if he would always carry one with him. I couldn't decide if it was worse to sound like I was pushing him to have sex or to take a chance on his getting caught up in the moment and not having one."

"You made the right choice," she said. "I'm sorry about the other night. I had no right to blame Luke the way I did. I think I was looking for someone other than myself to blame, and—"

"It's okay," he said softly, and stopped her from saying anything further by kissing her again. Candlelight danced across their skin, and she grew warm with longing. Ian reached for the hem of her sweater and pulled it over her head. Beneath it, she wore a white cotton blouse. He undid the buttons and brushed it open with the back of his hand, revealing the lacy white bra beneath.

His fingers trailed the length of her jaw, hesitated at the tip of her chin, then made a line down her throat, stopped at the hollow between her breasts, his thumb rotating over the soft flesh.

Colby's head dropped back, and a sigh of pleasure escaped her parted lips. He kissed the column of her throat, his mouth following the same trail his fingers had just taken. Her need for him grew more intense, and she began unbuttoning his shirt, the backs of her fingers grazing the hair-roughened skin of his chest. Halfway down, she yanked the shirttail from his pants, then undid the last few buttons and pushed it from his shoulders.

She let her eyes have their fill of him. He was a beautiful man. There was no other word for it. Fit and finely built. With wide shoulders and narrow hips, the kind made for blue jeans. His skin was still brown from the work he'd been doing outdoors in the fall.

Unable to resist the temptation, she ran the back

of her hand across his chest and then down to the waistband of his jeans. She heard his indrawn breath and took pleasure in knowing that she could affect him in the same potent way he affected her.

They kissed again, and his hand found the catch at the front of her bra. Once it was undone, he slipped it off. A wave of self-consciousness assaulted her. It had been a long, long time since she had been with a man. What if he didn't find her attractive? What if...

"You're so beautiful."

Renewed confidence blossomed inside her. Under his appreciative gaze, she *felt* beautiful. And powerful in the way a woman feels when a man looks at her with desire in his eyes. It was a feeling she had never known this intensely, but innately understood.

This time, she kissed him. She wrapped her arms around his waist, her breasts pressed to his bare chest. An orchestra of feeling struck up inside her. Need of the most overwhelming kind lent urgency to their movements and sent them toppling back onto the bed behind them.

The mattress dipped, their clumsiness lightening the intensity between them. They both laughed, breathless, eager. Their laughter faded, and they watched each other, assessing, appreciating. His hand found the snap of her jeans, and they somehow divested themselves of the rest of their clothes, their movements hurried and increasingly frantic.

He pulled her to him and kissed the side of her neck. "You scare me, Colby. You're everything I've ever wanted, even though I never realized it until I met you. I'd like to believe that maybe that means we were meant to be."

"Oh, Ian." She pressed her lips to his temple and closed her eyes, tears seeping through her lashes.

"I love you," he said.

"I love you, too."

He pushed a strand of hair back from her forehead, his fingers lingering in a gentle caress. He lay on top of her, shifting, getting acquainted, finding their fit. He held her gaze all the while, his hands twining through her hair. How good it felt to be this close, to know the weight of him, the lines of his body. She massaged his shoulders, near his collarbone, then farther down his arms.

He made a sound of longing and took her mouth again, while the music from the stereo played on. He moved against her, leading her now in a dance of a different kind, a dance that spoke to the furthest depths of her being, that made her rise and fall with each ebb and surge of his body. He led and she followed, the scent of honeysuckle all around them, and nothing, nothing mattered except this dance of the heart.

And there, in the candlelit room, they made love in the truest, most complete sense, writing their own song, testing and finding their own rhythms, following their own hearts and filling each other with the profound happiness that only comes with loving and being loved.

# CHAPTER SEVENTEEN

LENA WAS BUMMED.

Millie had gotten sick at the movie, a virus or something. Mrs. Mitchell had driven Lena home, since there wasn't much point in her staying the night if Millie spent most of it in the bathroom. Ever since Lena had confronted her with spreading gossip about Luke, Millie had been working overtime to make up for it. She'd felt terrible about ruining their afternoon. Lena had agreed not to hold it against her as long as she kept her word from now on.

Lena arrived home to find a note from her mom on the kitchen counter saying that she'd gone out to the lake to pick up Phoebe. That was just like her mom. Lena wasn't even supposed to be home tonight, and she'd still left a note just in case she came by and wondered where she was. How many kids had moms like that? A yearning for things to be the way they used to be swept over her. She thought about what Luke had said at the party last night. Maybe he was right. Maybe she hadn't handled things the way she should have. Was knowing her father worth ruining the relationship she'd had with her mom?

The question nagged at her as she went into the den and looked for the TV section of the newspaper.

It wasn't in any of the usual places. She peered out the window and saw the paper sticking out of the box. She put on her shoes and sprinted outside to get it. While she was there, she checked the mailbox and found several letters inside.

Just as she turned to head back up the driveway, she spotted the corner of an envelope sticking up from the edge of the brick flower bed that served as the base of the mail box. She bent down and picked it up, then threw it on top of the other mail. In the house, she tossed it all on the kitchen table and leafed through the paper until she found the TV section. Bummer. Nothing on worth watching.

She put down the paper, the letter on top of the pile of mail catching her eye. It was in a plain white envelope, addressed to her mom and marked Personal and Confidential. She picked it up and held it to the light. No return address.

It was wrong to open it. The last time she'd read something that didn't belong to her, she'd wished she'd left the letter where she found it. A strong voice told her to leave the letter alone. But like Pandora, she couldn't help herself. It was from her father. She knew it as surely as she was sitting here.

She got a pot out of the bottom of the stove and put some water on to boil. The minutes ticked by like molasses from a cold jar until finally enough steam rose from the pot to loosen the seal on the envelope. She slid the letter out and unfolded it, her heart thumping too hard, her hands clammy.

Colby,
I know I'm a coward for getting back to you

this way. But, as you know, confrontations were never my strength. I've gone over and over this during the past weeks, and I keep coming to the same conclusion. Lena is your daughter. I have a family of my own, and I can't bring myself to jeopardize what I have by telling them that I have a daughter they never knew existed.

I think it's best if we just leave things as they've been. Since Lena has never met me, she can't be hurt by my decision. I trust you to explain this to her in the best way you can.

Doug

Lena flung the letter away from her as if it had scorched her. It fluttered to the floor like a fallen angel, and she stood there staring at it, unable to believe what she'd just read.

He didn't want anything more to do with her now than he had sixteen years ago. Her stomach heaved. She ran to the bathroom and threw up until dry retching sounds echoed the emptiness inside her. She sat on the cool tile floor, her left arm and forehead resting on the side of the bathtub.

What was wrong with her? What had she ever done to make him hate her so much?

She sat there for a long time, miserable and crushed. When she finally got up from the floor, she wiped her face with a cool washcloth and then went into the kitchen and stood staring out the window at the backyard where she'd played and done much of the growing up that her father hadn't wanted to witness.

The pain inside her was so great that she wanted

nothing more than to make it go away. If not forever, then just for a little while.

She remembered the bottle of gin someone had given her mother for a Christmas present a year or two ago. She pulled a chair out from the kitchen table and scooted it over to the cabinet above the sink. She opened the door, and sure enough, there it was, in the back, unopened. Lena reached for it, then got down and poured herself a glass.

The first sip was awful. She nearly gagged, and when it hit her throat, still sore from being sick, it felt like fire blazing a trail to her stomach.

She went to the refrigerator and grabbed the orange juice container, watering down the gin with it. Still awful, but not quite so bad.

Taking the bottle and the glass with her, she went into the living room, sat on the couch, and, for the first time in her life, proceeded to get drunk.

SHE WAS DRUNK.

Luke knew it as soon as he answered the phone.

"H-he doesn't want me."

The words were slurred and hard to understand. "Lena, who are you talking about?"

"He sa-said I wouldn't c-care 'cuz I never met him. But that's not true."

Her father. She must be talking about her father. "Where are you, Lena? Are you at home?"

Her answer was barely audible.

Luke knew her mom wasn't there, because Mrs. Walker had called earlier to say his dad had gone out to the lake to meet Colby. "Lena?"

No answer this time. He heard the receiver drop

to the floor and felt his heart fall with it. "Lena, I'll be right there!" he yelled, hoping she could hear him. He grabbed his keys off the kitchen counter and lunged out the door.

IAN LAY AWAKE, looking down at this woman who had come to mean everything to him. They'd lost track of time, making love again, this time even better than the last as they learned about each other's bodies and the pleasures to be found in that familiarity. Her eyes were closed now, her thick, honey-colored hair fanned across the pillow. She was beautiful. Physically, yes. His immediate and continual response to her was proof of that. But he found her beautiful in so many other ways as well. She had simplified life for him, brought into focus everything that was important, screening out the things that were not. Her innate goodness became more clear to him with each moment he spent with her. His heart belonged to her, and he could not imagine a future without her.

She stirred and opened her eyes to stare up at him with the expression of a sated woman. The sight of it filled him with an almost primitive gladness that he had been the one to put that look in her eyes.

She stretched beside him, her legs entwined with his. He still wanted her as much now as he had a few hours ago. "You can't expect to look at a man like that and get away with it," he said, trailing a finger across the flat plane of her belly.

She wrapped her arms around his neck and kissed him with renewed heat and a good measure of lust before saying, "I don't intend to."

And he made sure that she didn't.

THE ENORMOUS TUB in the bathroom was too inviting to resist. Colby took the candle from the nightstand and set it on the sink counter. She filled the tub and added some of Phoebe's bubble bath. The bubbles tickled her chin as she sank beneath the water and leaned against the wall of the tub, more content than she could ever remember being.

Ian appeared in the doorway, a towel wrapped around his waist.

"Better come in. The water's fine," she said.

"It looks fine," he said, his gaze openly admiring.

She smiled up at him. He dropped the towel and slid in behind her, gathering her against him. He tucked his chin into her shoulder and kissed the side of her neck. "Is this real?" he asked.

"I keep thinking I'm going to wake up and find that it isn't."

"Me, too."

They were quiet for a while, just holding each other, while Colby thought how incredible it was that there could be such pleasure in companionable silence. It was almost too perfect to believe it could last. "What are we going to do about this?" she asked, and immediately wished she could take the question back. It was too soon. He'd just broken his engagement, and she didn't want him to think she expected something more from him.

"You mean what happens when the school year is up?"

She nodded.

He didn't say anything for a few moments. "I think that's something we need to talk about."

The phone rang. She sat up, wrapping her arms around herself.

"Think that's Phoebe?" Ian asked.

"I can't imagine she would call," she said, frowning.

The ringing stopped. A couple of seconds later, it started again.

"We'd better get it in case something's wrong," he said. He got out of the tub and grabbed a towel from the rack by the door.

"I think the phone's in the kitchen," she called after him. She watched him disappear around the corner, wishing she hadn't said anything about the future. She'd gotten so caught up in what had happened between them that she'd let herself forget he had another life in another world. He was no longer engaged, but that didn't change the fact that his stay in Keeling Creek would be temporary. He'd said he loved her, but she'd long ago learned the lesson that love didn't mean forever.

His footsteps sounded in the hallway. She looked up to find him standing at the door, his jeans in his hands, his face creased with worry.

"What is it?" she asked, knowing immediately that something was wrong.

"We have to go back. Luke and Lena have been in an accident."

ALL THE WAY back to town, Colby prayed. Harder than she'd ever prayed in her life. It had been Phoebe on the phone. There had been an accident, Ian had said. Phoebe had known next to nothing. Frank had heard about the accident on his police scanner, and the two of them had been on their way to the hospital when she'd called.

Ian held on to her hand as the Mercedes roared down the driveway, his grip firm enough that she knew he was suffering the same agonies as she.

It seemed like hours before they reached the emergency room door. As soon as Ian stopped the car, Colby was out and running. He was right behind her. Colby stopped the first nurse she saw. "Our children, they were brought in a little while ago. Lena Williams and Luke McKinley. Can you tell us where they are?"

"Certainly. Just follow me."

Ian took Colby's hand, and they anxiously followed the woman to an examining room, where both Lena and Luke lay in separate beds. The blood drained from Colby's face. Lena looked as white as the sheet covering her. Her eyes were closed, and there was a nasty-looking gash on her forehead which a doctor was stitching up.

Luke was on the other side of the divider curtain. Bandages encircled his hands, and white gauze covered the center of his forehead. His eyes were closed, and a nurse was adjusting the IV taped to his hand.

"Oh, thank God, you're here."

Colby swung around to find Phoebe and Frank hovering in the doorway. Phoebe had a stricken look on her face.

"They're going to be all right, aren't they?" she asked, hearing the fear in her own voice.

Phoebe nodded and waved them outside the door,

where she said, "Oh, Colby, I'm sorry. I feel as if this is all my fault. If I hadn't sent you two off to the lake, maybe this wouldn't have—"

"Phoebe, what happened?" Ian interrupted gently but with a distinct note of urgency.

Frank squeezed Phoebe's shoulder and said, "They were hit by another car, and...apparently, they had been drinking."

"Who had been drinking?" Colby asked, incredulous.

"Lena and Luke."

Ian leaned against the wall behind him and dropped his forehead onto the heel of one hand.

Colby knew what he was thinking. If Luke had been drinking when the accident happened, he would be in violation of his probation. She prayed that there had been some kind of mistake.

"They've both been out of it since they got them in here, so nobody knows anything for sure," Phoebe said. "And the blood work's not back from the lab yet."

"Did you call my mom and dad?" Colby asked, her voice raspy with shock.

"No. I thought you'd want to do that after we knew more."

"Good." Colby and Ian went back inside and talked to the doctor who had just finished with Lena. He assured them that they would be fine. He'd given them something for pain, and they would both probably sleep for a while.

As soon as the doctor left the room, Colby slid back the curtain that divided the two beds. She and

Ian stood between them, she holding Lena's hand, he holding Luke's, their own joined in the middle.

LUKE WOKE UP first. His eyes opened, and he made a visible effort to focus.

Relief flooded through Ian, making him weak with gratitude. "Luke?" He sat down on the edge of the bed and pressed his hand to his son's face. "I'm right here. You're going to be all right."

"Where am I?" Luke asked, still groggy. Before Ian could answer, the boy sat bolt upright and said, "Lena! Where's Lena?"

"She's right here next to you," Ian assured him. "She's going to be fine. Everything's okay. Just relax, all right?"

Luke sank back on the pillow, one hand pressed to his temple.

Colby came around to the other side of the bed. "How are you feeling?"

"Not too great right now."

"What happened, son?" Ian asked.

"We…the car…it came out of nowhere. I was trying to get Lena to the hospital."

"Lena. Why?" Colby asked, her hands clasped together.

"She called me. She…was upset about her dad, and I could tell she'd been drinking. I rushed over to your house, and she was passed out. I couldn't wake her up, so I was taking her to the hospital when—"

"You weren't drinking, son?" Ian interrupted, relief flooding through him.

Luke looked up at him and shook his head with a

half smile. "With my track record, I guess it's understandable that you might think so. But after all the trouble you've gone through to reform me, I'm not gonna blow it that easily."

Ian smiled down at him. "I should've known that."

"Old Pokey won't ever be the same, though," Luke said.

"Don't worry about that old truck. It's probably had its nine lives, anyway. You just rest now. Everything's going to be all right."

LENA AWOKE A half hour or so later. Colby was sitting by her side when she opened her eyes and realized where she was. Tears rolled down her cheeks, and she said, "Oh, Mom, I'm sorry."

"Oh, baby." Colby leaned down and took her into her arms, holding her as tightly as she could without interfering with the tubes attached to her.

Ian pulled the curtain between the two beds, while mother and daughter held each other for several long minutes, reestablishing the precious bond that had been threatened in the past few months.

Colby finally pulled back and smoothed a hand across Lena's hair. "What happened, sweetie?"

"I sh-should have left it alone." Tears welled up in her eyes again, and she bit back a sob.

Colby waited for her to go on, knowing she needed to get it all out.

"A letter came for you today. It was marked Personal, but I opened it. I shouldn't have. It was from—" Her voice broke, and fresh tears made their way down her cheeks.

"Oh, Lena." Colby's heart fell as she realized who the letter had been from and what it must have said. She pulled her daughter close again, wishing she could absorb her child's pain. But she couldn't. For so long, she had tried to protect her from this, and she had failed.

"How could he not ever want to know me, Mom? What did I do to—"

"You did nothing, honey. Nothing. He's the loser in all this. Not you. You've got to believe that."

"I've been so awful to you, Mom. I just couldn't believe that he wouldn't want to see me if he knew about me. I wanted to blame you for it, to believe that you were the reason. I couldn't face the fact that he actually didn't care about me."

"Oh, Lena." Colby held her tight, rubbing her back, her own voice wavering when she said, "You don't know how I wanted to spare you this."

"I know you did, but I asked for it."

Colby drew back and looked down into her daughter's eyes. "You didn't ask for any of this. You've done nothing wrong, my precious girl. From the moment I felt you move inside me, you've been the joy of my life. And you always will be."

Lena buried her face in Colby's shoulder, crying silently and clinging to her. Colby held her as close as she could and sent up a silent, grateful prayer of thanks for her safety.

COLBY DECIDED TO wait until morning to call her parents. Since the kids were all right, there was no point in getting them out of bed at 2:00 a.m. The doctor wanted to keep both Lena and Luke overnight for observation.

Colby and Ian stayed with them. Phoebe went home around 3:00 and surprised them by never even asking how their evening had gone.

Lena and Luke were both awake off and on, so conversation between Colby and Ian was limited. In fact, there was no chance for them to talk alone at all.

Colby called her parents about 7:00 that morning, and they arrived within half an hour, hovering over Lena to make sure she was all right. Even though they had met once at the church breakfast, Colby introduced them to Ian and Luke again, and she could see that both her mom and dad were more than a little impressed with them.

The doctor released both Lena and Luke when he came to check on them around 8:00. It was after nine by the time they got the paperwork taken care of and checked the two of them out.

At the hospital exit, Colby's father insisted on driving Lena and her home.

Ian shook hands with her parents. "I hope to see you again soon," he said, and then turned to Colby. "I'll call you later."

She nodded and watched him help Luke into the car, then pull away with a wave.

At the house, they got Lena settled into her bed, where she fell asleep within minutes. After assuring herself that her daughter was all right, Colby went back downstairs and found the letter from Doug lying on the coffee table in the living room. She picked it up and read it, her heart aching for the pain it had caused Lena. How could anyone be so cruel and callous? Even though she knew Doug had never intended for Lena to see the letter, anger propelled her toward the kitchen. She picked up the phone and began punching in his number, the letter still in her hand.

"He's not worth it, you know."

Colby swung around to find her mother standing in the kitchen doorway. She hung up the phone and pressed her forehead to the receiver. "She could have been killed, Mom. And Luke, too."

"I know." Emma came forward and put her hands on Colby's shoulders, pressing her cheek against her back. "I know. But you have to let this go. Whatever happens between Lena and her father will be between them. You tried to protect her and nearly lost her. Focus on what you can control—your relationship with her—and leave the rest alone."

Colby turned around and hugged her mother. "How'd you get so wise?"

"It comes with the crow's-feet," she said, her eyes shining with love. "I'm so proud of you, Colby. You're a wonderful mother. Don't ever forget that."

"I had a wonderful role model," she said. "And you're right." She opened the drawer beside her and pulled out a book of matches. Moving to the sink, she lit one and held it to the edge of the letter. The paper went up in a quick blue flame, then crumpled and turned to ash.

Emma squeezed her arm. "She'll be fine, you know. She's strong like you."

"I hope so."

They were silent for a while and then Emma said, "He's awfully nice."

"You mean Ian?"

Emma nodded. "Is it serious?"

Colby hesitated, not sure what to say. In the hours since she and Ian had separated, she'd been bombarded by doubts, wondering if the things they'd said to each other last night would last through the light of day. "After all these years of thinking I'd never find someone who—"

"—was worth risking your heart for?" her mother interrupted softly.

"It's terrifying."

"There's always risk in loving someone, honey. And if he's the man I know he must be for you to care for him, then he must be worth it."

COLBY'S MOTHER AND father stayed until after lunch, just to make sure Lena was all right.

While Lena took a nap, Colby put together a batch of her favorite cookies. She'd just slipped the first pan into the oven when the doorbell rang. Wiping her hands on a dish towel, she made her way to the front of the house, Petey and Lulu at her heels. She opened the door to find Ian standing on the porch, dressed in gray wool pants and a blue-green wool sweater. Lord, he looked good. Memories of last night flashed through her mind, and she met his gaze with difficulty.

"You have flour on your nose," he said, reaching out to rub it off.

His touch sent a thousand shock waves through

her. "I was baking Lena some cookies. I was going to send some to Luke. How is he?"

"Mabel's with him. She may mother him to death, but other than that, he's fine."

Realizing he was still standing outside in the cold, she stepped back and waved him inside. "Come in, please."

Inside the foyer, Petey and Lulu greeted him by nearly knocking him down. "Whoa there, guys," he said, smiling and then bending down to pat their heads.

"Okay, you two, scoot now," Colby said.

Looking disappointed, the two dogs slunk into the den and plopped down on the rug.

"I have to finish the cookies," Colby said, heading toward the kitchen, where she picked up a spoon and stirred the remaining batter just so she wouldn't have to look at him.

"Mmm. They smell good. What kind?" he asked.

"Chocolate chip."

"My favorite."

"Lena's, too."

"Good. That's one more thing we'll have in common."

Colby looked up, afraid to wonder what he meant by that.

"Want to know what the other is?" He moved closer and tilted her chin toward him.

"What?" she asked, her voice little more than a whisper.

"Loving you."

Colby's chest tightened. She couldn't breathe normally. "When you didn't call today, I thought maybe—"

"Hey," he said, shushing her with a finger on her lips. "You're messing up my plan here."

She looked up at him, shaking her head. "What plan?"

"The one where I ask you to marry me."

It took a couple of seconds for the words to register. She folded her arms across her chest and smiled up at him. "Oh, that plan."

He grinned, then reached into his pants pocket and pulled out a little black box. He opened the lid.

"Oh, Ian," she whispered.

"You'd be surprised what it took to get Gentry Saunders to open his jewelry store today. His wife had a baby in the middle of the night. I had to promise him free vet services for his potbelly pig."

Colby looked down at the ring. Every bit of two carats, it might not have been the most practical piece of jewelry for a small-town veterinarian to wear, but she wasn't immune to feminine vanity, and she marveled at the size and sparkle of it. "It would be hard to get you out of a verbal contract like that," she said, emotion making her voice hoarse.

"Yeah, and I hear he's in pretty tight with the Better Business Bureau."

She smiled up at him, tears of happiness in her eyes. "Is that right?"

He nodded and pulled her to him. They held each other, renewing the bond they'd formed last night. He removed the ring from the box, took her hand and slid it on her finger. The stone sparkled in the light from the kitchen window. "Will you marry me, Colby Williams?"

Hope for a future she'd thought she would never have blossomed inside her. "Ian, are we kidding ourselves about this? You have a life in New York."

"I want my life to be with you. It may not be easy at first, but I'll find a way to make it work. I'm not the same man I was when I came here. Then, I couldn't have imagined permanently leaving the city or my work there. Now, I can't imagine going back. I want more out of my life than sixteen-hour workdays."

He tilted her chin upward. "I called my partners this afternoon and told them I want to sell my interest in the firm. I still have some thinking to do, but I could work out of my office at Oak Hill. I have a few clients I think would be willing to stay on with me. Enough to keep me busy and still allow time for you and Lena and Luke. I might even try my hand at putting away some hay for Matilda."

"With the tractor?" she asked, a tearful smile in her voice.

"Only if you agree to give me driving lessons."

"I guess I could do that. For the safety of the community."

"Think a city slicker like me could ever get the hang of it?"

"With a little practice."

His eyes grew serious again. "So how about it, Dr. Williams?"

"Yes," she said, a smile on her lips. "Yes."

He pulled her to him, and they kissed with a hunger last night had only begun to satisfy. Colby was again filled with the sense of utter completeness she found only in his arms. It still amazed her that she could know with such certainty that this was the man she had been meant to find. The right one. The only one. And she realized then that it wasn't marriage she had feared all these years. It was the fear of ending up with the wrong person: someone like Doug who would decide that he didn't love her as soon as the going got rough. Certainly there would be bumps along the way. Like the not-so-smooth road she and Ian had traveled as parents. Life would deal them a wild card now and then, but with Ian, she knew in her heart that he would be right there beside her, dealing with the bad right along with the good.

"Hey, Mom, who was that at the—"

Still wrapped in each other's arms, Colby and Ian looked up just as Lena stopped in the kitchen doorway and said, "Oh."

Remaining in the loose circle of Ian's embrace, Colby said, "Come here, honey."

Lena crossed the room, and Colby took her hand in hers. "Ian just asked me to marry him. What do you think about that?"

A smile broke across Lena's face. "Really? Well, yeah, that's great! But, gee, Mom, you really know how to kill a girl's love life."

Both Colby and Ian broke into laughter. Ian put a hand on Lena's shoulder and said, "I hope you and I can work on being friends. You and Luke knew each other before we ever decided to get married, so I don't see why you have to start acting like brother and sister. But the four of us will have to sit down and have a serious talk about things. Deal?"

"That's cool. But I sure don't want to think of him as my brother."

Colby pulled her daughter close and hugged her, with Ian's arm still around her. Lena still had pain to deal with. Colby would be there for her in every way she could. This new family they were creating wouldn't be a family in the traditional sense of the word, but it would be a family, nonetheless, and that filled Colby with a joyful satisfaction.

"Don't you think we should go see what Luke thinks about all this?" Colby asked, smiling up at her husband-to-be.

"I think we'd better. Phoebe might get wind of it, and the rest of the town would find out before he does," Ian said, chuckling.

"Let me get dressed first," Lena said, trotting off for the stairs.

"Are you sure you feel up to it, honey?" Colby called out.

Lena popped back around the corner. "My head still hurts, which I deserve. But I'm not about to miss this." She was off again, only to add from the bottom of the stairs, "Don't forget the cookies, Mom. Luke likes chocolate chip."

"I won't, honey," Colby said, smiling. "I won't."

# EPILOGUE

"WAKE UP, sleepyhead. Today's the day."

Colby rolled over and stretched alongside her husband, naked beneath the sheet. The bedroom was cool with the onset of January. Oak Hill was Colby's dream house, but they still had a lot of work to do, including installing a new furnace. But she didn't mind the cool room with Ian here to keep her warm. She didn't think she would ever quite get used to waking up next to him. Or to having him wake her in the middle of the night with kisses and loving. Now that she had him, she couldn't remember how she had ever lived without him.

"What's today?" she asked, her voice still husky with sleep.

"The day you get your wedding present."

They'd been married three weeks before at the First Baptist Church of Keeling Creek with Luke as best man, Lena as maid of honor and the front pews filled with her parents, Phoebe and Frank, and Mabel, none of whom managed to get through the ceremony with dry eyes. They'd decided to put off their real honeymoon and had gone to Manhattan for a short one right before Christmas, spending a few days at Ian's apartment—if something that elaborate could be called an apartment—in blissful solitude. He had decided to hang on to the place for a while, since he would occasionally need to stay in the city. When they returned to Keeling Creek, Phoebe had planned a moving party one Saturday afternoon to help move Colby and Lena out to Oak Hill.

Christmas had been like a fairy tale. They'd gone in search of their own tree and decorated the house with white pine wreaths and candles in the windows. Colby couldn't have imagined a more fulfilling holiday. They had a full house—Luke and Lena, along with Critter, Petey and Lulu, U-2 and Rebel. Ian had even insisted they bring Don Juan home from the clinic. What was one more dog when they already had four? he had asked her on Christmas Eve.

If possible, Colby's love for him had taken on new dimensions at that moment.

After the holidays, she and Ian had taken on the project of renovating the old place together. And she was enjoying every minute of it.

She slipped her arms around her husband's waist now and pressed her cheek to his chest. "So, how much longer do I have to wait?"

"Just how anxious are you to see it?" he asked, slipping his leg between hers and running his hand up her thigh.

"Welll," she said, pretending intense concentration while the now-familiar hum began inside her and love for him played through her like the sweetest of songs. "I think we could put it off a bit longer."

He grinned. "As much as I would like to take you up on that, I'm going to be in serious trouble if I don't get you out of this house within the next twenty minutes."

Thoroughly intrigued now, Colby gave him a protesting kiss before getting out of bed and heading for the shower. A little while later, she followed him out to the car, begging for at least a hint. He was stubbornly closemouthed for the duration of the drive. A mile or so down the road from the house, Ian made a right-hand turn at the edge of a cornfield that was part of Oak Hill property. Since it was on the back side of the farm, Colby rarely drove past it, but she noticed now that a road had been cut through the field and covered with gravel.

"Did you do this?" she asked, more curious than ever.

"Maybe," he said, looking at her with a smile.

"But what on earth for?"

"Patience," he said.

The road wound on for several hundred yards and then curved to the right. Just around the bend, she saw Lena and Luke. They were both wearing face-splitting smiles, one on each side of a sign that read:

### The Oak Hill Home For Animals
*Permanent Housing for Pets Waiting to be Adopted*

Colby stared at it, unable to believe what she had just read. Behind the sign sat a bulldozer with Davis Construction emblazoned on the side.

Colby's eyes filled with tears. She turned to look at Ian. "This is…you did this for me?"

He got out and came around to the other side of the car, took her hands and pulled her out. He put his arms around her waist and kissed her forehead. "Just for you," he said.

"Oh, Ian." She put her arms around his neck and hugged him, unable to think of any words eloquent enough to express what she was feeling.

But he understood. She could see it in his eyes when she pulled back and looked up at him. "Did I tell you I love you?"

Ian glanced at his watch. "Not in the past hour or so."

"I do," she said. "I do."

He kissed her, the gesture assuring her of his love more than words. A few moments later, he said, "I wanted to tell you about this sooner, but I had to make sure I could get the building permits and that sort of thing first. It's been a real challenge making sure those two didn't spill the beans."

She sent a teary glance toward the boy and girl in question, still standing by the sign, thoughtfully giving them a moment of privacy.

"When you two get finished with that," Luke called out, "we've got a building site to show you."

Colby looked up at her husband and smiled. "These teenagers. They don't know a thing about patience, do they?"

Ian shook his head. "That comes with age."

"And a lot of other good things."

"And a lot of other good things," he repeated, a not-so-innocent look in his eyes.

With their arms around each other, they made their way toward the son and daughter who couldn't wait to tell Colby all about her very special wedding gift.

# *Heartbreak* RANCH

Four generations of independent women...
Four heartwarming, romantic stories of the West...
Four incredible authors...

## Fern Michaels
## Jill Marie Landis
### Dorsey Kelley
### Chelley Kitzmiller

Saddle up with Heartbreak Ranch, an outstanding
Western collection that will take you on a whirlwind
trip through four generations and the exciting,
romantic adventures of four strong women who
have inherited the ranch from Bella Duprey,
famed Barbary Coast madam.

Available in March,
wherever Harlequin books are sold.

HARLEQUIN ®

Since the turn of the century the elegant and fashionable
DeWilde stores have helped brides around the world
turn the fantasy of their "Special Day" into reality. But now the
store and three generations of family are torn apart by the
separation of Grace and Jeffrey DeWilde. Family members
face new challenges and loves in this fast-paced, glamorous,
internationally set series. For weddings and romance, glamour
and fun-filled entertainment, enter the world of DeWildes....

## Watch for *I DO, AGAIN,* by Jasmine Cresswell
## The final installment of Weddings by DeWilde
## Coming to you in March, 1997

Grace DeWilde's ambitious cousin, Michael Forrest,
represented everything Julia Dutton emphatically wished to
avoid in a man. Julia had been earmarked "perfect little wife"
material, while Michael's high-voltage sexuality attracted
glamour like moths to a flame. They could barely stand to
be in the same room together. So how was it possible that
one charged evening could make teaching French at the
Kensington Academy for Girls suddenly seem so dismal,
while the chance to assist in developing Michael's new
Berkshire Forrest Hotel loomed as the chance of a lifetime?

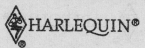

**HARLEQUIN®**

## HARLEQUIN SUPERROMANCE®

### There's more to the story...

Every now and then comes a book that defies convention, breaks the rules and still offers the reader all the excitement of romance. Harlequin Superromance—the series known for its innovation and variety—is proud to add this book to our already-outstanding lineup.

## #733 SOMEWHERE OUT THERE
### by
### Connie Bennett

Kit Wheeler doesn't believe in UFOs or aliens or government conspiracies. The former astronaut and now respected TV science correspondent wants nothing to do with the crackpots and their tales. Then an air-force jet mysteriously crashes, and Brenna Sullivan, an expert in her own right, has a convincing theory.

*Whether you believe or not, you'll enjoy this wonderful story of adventure, romance and the endless possibilities that exist...somewhere out there.*

Available in March wherever Harlequin books are sold.

# HARLEQUIN®

Don't miss these Harlequin favorites by some of our most distinguished authors!
And now, you can receive a discount by ordering two or more titles!

| | | |
|---|---|---|
| HT#25645 | THREE GROOMS AND A WIFE by JoAnn Ross | $3.25 U.S. ☐<br>$3.75 CAN. |
| HT#25647 | NOT THIS GUY by Glenda Sanders | $3.25 U.S. ☐<br>$3.75 CAN. |
| HP#11725 | THE WRONG KIND OF WIFE by Roberta Leigh | $3.25 U.S. ☐<br>$3.75 CAN. |
| HP#11755 | TIGER EYES by Robyn Donald | $3.25 U.S. ☐<br>$3.75 CAN. |
| HR#03416 | A WIFE IN WAITING by Jessica Steele | $3.25 U.S. ☐<br>$3.75 CAN. |
| HR#03419 | KIT AND THE COWBOY by Rebecca Winters | $3.25 U.S. ☐<br>$3.75 CAN. |
| HS#70622 | KIM & THE COWBOY by Margot Dalton | $3.50 U.S. ☐<br>$3.99 CAN. |
| HS#70642 | MONDAY'S CHILD by Janice Kaiser | $3.75 U.S. ☐<br>$4.25 CAN. |
| HI#22342 | BABY VS. THE BAR by M.J. Rodgers | $3.50 U.S. ☐<br>$3.99 CAN. |
| HI#22382 | SEE ME IN YOUR DREAMS by Patricia Rosemoor | $3.75 U.S. ☐<br>$4.25 CAN. |
| HAR#16538 | KISSED BY THE SEA by Rebecca Flanders | $3.50 U.S. ☐<br>$3.99 CAN. |
| HAR#16603 | MOMMY ON BOARD by Muriel Jensen | $3.50 U.S. ☐<br>$3.99 CAN. |
| HH#28885 | DESERT ROGUE by Erine Yorke | $4.50 U.S. ☐<br>$4.99 CAN. |
| HH#28911 | THE NORMAN'S HEART by Margaret Moore | $4.50 U.S. ☐<br>$4.99 CAN. |

(limited quantities available on certain titles)

| | | |
|---|---|---|
| | **AMOUNT** | $ |
| **DEDUCT:** | **10% DISCOUNT FOR 2+ BOOKS** | $ |
| **ADD:** | **POSTAGE & HANDLING** | $ |
| | ($1.00 for one book, 50¢ for each additional) | |
| | **APPLICABLE TAXES*** | $_____ |
| | **TOTAL PAYABLE** | $_____ |
| | (check or money order—please do not send cash) | |

To order, complete this form and send it, along with a check or money order for the total above, payable to Harlequin Books, to: **In the U.S.:** 3010 Walden Avenue, P.O. Box 9047, Buffalo, NY 14269-9047; **In Canada:** P.O. Box 613, Fort Erie, Ontario, L2A 5X3.

Name:_____

Address:_____ City:_____

State/Prov.:_____ Zip/Postal Code:_____

*New York residents remit applicable sales taxes.
  Canadian residents remit applicable GST and provincial taxes.
Look us up on-line at: http://www.romance.net

HBACK-JM4

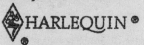

## HARLEQUIN SUPERROMANCE®

# PROTECTING MOLLY McCULLOCH
## by
### Dee Holmes

### Superromance #732

Hunt Gresham left the police force after deciding that he was no longer in a position to protect anyone. But the indomitable Molly McCulloch has a way of getting to him. When Hunt learns her newfound brother is a hit man for hire, he knows it's time to bury the past and mount his charger one last time.

But with Molly, once is never enough....

Look for *Protecting Molly McCulloch* in March wherever Harlequin books are sold.

Look us up on-line at: http://www.romance.net

Loving
DANGEROUSLY